The Palace

The Palace has stood for seven hundred years, a fortress on the eastern plain. Down the centuries it had resisted the attacks of countless invaders: Ghengis Khan himself had turned from its walls to find easier prey in the barren countryside around. Successive generations of kings and princes had added to its barbaric splendour, contriving finally a structure greater than they, greater than the sum of its parts, a monstrous symbol of their oppression. With revolution the gaudy oppressors were swept away, replaced by grey men, scuttling politicians ignorant of the building they were to inhabit. But the passions it forced on them made nonsense of their small expediences. The man who would rule the country must first rule the Palace and himself.

The Palace

by

D. G. COMPTON

HODDER AND STOUGHTON

The characters in this book are entirely imaginary
and bear no relation to any living person.

Copyright © 1969 by D. G. Compton

SBN 340 10968 8

First printed 1969

Printed in Great Britain for Hodder and Stoughton Limited
St. Paul's House, Warwick Lane, London, E.C.4
by Willmer Brothers Limited, Birkenhead

For
ANNE MARIE
with my love

He was a braw fellow,
And he played at the ring;
And the Bonnie Earl of Murray
He might ha' been the King...

Old Scottish Ballad

Part One

NOVEMBER

One

Approaching across the barren plain on the eastern side of
the river, especially when the sun had just risen above the
Yahla mountains behind one, it was possible to see the
Palace from a distance of twenty kilometres. It would first
be distinguished from the wooded ground rising behind it
by means of the three great gilded domes: one on the
Cathedral of the Blessed Virgin, and two situated at either
end of the former King's Residence – now drably called the
Government Building. The motor road across the plain took
two near right-angled turns to avoid large areas of marshland,
and thus for three kilometres of its course lay parallel both
to the river and to the outer wall of the Palace. Accidents
on this stretch of the road often occurred by reason of the
motorists' eyes being drawn away to the left by the magnificence and improbability of the view presented.

For six months of the year the intervening marshes would
be frozen, sharp grey ice showing occasionally among wide
expanses of rushes and blackened moss. At road level the
dividing river would be out of sight, so that the outer wall
of the Palace would seem to spring straight from this pitiful
terrain, a wall in no place less than twenty metres high,
surmounted with towers and inhumanly gigantic battle-
ments, its grey granite sallow in the early morning light.
Now, at a distance of scarcely six kilometres, the windows
of the Palace buildings themselves, behind the outer walls,
would gleam blackly, and also the gilt along the mouldings

of the neo-Classical pediment which was one of the few tasteful additions made by Gustav III. The other turrets and towers and domes and spires would be clear now against the black-green forest, their colours, brilliant blues and greens, muted in the thin sunlight. Winter sunrises were usually clear, for the bitter marshes retained nothing of the day's tiny heat from which to spin mists against dawn's coming. In this pale clarity every eastward-facing feature of the Palace would be visible from the road: the huge blank bulk of the Arsenal, the Eternal Flag of the Revolution that was never lowered, the balconied Royal Walk from which George I had watched the execution of the Princess Irene, even the outline of the River Gate walled up in the siege of 1740 and never reopened. On a winter's morning the details of the Palace were cruelly precise, a structure showing fearful solidarity, a mass that grew like a fantasticated mountain out of the frozen plain. It was harsher by far than the successive regimes for which it had served as outward symbol. Even the present administration, pledged to outlast mankind itself, seemed weak and ephemeral by contrast.

Even to a man who knew and loved every smallest detail of the Palace, this view on a grey November morning was disturbingly malign. So heavy was the weight of menace that settled over Major Kohler as he approached and turned the first corner to bring his car parallel to the Palace's eastern wall, that he drew in to the side and stopped. Making the forty kilometre drive back after a week-end pass in the neighbouring city of Dorlen, his explanation to himself for having stopped was that he needed to stretch his legs and relieve himself. Nevertheless, these two tasks completed, he still found himself lingering in the bitter air, staring gloomily across the marshland at his destination. With no sun to help them, the walls were the colour of dull lead. The red flag above the Guard Barracks seemed not red but black. And above the northern end of the Palace a heavy cloud of dark smoke rose slowly from the unseen chimney of the Palace bakery. They burned straw in the early mornings to raise quickly the temperature of the ovens, straw from the Palace stables. Major Kohler thought of other fuels that had gone into the oven furnaces, the bodies of those who had displeased Royalty, and in the end the body of Royalty itself.

As an army engineer, a graduate of Orstak University, Major Kohler was accustomed to the grey look of barracks, of prison blocks, of the dark local stone that was used in official buildings all over this part of his country. Nevertheless, the Palace depressed him. He lingered by his car, hunched his shoulders to light a cigarette, stamped his feet, smoked his cigarette through, tossed the stub away onto the thin crust of snow that had fallen three weeks before and frozen as hard as sugar. Only then, his mind concentrated on his duties in the day ahead, did he climb back into the car, start the engine, and drive on.

He was not a man who practised analysis, either of himself or of others. His intellect was at its best when calculating stresses, turning moments, coefficients of expansion. He reasoned now that his week-end in Dorlen had been good, that no man liked the prospect of returning to work, especially to the unpredictable rages of the Engineer Colonel. The Palace, he thought, was like a good whore – the exterior might be a bit rough, but once you got inside . . . well, you were probably in for a hell of a surprise. So he drove steadily neither hurrying nor dawdling. His short break out in the morning air had chilled him, and he eased his fur jacket open as he drove, letting in the warm air from the car heater. There was another chill, however, that remained.

After the second right-angled turn the road to the Palace ran as straight as a gun barrel. This last section was lined with large notices : warnings of traffic restrictions ahead, Party exhortations, brief summaries of Palace history for the benefit of tourist bus-loads. Major Kohler knew them all by

13

heart. He had been stationed at the Palace now for seven years. As he approached the river he slowed – he did not recognise this action, nor the reason for it. The river represented freedom to him, and dignity : the freedom of nature. His life went on within another, perhaps more limited, level of freedom – the freedom of man with man, of socialisation, of conscience, of respect and love and duty, the freedom man's mind constructs and at the same time controls. Which has its own dignity. For the river none of this irksome structure existed or was necessary, so Major Kohler would slow each time he crossed it, and snatch quick glances to left and right, up and down its yellow water. When in the depth of winter its surface froze, he never joined his fellow-officers in their skating or riding motor bicycles across it. He gave no reason and knew of none : the sense of violation he felt remained unshaped, denied even.

This particular November morning he drove even more slowly than usual : the river was still in spate from recent snowfalls on the foothills of the Yahla mountains, swirling through the reddish sticks of the willows, its surface broken here and there with tangles of brushwood and occasional tree trunks that had eluded the hooks and poles of the vigilant peasants. Major Kohler slowed his car to walking pace. Downstream his eye was drawn to the new section of embankment whose construction he was supervising. The temporary shuttering was holding well – the army divers had done good work under particularly difficult circumstances. He engaged a lower gear and drove on. His mind was looking ahead now, to the details of his morning's work. At the Mantua Gate he stopped and showed his pass to the guard. The Cathedral clock had just finished striking seven.

In the Officers' Quarters he washed and shaved again and changed into the fresh uniform his batman had laid out for him. A very dark-jowled man, the shave he had had three hours earlier before leaving the brothel in Dorlen would never last him through to the end of his duty tour. The Engineer Colonel was quite capable of calling him out in front of the men to account for his unshaven appearance. The Engineer Colonel's batman had told his batman (who in his turn had passed the information on) that the Engineer Colonel set a no higher standard for his subordinates than he did for himself.

Major Kohler breakfasted in the Officers' Mess. The food was good: a spiced liver pâté spread thickly on black bread, peppered with turmeric, and grilled. The coffee also was good: black, and pleasantly gritty. He finished his meal with a green Thai orange. Messing in the Palace was like nowhere else in the service. In compensation for the other rigours of Palace life, perhaps.

His fellow officers were not communicative. For those not on duty the previous night there had been the usual drinking party, the songs and the toasts lasting till most of them could no longer stand. A few of the younger subalterns came in chattering, still needing to prove their resilience and manhood, but they soon hushed under the silent disapproval of their superiors. The chandeliers were unlighted. Except on Mess Nights the hall was illuminated by wall brackets of post-Revolutionary simplicity.

At eight o'clock Major Kohler reported to the Engineer Colonel. The older man never drank with his subordinates. None the less, his condition that Monday morning was worse than theirs. It hushed the stridency of his voice and made it painful for him to lift his eyes from the fine morocco surface of his desk. The Engineer Colonel was an old man, his liver even older.

"Back from another of your week-ends, Kohler?"

Major Kohler had had no leave of any kind for nine weeks previously. He stood stiffly to attention and waited.

"Well, Kohler, and how were the bright lights? You did go to the city, didn't you? How were the bright lights? Squander all your money, did you?"

"A pleasant week-end, thank you, sir."

"And now you're ready to get down to some work, eh, Kohler?"

"The new stretch of embankment, sir. I was gratified to see how well it – "

"I have under my command lunatics, Kohler. Worse than that, they are interfering lunatics."

The Engineer Colonel eased a short memorandum out of his tray at his elbow and flung it across the desk at Major Kohler.

"For a few hours this morning, Kohler, the embankment project will have to get along without you. That *is* possible, you know. Send Lieutenant Dzek – he can keep the men busy grading ballast for the filling. From you I want a negative follow-up report on that damnfool memorandum."

Major Kohler read the five lines of neat typing. They were signed by Lieutenant Mandaraks and described cracks and signs of stress that the young lieutenant had found – or thought he had found – in the ceiling of the Paul VII Passage. The memorandum was dated the previous Saturday: indeed, its presence on the Engineer Colonel's desk at all depended on its bearing that date. On any other day Lieutenant Mandaraks would have come to him, Major Kohler, and none of it need ever have been committed to paper.

Pieces of paper were intransigent – they did not disappear when the Engineer Colonel shouted. Worse than that, they bred carbon copies that circulated to other departments, that brought back queries from other sources on the action taken, that caused flutters of general excitement around the Palace and resulted in too many right hands knowing what too many left hands were up to. The Engineer Colonel hated pieces of paper and feared them. Officers even nearer to retiring age than he had been discredited, lost rank, reputation and pension on account of injudicious pieces of paper. One of Major Kohler's duties, therefore, was to protect the Engineer Colonel from all such. Hence the heavy comments on the subject of the Major's week-end pass. If he had not been away in Dorlen none of this need ever have happened.

The Major folded the piece of paper carefully, put it in his pocket and returned to the position of attention.

"Mandaraks is full of ill-informed notions," said the Engineer Colonel. "Most of these youngsters are. Two years at some provincial college and they think they know it all."

Major Kohler recalled that the young lieutenant had attended the finest Mining Institute in the country. He remained silent.

"I'd go myself," said the Engineer Colonel, "if my day weren't so fully booked."

He thumbed vaguely through his desk diary, careful not to open it at the right page. He lifted his eyes laboriously up to Major Kohler's face.

"Your lanyard, Major Kohler, is a symbol of rank, not a whore's shoulder strap."

Major Kohler remained at attention.

"Five copies of your report, Kohler. And see they're circulated. Rumours like this need scotching. I rely on you, Kohler, to investigate thoroughly. Your report must show a complete grasp of the technicalities involved. This foolish business might come to the attention of the Minister. I want no doubt to be left in his mind whatsoever."

Major Kohler saluted and turned to go.

"Is there something the matter, Major Kohler?"

"Sir?"

"I asked you about the bright lights of Dorlen. I don't remember that you answered."

"They were bright, Engineer Colonel."

In private Major Kohler could be pushed so far and no further. In public his concern for the shows of discipline was so great that he made no such limits. The Engineer

Colonel was aware of this quality in the man and treated him accordingly.

"Bright, were they, Major Kohler? I'm glad to hear it. Glad to hear it."

Major Kohler went out, closing the door quietly behind him. In the mirror beside the door – a mirror placed so that all subordinates could check their turn-out before going in to see the Engineer Colonel – he inspected the lie of his major's crimson lanyard. It was, of course, immaculate.

The Engineer Colonel's offices were on the ground floor of the building that had housed the Cathedral clergy during the old regime. The niches along the bare corridors that had once contained gilded icons and holy water stoups were now occupied with fire extinguishers and buckets of sand and water. Throughout the Palace the danger of fire was always present. It was the frequency of disastrous fires in the past that had given the Palace its rich variety of architecture, each king rebuilding in the highest mannerism of his reign.

Passing along cold corridors floored in contrasting octagons of indigo and green and white marble, Major Kohler made his way to the Orderly Room where he instructed the sergeant to send a runner for Lieutenant Dzek. Then he sat down and glanced through the papers that had come in over the week-end. Looking steeply up out of the window of his office it was possible to see the red onion dome of the Prince's Tower, and a patch of heavy grey sky beyond. If the temperature rose sufficiently, snow would fall.

Lieutenant Dzek was not pleased by his change of duty. His previous detail for the morning had been to measure the comfortably warm kitchens for the new equipment soon to be ordered. This whim of the Engineer Colonel would cause him to stand for several hours in the open, fully exposed to the rising easterly wind, as he watched a platoon of pioneers from some barbarous province shovel stones monotonously through coarse wire sieves. They would at least have their work to keep them warm – for him the only exercise possible was to bully them without cease. He felt sorry for the poor bastards, but what else could he do? All this he confided to the Orderly Sergeant while Major Kohler was in his office making out requisition forms for the equipment he would need in his inspection of the Paul VII Passage. The Orderly Sergeant tactfully advised Lieutenant Dzek to hurry – the men paraded at eight fifteen and he was late already.

For his assistant on the tour of inspection Major Kohler chose a young sapper, Fasch, who worked in the Engineer's Stores. He knew about Fasch from the Personnel Officer – as a student he had missed going to university through an unlucky illness, and he was now working for a degree in his spare time. Among the barely literate soldiery his life could not be easy. Major Kohler was in the habit of taking Fasch with him whenever he thought the journey was likely to be instructive.

They went together to the Drawing Office and Major Kohler signed for a photostat map of the catacombs. The map was incomplete and in places frankly conjectural – the Engineer Colonel had once begun to organise a complete new survey of the passages and storerooms under the Palace, but the scheme had met with such a lack of enthusiasm from higher quarters (on the grounds of more pressing priorities) that he had tactfully shelved the matter. But the Paul VII Passage was in a well-used area and the photostat would indeed hardly be necessary. As they came out onto the steps in front of the old Archbishop's Residence there was a commotion in the courtyard below. Two motor cycle outriders roared by. The heavy black limousine behind them carried presidential pennants. Fasch stood to attention as well as he could beneath his various burdens, and Major Kohler saluted. Through the windows of the car they had a brief glimpse of the President's wife and two or three other Central Committee wives. The second car contained food baskets, a pile of extra clothes, and a neat rack of skating boots. Behind it came two further outriders, their intercoms rasping unintelligibly. The courtyard cobbles had been swept clear of snow two weeks before and the tyres of the small convoy left damp black lines.

"A skating party to Novellnyi," said Major Kohler, watching the last motor cyclist turn sharp left in the direction of the northern Partiot's Gate. "The snow must be going to hold off then. For the women's sakes I hope the forecasters are right."

"They usually are." Fasch stood at ease. "I didn't notice Comrade Korda, did you, Major?"

Kohler looked at him sharply.

"The Minister of Education is a busy man." Major Kohler wondered if he should pursue the matter further. "You have inside information, Fasch, that makes you surprised that Comrade Korda is not a member of the skating party to Novellnyi?"

"None at all." Fasch busied himself clipping the map onto the map board. "Central Committee members do sometimes take a morning off to go skating. Perhaps my remark was caused by a little jealousy."

Major Kohler walked quickly away down the steps. Of course the soldiers gossiped – it would be ridiculous either to pretend they did not or to try to stop them. The closed life of the Palace made such talk inevitable. If it did not interest him personally this was probably because he felt safer with things than with people. He led the way to the Judiciary Building, in the foyer of which was the most used entrance to the catacombs. At the head of the staircase down he identified himself and his companion, and told the guard their business.

Sections of the catacombs were open to conducted tours, thick white ropes on brass staunchions fencing off the more exclusive parts. Other areas were used for movement about the Palace during bad weather. Every entrance was carefully guarded, however – when the ground beneath a centre of government is honeycombed with passages of doubtful extent it is wise to take every possible precaution. At one time secret tunnels from inside the Palace had emerged at several places in the surrounding countryside. These had been found and sealed, or so it was generally believed. Major Kohler suspected otherwise. He had read the Palace histories. Certain events – the escape of the Bulgarian spy in 1951 for example – could only be explained by the presence of tunnels as yet undiscovered. One day he would re-open the question of a comprehensive survey. One day, when the political moment was right. But Major Kohler was a soldier and an engineer, and nothing more. For him political moments were a closed book. The comprehensive survey would never be made in his lifetime. But at least in a few weeks' time he would understand why.

The Paul VII Passage was to the left of and at a lower level than a large show cellar – the cavern where in the Great Famine of 1811 the Royal Family's private store of grain had been raided by the desperate garrison. The King himself, Georg III, had come to the defence of his granary, and tradition named a certain raised part of the floor as the place where he had personally decapitated the leader of the mutineers and tossed the dripping head to its followers. Major Kohler and his assistant crossed the silent cavern – conducted tours took place on Saturdays and Sundays – stepped over the boundary ropes and entered a less well-lit corridor that sloped steeply downwards. This terminated in a vertical ladder descent and brought them directly into the Paul VII Passage.

As he jumped the last three rungs of the ladder and landed on the rough stone floor of the passage, Major Kohler became immediately aware of a change in the atmosphere: a drop in the temperature and also a curious pressure, not quite a sound, in his ears.

He waited at the foot of the ladder and helped Fasch down with the instruments. These less frequented areas were lit by regulation wall fittings at five metre intervals. They were inspected in strict sequence – for Lieutenant Mandaraks to have been down there the previous Saturday morning represented a curious break with routine. That the Engineer Colonel had failed to comment upon this could only be attributed to the poor state of his health – solitary drinking played hell with any man's constitution, in the opinion of Major Kohler. He took the map from Fasch and examined it carefully. There was no elevation. Certain spot depths were marked and rough indications given of the gradients joining them. Minor changes in angle or direction were impossible to detect.

"Well, Fasch, what do you think?"

"I don't like it, Major."

"Neither do I. But give me your reasons for not liking it."

"That light, Major – the sixth one along. It's out of line."

The passage ran straight for fifty metres. Wherever possible the lights were mounted to constitute a datum line. They provided a very approximate check.

"These lights have been here for twelve years now, Fasch. Minor subsidence in a tunnel as ancient as this is bound to occur."

"And there's a noise, Major. Can't you hear it?"

Not quite a noise. Something between a noise and a sensation. Major Kohler had experienced it once before during a special course down the mines near Pol. Then it had been expected and accounted for – down here in the Paul VII Passage it could only mean danger. Many sounds under the earth were normal – soil moved, rocks creaked against one another, clay that worked made a curious gulping sound. These and others would be lived with. But the sound of running water – no matter how faint – where no running water should be, brought fear to even the most experienced miner.

22

He set up the tripod. "What can you hear, Fasch? Tell me about it." It was essential to make a survey of every inch of the passage. Only by means of this would any future changes in the structure be measurable.

"I don't know . . . It's too faint. I thought at first I was imagining it. Can't you hear it, Major?"

Kohler avoided answering. "Take the rod and measure, boy. Stop off at twenty metres and give me a vertical."

While Fasch was paying out the tape Major Kohler referred again to the map. Certainly they were under the eastern, riverside sector of the Palace, but the nearest point of the river bed itself was still more than three thousand metres away. Impossible that the sound of a river even in spate could be travelling through earth that distance. He saw below the Paul VII Passage the line of another tunnel leading out under the river. It was marked as having been mined and sealed in the consolidation operation shortly after the war. The water must be penetrating at a higher level, he thought, somewhere between the –

"Twenty metres, Major."

"Any sign of seepage, Fasch?"

"None at all, sir."

Their voices resonated unpleasantly, shrill as if mechanically reproduced.

"Right, boy. We'll take the vertical."

They worked on the one stretch of ancient vaulting for more than three hours, plotting the smallest variations. Major Kohler built up a minutely-detailed three-dimensional picture of the tunnel. He found the cracks Lieutenant Mandaraks had described, and stress crazing on several of the filler stones. The signs were minute – unless Mandaraks had been looking for them specially he would never have found them. He decided to have a word with the lieutenant as soon as possible.

He took flashlight photographs of three cracks from three different angles and measured them again to be quite certain. In pairs the photographs could be viewed to give a stereoscopic impression. From Mandaraks' description there seemed to have been no significant changes since Saturday, but that was proof of nothing but itself.

Fasch was reeling in the tape measure and packing the instruments away. Major Kohler walked to the far end of the tunnel, feeling the air, watching the rhythmic passage of the barrel vaulting above his head. In some manner he was able to share in the stresses of the stones above him, experience their strange unease, a restlessness perhaps long overdue. To stand for three hundred years was enough. In the mines near Pol he had seen a whole siding fall. The sudden release of energy had left him almost exultant, not knowing why. There was the edge of that same feeling showing now as he turned at the end of the passage and gazed up the narrow perspective to the figure of Fasch bent over the buckles of his instrument case. The boy seemed unnaturally small. Between them the water rustled, straining rock against rock . . . He wondered how long it would be before he and Fasch were missed, should anything happen. He paced slowly back between the stooping walls: there was strength in them yet, for weeks or months or even years. For just how long was a calculation no man could make. The masons serving the sickly Paul had worked well – death had intervened before the underground chapel this passage was to reach had been started, but the passage itself remained when many others under the Palace, younger, had caved and disappeared. He felt safe down there, safer than on open ground.

Major Kohler took a last look down the tunnel and then climbed the ladder to the next level. He took the equipment as Fasch handed it up to him. Along in the granary cavern he paused.

"This is a matter needing discretion, Fasch," his voice not loud enough to rouse echoes. "It might be serious. It might, on the other hand, be no more than the sort of settling inevitable in masonry of such great age." He made no mention of the water, leaving Fasch to interpret the sound in whatever way he chose. "It would be a pity, Fasch, if certain sections of the Palace administration were to be alarmed unnecessarily."

Caution was essential. It was a question of simple self-preservation to shape every event into an acceptable whole before passing it on. Incompleteness bred anxiety, and anxiety bred reprisal. The result of such shaping, Major Kohler believed, was tidy administration and a lack of large-scale panic.

"I quite understand, Major."

"I hope you do, Fasch. In the circumstances you would be well advised to know nothing. If anybody should ask you – there's no reason why they should, of course, but it's best to be prepared – it will be easy for you to say you were only the sapper, that I didn't take you into my confidence."

"No more you did, Major."

"No more I did."

And, looking back on it, that was indeed so. He had kept his thoughts to himself. It was a wise habit.

After returning the instruments to store Major Kohler dismissed Fasch and himself took the map back to the Drawing Office. The captain in charge happened to come into the outer office as the orderly was signing for the map. He glanced at the entry book.

"Uncovered a plot to blow up the Palace, have you?"

"I'm afraid I don't understand you."

"Mandaraks on Saturday, and now the Engineer Colonel's watchdog. What's down in that corner of the catacombs to interest you so?"

Major Kohler knew he would be expected to pull rank. To do otherwise would make the other suspicious.

"A minor departmental project, Captain. Nothing you need concern yourself with."

"Of course not, Major Kohler." The captain buttoned his jacket which had been hanging open. "Not that I've not got plenty of worries of my own, I can tell you. Our photocopier has broken down. Some fault in the timer and the electronics men can't seem to find it. I'm going to have to ask for an engineer to be flown in from Dorlen. You know how the Senior Draughtsman detests involving other departments."

"The failure is Electronics' responsibility. I don't see that you have to worry."

Major Kohler needed to make a discreet telephone call. He left the Drawing Office and rang his Orderly Room from the Archives Department across the corridor. He was told that Lieutenant Mandaraks was supervising a conduit clearing operation near the Maria Irene Gate. He fetched a motor bicycle from the Pool and drove across.

The Maria Irene Gate was a late-nineteenth century structure built on the foundations of one of the earliest towers in the Palace. Queen Maria Irene, wife to Michael I, had been canonised during her lifetime for the frequency of her holy visions and the purity of her life. Her canonisation represented a successful attempt on the part of the Early Church to stabilise the stormy natures of the Royal Family – once his wife had been publicly proclaimed a saint it was impossible for Michael to question the legitimacy of her children. In this way the succession was assured for at least one generation : a trick worth knowing but not one easily repeated.

Lieutenant Mandaraks had his men working in a deep gully beside the roadway. They were shovelling mud onto a powered conveyor that lifted it up to a waiting lorry. Major Kohler noticed that the mud was yellow. He called the lieutenant to one side.

"Lieutenant Mandaraks, I have been detailed by the Engineer Colonel to follow up your memorandum on the Paul VII Passage. Would you please begin by telling me

26

how you came to be so far from your usual area of duty?"

"I'm not sure, sir." Mandaraks was expecting praise. "I suppose you might call it intuition, sir."

"I don't believe in intuition, Mandaraks. Intuition is another word for unconscious deduction."

"Yes, sir." Mandaraks beat his arms against his sides to warm himself and conceal his disappointment. "Well, sir, it started with the yellow mud in this conduit, sir. It seemed to me obvious that it was coming from the river, and therefore that the — "

"There are other possible sources, Lieutenant."

In one step he was dangerously near the truth.

"I know, sir. But I discounted them. The volume was too great, I thought. I see now that I was quite mistaken, of course."

"Mistaken?"

"You see, Major Kohler, I studied the maps and I decided that the river must somehow have broken through into the Paul VII Passage and be bleeding from there along a fault into one or more of the branch sewers."

Near the truth, but unaware of it after all.

"A rather dramatic conclusion, Lieutenant. One hardly supported by the facts at your disposal."

"I know, sir. But it seemed so certain at the time."

Major Kohler smiled slightly. He could picture the young officer, full of enthusiasm for his theory, seeing himself the saviour of the Palace, rushing down into the catacombs only to find the Paul VII Passage bone dry and apparently undamaged. No flood, no dramatic collapse, no water lapping the lower rungs of the ladder. It was the intense disappointment of Lieutenant Mandaraks that had driven him to pick over the surface of the tunnel in the sad hope that some small justification might be found. In Mandaraks' case it was disappointment rather than an unusually acute sense of hearing.

"The cracks you found were very small, Lieutenant

27

Mandaraks. You thought carefully before you decided them worth a written memorandum?"

"You were on leave, Major, and I thought – "

"You thought my absence gave you an opportunity to show the Engineer Colonel the excellence of your initiative. But initiative is like any other human quality, Mandaraks, it needs to be disciplined. In your case the man you need to impress with your initiative is not the Engineer Colonel but myself. He, as it turns out, is not in the least impressed. He called you an interfering lunatic."

"I'm sorry, Major Kohler. I – "

"It's no use being sorry, Lieutenant, and well you know it." Major Kohler turned to go, then paused. "Look for the source of your mud around the rebuilding operations at the north end of the stables, Lieutenant. You may find the men are disposing of the spoil down the conduits there."

This was a not implausible suggestion. And it would give Lieutenant Mandaraks' over-inquisitive mind something to work on for the next few hours. Major Kohler saw now that the situation was worse than he had at first imagined. If river water was finding its way under the Palace in sufficient quantities to bring mud with it, then it could only be doing so via one of the main sewers. And if there was enough mud to leave a deposit even in one of the open overflow conduits, then the deposits being left in the sewer itself must already be of dangerous proportions. Yet in spite of all this, the Engineer Colonel was expecting a negative follow-up report. Kohler suspected that general reality had long ago ceased to have any significance to the Engineer Colonel. The only reality that concerned him was his coming retirement and the smooth passage to it that he felt he deserved. The man who attempted to deny him this smooth passage committed something very near to treason.

Major Kohler drove thoughtfully back to the vehicle pool. The noise of his machine rebounded harshly between the cliff-like buildings on either side of the narrow cobbled streets. There was seldom room for two vehicles to pass, even along the routes that had originally been laid out for ceremonial and religious purposes, and for this reason a complicated one-way traffic system had been devised. This gave any journey within the Palace walls something of the quality of a children's maze, being designed apparently to cause the utmost frustration. In addition to this there was the foot traffic – always in a hurry in the cold weather – to contend with. So that by the time Major Kohler coasted in under the intricately moulded archway to the Palace garage he had plenty of time to decide what he should do next.

On Monday afternoons it was the Engineer Colonel's duty to attend the office of the Minister of State Building, both to report on the previous week and to receive his orders for the week to come. If the business of the meeting could be finished quickly – as was usually the case – the Minister would then invite the Engineer Colonel to stay for a short drink. This drink had been known to last until five in the afternoon, for the Minister was a compulsive raconteur and the Engineer Colonel – so near to his pension – made a dutiful listener.

If Major Kohler could dare to intrude upon this tête-à-tête at some little time after three – offering the urgency of the situation as excuse for this break with protocol – he would gain a threefold advantage. First, in the presence of the Minister the Engineer Colonel could hardly give full vent to his rage at Major Kohler's report not being of the reassuring nature he had specifically ordered. Second, the Minister's impression of Major Kohler and of Major Kohler's zeal would be extremely favourable. And third, by delivering a verbal report to the ear of the Minister himself, Major Kohler made sure both that the information did not get blocked by the Engineer Colonel as being inconvenient, and also that he achieved his purpose without actually putting anything in writing – which was always a tactical error.

Accordingly Major Kohler sought for a way of keeping out of the way until the Engineer Colonel was safely in conference with the Minister of State Building. He thought at once of Lieutenant Dzek with his working party down on the bank of the river.

During the short hours of winter daylight all outside working parties went without their lunch breaks. As they were dismissed from duty as soon as darkness fell, which was at times as early as three o'clock, this was in fact only a small hardship. Nevertheless, Major Kohler felt sure that Lieutenant Dzek would be grateful if he were taken a flask of hot soup, and would be even more grateful if the soup bearer stayed with him under the shadow of the eastern wall for an hour or so, easing the tedium of the afternoon with conversation about the Imperialist threat and the role of their country as mediator between East and West. This decided, Major Kohler quickly took two flasks and went unobtrusively to the side door of the Officers' Mess kitchens.

Two

FROM OUTSIDE THE Palace was given an appearance of unity by the continuous curtain wall. Once through one of the five gates in that wall and the true nature of the Palace, that of a tiny, haphazard medieval city, was immediately clear. The only historical unity within the walls was that of purpose — everything devoted to the service of the King, of his family, and of his favourites who made up the country's government. Church buildings proliferated; there were stables, barracks, arsenals, royal residences, quarters and offices for the various ministries. There was also a tiny school building where the King had allowed royal tutors to instruct the children of more senior Ministers. There were, of course, no shops or market places : local traders wishing to transact business had been obliged to do so in a cleared area outside the Palace walls.

At various times down the centuries encampments had grown up around this trading area, and even quite substantially built wooden houses. Fairs had been brought there for the entertainment of the Palace servants, and often contingents of the Palace Guard had been quartered there to relieve congestion within the walls. These settlements had proved themselves sadly vulnerable to attack, especially since at the first sign of danger the Palace closed its gates on friend and enemy alike. In the two hundred years of Mongol depredations alone, more than thirty such settlements had been razed to the ground, their inhabitants slaughtered or carried away to slavery.

The Palace itself had never fallen. The countryside around was not conducive to long sieges and its inhabitants preserved a perverse loyalty to their feudal ruler. Also invaders found that by the time they reached the Palace their lines of communication were too long to sustain a lengthy siege. Only the Tartars, whose fighting men seemed able to live on moss and bog-water for months on end, stayed long enough to bring serious privation within the Palace walls, and their visits were always cut short before the point of victory by the presence of easier, if not richer, prizes in the neighbourhood. The Tartars waged war not for the conquest of nations but out of a native restlessness and a desire for loot. The Palace was never considered worth the immense trouble involved in taking it.

The German invasion of 1943, which looked like providing a break with this tradition, was dealt with in a common-sense manner by the reigning monarch, Georg III, who surrendered his entire country roughly forty-five minutes after enemy troops had crossed its borders – this being the time required to get him out of bed with news of the attack and to convey his reaction to the German High Command. The peace that he negotiated placed the country at the disposal of the invaders while preserving the Palace inviolate. More than anything else it was this act of sophisticated treachery that brought his country to revolution the moment German strength was removed.

This ended the rule of a Royal Family that had remained in sole and ill-deserved control for nearly a thousand years, collecting during that time a fortune in gold and jewels and precious things impossible to catalogue. When the revolutionaries came, they struck so sharply and decisively against the leisurely Palace authorities that they were able to keep the treasure unplundered and virtually intact. Once again the King surrendered peacefully, this time in the hope of gaining later help from abroad. He and his entire family were quietly shot.

Only the Grand Salon was seriously damaged. Here a group of mutineers, separated for a short time from the discipline of their officers, lighted a bonfire of gilded chairs on the marquetry flooring. Fortunately their enthusiasm was ill-judged, for when the chairs and other furniture were nearly consumed they piled on tapestries and brocaded hangings so that the fire went out. The men concerned were sentenced to fifty lashes, one of them subsequently dying of gangrene.

In this way the Revolution created an image of civilised government. The ground floor of the former King's Residence was turned into a museum, as was the Cathedral of the Blessed Virgin. Tourists, if organised into proper groups, were encouraged : it was rightly thought that the grotesque splendour of these buildings would reflect unfavourably on the way of life that had created it.

Above the ground floor of the Residence, the Revolutionary government had established its principal offices in the rooms previously used for the accommodation of visiting notables. These were approached by a brown marble staircase of particular magnificence, the risers of which being inlaid, ormulu fashion, with a fine silvery tracery. It was on this staircase that Paul IX, in the presence of many courtiers and foreign emissaries, had killed his own brother in a passing fit of temper. The brother had been younger, weak in the head, no possible threat to the throne, and therefore much beloved. He had made some ill-judged joke – no historian knew or cared to disclose exactly what – while the Royal Family was on its way down to dinner, and the King, suddenly enraged, had struck him below the ribs with his jewelled ironwood staff. Blood had unaccountably spouted from the poor brother's mouth and he had rolled the length of the marble staircase, dead. At this the King's rage departed, leaving him broken-hearted, ravaged by grief.

Seeing it as an act of God's vengeance for the neglect of His Church in the land, the King summoned three thousand clerics to the Palace, berated them, and publicly burned one in ten in the square outside the Cathedral of the Blessed Virgin. In this way his brother became a martyr for the truth, and the staircase upon which he had died was officially named The Martyr's Staircase. Since the Revolution, it had been renamed The Murderer's Staircase.

The Murderer's Staircase was guarded night and day by six soldiers in revolutionary uniforms – suitably sombre after the theatrical excesses of the Royalist Guard. The French Ambassador once described these impassive guards to a friend as resembling six grey serge ant-hills. The staircase led to a first floor reception area panelled in oiled cedarwood, its ceiling supported by heavy onyx pillars, and off this foyer corridors led to the public offices of the more important Ministries. During the long office hours the foyer was always busy with messengers and minor officials, but its size was so great – from the head of the staircase to the back wall was upwards of a hundred metres – that it never seemed crowded. The private offices of the Ministries, where most of the work was done, were on the floor above. And above that again were two floors devoted to the living quarters of prominent members of the Central Committee, including of course the President. These floors could be reached by a separate and unobtrusive elevator.

To term the chambers on the first floor 'offices' is perhaps to give the wrong impression. These had once been the reception rooms, dining rooms and private suites of the most respected court guests, and their decor was suitably magnificent. The Minister for State Building, for example, did much of his administrative work in an enormous room that was nevertheless rendered charmingly intimate by a ceiling tented in soft green velvet, by the beauty of its Persian silk carpets, and by the placing of exquisite pieces of Chinese Chippendale to arrest the eye and prevent it wandering aimlessly in the ambient vastness. The Minister himself sat at a desk of local design and workmanship, not large but sufficient for his purpose. He had big leather armchairs for his visitors, and when these were of lower rank and also appreciative of his patronage, he would frequently leave his desk and sit with them, dispensing interminable anecdotes from the cigar- and leather-scented depths. A savage eye remained always watchful, however, in case his favours might fall on ungrateful ears.

Like all other Ministers, whether of Central Committee status or not, the Minister of State Building had an Aide who worked in an office adjoining that of his master. The Aide's office was perhaps smaller, but no less magnificent. Boris Kils was a youngish man of little presence but great conceit. He inhabited his office much in the manner of a hen who has wandered into a lady's boudoir, strutting grandly round it, glaring ignorantly and suspiciously at the furnishings, and uttering short unpleasant little remarks, like turds. These remarks were gathered up via the intercom by his secretary in the next room, who composed them into suitable inter-departmental memoranda. These fertilised the entire system and kept it running.

His office was also in constant communication with the tape recorders and monitoring services of the Internal Security organisation of Marshall Tarsu. There was no secret about this. Like everyone else in the Palace, Boris had learned to run his life accordingly.

This afternoon he stood with a letter in his hand and glared resentfully out of one of the two huge windows that lit his office. From this, the second floor of the Government Building, it was still impossible to see properly over the Palace walls, so his view was limited to the small deserted parade ground below. The uncleared snow on it had been scuffed and dirtied by endless drill parades. At one side there was a neat saluting dais, and for a moment this drew the Aide's attention away from the irritating contents of his

35

letter. He despised the Military. Men ought to be like himself, able to command respect and obedience without uniforms and service hocus-pocus. The thought cheered him briefly.

But the view was grey; dark grey snow on darker grey asphalt, black grey walls framing blacker grey windows, and over it all a grey sky heavy on the rooftops. It was getting ready to snow again the moment the temperature rose ... At the far corner of the parade ground an army officer appeared, walking briskly, a briefcase under one arm. Grey again. At that distance even the briefcase looked grey.

Boris turned back into the room. Even at two in the afternoon the light over his desk was switched on, and the one illuminating the Revolutionary Heroes. He walked to a side table and poured himself a glass of water.

"Some people ought to be pole-axed."

He drank the water. His stomach was troubling him. The heating in the lower offices dehydrated his very bone marrow, he thought. The humidifiers worked nowhere near as well as on the floors above.

"Or thrown to the people of the north and their dogs."

He smoothed his letter but did not re-read it. He knew every word, every innuendo.

"Whom precisely does Comrade Poldi think he is fooling?"

He circled the room, pecking scornfully at the furniture as he passed. At least it distracted him from Comrade Poldi.

"Artifacts of noble peasant origin." Peck. "Symbols of noble peasant aspiration." Peck. "Decadent propitiations from pampered Royalist lackeys, more like."

The words pleased him. Every time.

"Decadent propitiations from pampered Royalist lackeys."

He sat down at his desk.

"The Poldi file," he said in a quite unchanged tone of voice. It pleased him that the loudspeaker on his desk should provide an immediate reply.

36

"I have it in front of me, Comrade. I'll bring it through at once." Anna knew her job. She listened to every word. And read every document. Anna served more than one master. "And I have the Engineer Colonel here, Comrade. Here to see the Minister."

"Don't keep the Engineer Colonel waiting. Show him in at once."

His tone of voice flattered, his eyes did not. One half of the great double doors opened and the Engineer Colonel came in, his briefcase held almost protectively in front of him, smiling pensionably. The secretary followed him in, put the Poldi file on his desk, and went out again.

"My dear Engineer Colonel . . . so Monday has come round again. And – thanks to your stalwart efforts – our great and historic Palace still stands."

"A staff effort, Comrade Kils. I have good men under me. Very good men."

"All the same, Colonel, we all know what importance to attach to good leadership."

Boris always had a mild little game with the Engineer Colonel – flattery, he had discovered, was the one thing that unnerved the old soldier more than anything else. On this occasion, however, the Engineer Colonel seemed hardly to be listening, absorbed in anxiously trying to read the upside-down papers on the Aide's desk. It was as if he expected some particular item to be there but fervently hoped it was not. Boris watched keenly: the Engineer Colonel was worried about something, and insecure.

"Kind of you to say so, Comrarde. But if an officer hasn't learned to lead by the time he gets to my age, then – "

"But you don't look quite yourself, Colonel. Not ill health, I hope?"

"Certainly not. My health is excellent. Excellent."

It had to be. Six more months to retirement on a full General's pension.

"Then perhaps something is worrying you?"

"I don't think so, Comrade." An attempt at humour. "Should it be?"

"If I were in your position, Colonel, I think I'd be worried all the time." Boris kept his attack wide, to cover all possibilities. "Responsibilities such as yours would not sit lightly on my shoulders, I can tell you. But then, I have not your wide experience. And perhaps I am unfortunate enough not to be able to place such great faith in my subordinates."

Boris Kils was not a subtle man. His remarks were so heavily loaded as to be ludicrous. But to the anxious Engineer Colonel they meant one thing – all was lost. Into the office, seething with anger at Lieutenant Mandaraks' memorandum, he had come empty-handed. He tried to raise his own indignation at Major Kohler whose inexplicable disappearance had forced him into this impossible situation, but he knew that this was one of the few occasions when blaming others would be useless. With a memorandum of such potential importance he should have made the inspection himself. And so he would have done, if . . . if he hadn't felt so bloody lousy. He prepared to make a full confession.

At that moment the doors into the Minister's office were suddenly flung open, revealing the Minister himself. This was a gesture that might occur at any time, and partly accounted for the Aide's henlike jumpiness.

"My dear Grigor – so here you are. Boris hasn't been keeping you waiting, I hope?"

"Certainly not. He's been most kind. Most complimentary."

"But my dear Grigor, why should he not be? It is thanks to you entirely that we continue to enjoy immunity from the elements on this barren and unkindly plain."

The Minister was not a circuitous man. If the memorandum had reached him his greeting would have been very different. The Engineer Colonel adjusted his attitudes. The memorandum was being held at a lower level, had vanished into some pending tray perhaps, or had been totally lost even. This did happen to memoranda, the Engineer Colonel was sure of it.

Immediately the doors had closed upon the Minister and the Engineer Colonel, Boris forgot about the game he had been playing with the old man. You prodded a tortoise, it moved. It stopped moving, you lost interest. He returned to the file brought in to him by the secretary. The Poldi file.

Comrade Poldi was a building contractor with his headquarters in Dorlen. Heavy duty earth-moving equipment, pumps, cranes, cement mixers, any large machines that the Palace engineers did not think worth keeping on permanent establishment, these had over the last five years been obtained on hire from Poldi. There had never been any question of putting the work out to competitive tender: Poldi was the only man in Dorlen with suitable machinery. And although there was another contractor in Lyck away to the north, Boris had been able to assure the State Estimates Committee that the extra distance – nearly a hundred kilometres – made employment of the contractor in Lyck wholly uneconomic. In return for this repeated assurance to the S.E. Committee, Boris Kils had over the years received from Poldi considerable sums of money. These were paid to an account number at the National Bank in Dorlen and provided a useful emergency fund for Boris should he ever find it necessary to leave government service.

Nothing in this world, however, remains stable. Comrade Poldi now considered his position so secure that he had decided to do without his influential friend. The letter that Boris had been holding told him – by inference – so. "In future," ran Comrade Poldi's letter, "cash rebates will *on no account* be paid." And although the letter went on to explain in grovelling terms that rebates for prompt government payment should instead be deducted at source, the italics in the first sentence left Boris Kils with no doubts at all as to their real meaning.

Boris glanced through the file brought him by his secretary. He was placed in a difficult position. If he retaliated by taking government business elsewhere, the State Estimates Committee would demand good reasons. Poldi was efficient: his machinery arrived on time, did not break down, and was removed the moment any particular job was finished. After five years of faultless service Comrade Poldi was in a strong position, and he knew it.

Boris considered the possibility of an ideological objection. Pressure in that direction was always useful. But in all their five years of co-operation Boris had heard nothing against the contractor, not even the faintest rumours of unorthodoxy. And to manufacture a case from scratch would involve outside people, and would be dangerous. The excellence of the previous arrangement had always rested in its total lack of middle-men. Besides, ideological smears had been known to rub off on others.

Boris returned to the file. He noticed that Poldi had a son of military service age. This was interesting: if the young man were ambitious then the threat of a posting to some isolated dead-end station on the northern borders might well be enough to make his father see reason. Although Boris had no influence over postings at all, there was no need to tell Comrade Poldi so ... It was not as if payments in the past had been excessive – the man must be making a fortune out of government contracts one way and another. Enlightened Communism, some people called it. Capitalist exploitation, more like.

"Poldi," he announced, the decision made. "Put me through to his office in Dorlen."

"At once, Comrade."

He got up, strutted back to the window. Three minutes passed. He watched them on the grey clock overlooking the parade ground.

"The Poldi number," he said sharply. "If you've fixed your face, that is."

"The exchange is doing its best, Comrade Kils. Lines to Dorlen are very busy."

"You can't possibly know that until you've tried."

"I'll try them again, Comrade. They may have forgotten."

At that moment the buzzer sounded from the Minister's office. His Aide waited long enough to appear busy, then went to the double doors and opened them.

"Minister?"

"A small point regarding the Library Extension, Boris. The Engineer Colonel has brought up the question of the building schedule. Refresh my memory."

"We're using the old Refectory adjoining, Minister. Plans were approved for an intermediate floor, windows to be cut in the wall overlooking the – "

"I'm aware of that. I was referring to the work schedule."

"Existing fittings to be removed by the end of this month, Minister. Also the exterior scaffolding to be erected. New floors to be in by December seventeenth, I believe."

The Minister looked across at the Engineer Colonel and raised his eyebrows. The Engineer Colonel was perched on the edge of his armchair, a sheaf of papers on his knee, one of the Minister's cheroots held awkwardly in his
Aide heard his telephone begin to ring.

"A tight schedule," said the Engineer Colonel. "I don't think I was consulted?"

"That is so, sir. But the Minister of Education insisted."

"Comrade Korda may have the interests of the administration very much at heart, Boris, but not even he can control the weather." The Minister stretched and yawned. "Did he not realise that in December it has been known to snow?"

"Average snowfall of 2·7 metres," put in the Engineer Colonel.

"And that the erection of scaffolding under such conditions is difficult, not to say bloody dangerous?"

"I've no idea, sir. You discussed the matter with him yourself, Minister, over – "

"We all know that Comrade Korda likes to make a splash, Boris. And that for prestige reasons he receives priority often when others are less fortunate. . ."

The Minister tailed off. Criticism of an official as successful and popular as Comrade Sigmund Korda was always a delicate matter. Boris heard the telephone in the office behind him stop ringing.

"It has hardly snowed at all so far," he offered. "Perhaps the – "

"Perhaps the Minister of Education has made a special arrangement with the elements. And perhaps he hasn't." The Minister frowned. "Get him on the phone for me, will you, Boris?"

"Will that be possible, sir? I heard on Saturday that he planned to join a skating party to Novellnyi today."

The Minister stretched again and did several pleasurable arms-bends. His personality seemed to expand with secret knowledge, filling even the vast twilit emptiness of his velvet-hung chamber.

"Wherever else Comrade Korda may be, Boris, he will not be out with the Novellnyi skating party. . ." He suddenly sat up straight. "So get him on the phone for me, will you? Unless of course you're shy of troubling so great a man. . ."

"At once, Minister."

Back in his own office, with the interconnecting doors closed tightly behind him, Boris stood silently for a few seconds, considering this latest development. In any clash between the Minister for State Building and Comrade Korda, he had no doubt at all who would be the winner. But the skating party to Novellnyi was a different matter. What could there be about Korda's sudden change of plan that gave the Minister for State Building so much evident pleasure? Boris knew he was missing something.

He returned to his desk and contacted the Department of

Education. Comrade Korda was just on his way up to the Council Chamber for a special meeting of the Central Committee, but was willing to spare the Minister of State Building a few moments. Boris put him through to the next office and closed the circuit. Listening in privately to ministerial telephones was too dangerous to be worth it – the tapping devices up in the Communications Centre registered if a third person were sharing the line. But at least there was no longer any mystery over the skating party – if a special Central Committee meeting had been called then of course Comrade Korda had been obliged to give up his trip to Novellnyi. Boris returned to the problem of Poldi.

The exchange, suffering from pique, perhaps, took even longer to get the Dorlen number on the second try than they had on the first. But at last Comrade Poldi came through.

"Comrade Poldi? The Aide to the Minister for State Building speaking."

"Afternoon, Kils. Good of you to ring. How goes the revolution?"

"Your letter of the seventeenth instant received, Comrade, and its contents noted."

"Glad to hear it. Only saying to my wife the other day – "

"You will be receiving official acknowledgement in due course. The renewal of your contract is naturally a matter for the Committee to decide. But I think I can – "

"That's all right, then. So you're all still in one piece. Every morning I switch on the wireless, expecting to hear that the whole bang chute's slid quietly into the river."

Poldi was attacking by means of aggressive friendliness. As a counter to cold formality it was effective. Boris decided to modify his approach.

"The Palace has been here a long time, Comrade – I wouldn't be surprised if it didn't outlast the lot of us."

"I expect you're right. I often say to my wife, 'These

43

buildings we're putting up today, how will they look in a couple of hundred years?' 'Why should we care?' she tells me. 'We won't be here to see them.'"

"And how is your wife?" The ideal opening. "And the rest of your family? All well, I hope?"

"No complaints, Comrade. And you?"

"Flourishing, thank you. Never felt better . . . The Minister was talking to me the other day, asking about your family. I told him your son was of military service age. That is right, isn't it?"

"Quite right. He was eighteen last birthday."

"The Minister can be very helpful in these matters. He wondered if he could use his influence in any way."

"And him so busy. All the same, I don't think – "

"A word in the right place can make a great difference, Comrade Poldi. In either direction, you know. In either direction . . . After all, an ambitious young man can so easily get stuck in some backwater where his talents go unappreciated."

There was a silence at the other end of the line. Boris smiled to himself and stared up at the green velvet ceiling. Two and two were undoubtedly making four.

"Thank the Minister for me, will you, Comrade? Unfortunately in this case his help will be of little use. In either direction." Comrade Poldi paused. "My son, you see, is severely spastic. You will thank the Minister though?"

"My dear fellow – I'm so sorry. Believe me, I never dreamt. . ."

The words came automatically. Boris sat forward, slamming the Poldi file shut. The whole world was against him. What right had he to be afflicted with a spastic son? Privilege was everywhere; protected minorities sprang up as quickly as revolutions mowed them down. He interrupted Comrade Poldi's protestations, not even having heard them.

"Forgive me, Comrade. The Minister is buzzing me. He hates to be kept waiting."

"The prerogative of the great, Comrade. They beckon and we run. It's – "

Boris replaced the receiver gently, almost lovingly – the one gesture of power left to him. He tapped the closed file. He felt he had been made a fool of and his anger turned against his secretary for offering him an incomplete file – obviously the screening of Comrade Poldi had been dangerously inadequate. He got up slowly from his desk, intending to go and speak to Anna, his mouth already beginning to quiver with the rage it was about to express. But as he approached the outer doors they burst open in his face. An army officer, an Engineer Major, stood in the doorway. The secretary hovered behind.

"What the hell – "

"I'm sorry, Comrade. It is important that I speak with the Engineer Colonel. Your secretary – "

"You have no right to force your way into ministerial offices, Major."

"I'm sorry. But your secretary said – "

"My secretary has orders to exclude all visitors who do not have appointments."

"And so she would, I suppose, even if the Palace were burning down around you."

The Minister's Aide controlled himself. Even army ranks as low as major occasionally wielded unsuspected powers – it was always wise to take the temperature, to dip your toe in, as it were, before committing yourself.

"I'm not in the habit of being shouted at, Major. Will you kindly remember your manners."

"I'm sorry. It's just that. . ."

Knowing now that he was safe, Boris turned away. One of Tarsu's men would never have said he was sorry, and so obviously meant it. Boris moved slowly round behind his desk and leaned his knuckles on its surface, feeling power travel up out of it to suffuse his whole person. Army men were dregs. Army men he spat on.

"Also remember the respect due to the Minister's personal assistant, Major." The officer's mouth shut in a tight, thin line. "Close the doors behind you, Major. Unless of course you prefer brawling in public."

"I have no intention of brawling, Comrade Kils. Merely of – "

"Close the doors, I said."

The Aide's voice cracked slightly, but the Major did as he was told. Out of good manners if nothing else.

"That's better. Name?"

"Kohler. Major Kohler."

"Engineer's department, aren't you?"

"That's right. I have important information for the Engineer Colonel."

"Information is seldom as important as people think, Major. I expect yours can wait."

Boris sat down very gently. This Major Kohler should not be allowed to think that his information gave him status. It was probably dreamed up, half of it, anyway.

"Your Commanding Officer will be available in due course. He's in conference with the Minister at the moment."

"I know. I was hoping to see them both."

"And the nature of your business, Major . . . Kohler?"

"It's a matter for the Engineer Colonel and the Minister."

"I am the Minister's personal assistant, Major."

"I'm afraid I must insist, Comrade."

"You are in a position to insist upon nothing, Major Kohler."

The Aide opened a file – it happened to be the Poldi file – and studied it for some time. In his peripheral vision he could see the Major fidgetting, angry but not daring to show it. The scene in his office at that moment was a microcosm of the whole country, of the whole world. The army might have the guns, but the power to make decisions, the leadership, was in the hands of civilians. Guns were not enough.

Shouting was not enough. True leadership demanded something more.

"Do I get in to see the Minister or don't I?"

"Have a word with my secretary on your way out, Major. She will be able to arrange an appointment."

"But it's vital that — "

"It's always vital, Major. These words get over-used, don't you think?"

Major Kohler stared at him, then turned away and made straight for the doors into the Minister's office. Boris opposed force with intellect. The size of the room made it possible for him to measure his voice very calmly and still intercept the Major while he was three or four metres from the doors.

"Those are cupboard doors, Major. You may certainly look behind them if you wish." The officer hesitated, afraid as even a soldier must be of making a fool of himself. "The Minister's rooms are across the corridor. You can force an entrance there if you really think it advisable."

Boris knew he was safe, for the Major's moment of courage was past. He took one more impulsive stride forward, not quite believing, his hand within centimetres of the doorknob. Then he turned away and abruptly left the office. He went straight through the outer room without pausing, and Boris heard the far door open and then close behind him. The Aide uncurled his toes inside his shoes. How delicate it was, the balance of power.

"A Major Kohler," he said at his intercom. "Get me his file from Central Information." Then he laughed. "No," he said, "don't bother. There won't be anything in it. The man is an open book and open books bore me."

For that brief moment he felt at one with his office, with the entire Palace, sharing in its magnificence, partaking of its glory. The Cathedral clock began to strike three.

Three

As WELL AS being reached by The Murderer's Staircase via the first floor, the top two floors of the Government Building were also served by an elevator and a private stair. The elevator had been installed in the shaft of what had once been a secret staircase buried in the wall at the corner of the King's Wing. Secrets come in two equally useful kinds – those known by nobody and those known by everybody. The staircase up to the King's Disrobing Room had been in the latter category ever since the reign of young Paul IX who, having recently acceded to the throne partly by means of foreign assistance obtained through an advantageous marriage with the aged Bulgarian Princess Alicia, saw in the staircase a marvellous way out of his most pressing difficulty. It was during his reign that the staircase became known as the Virgin's Stair or the King's Relief.

The only person in the district who did not know of its existence, or who wisely feigned ignorance, was the Queen herself. It was during her reign that the separate Queen's Residence was built within the Palace Walls – it is not known at whose insistence.

After the Revolution the top floor of the King's Residence – now known as the Government Building – was divided into suites for the four most senior members of the Central Committee and their families. The President lived there, the Minister for Internal Security, the Minister for External Security, and the Minister of the Arts and Education. The inclusion of Sigmund Korda in such elevated company was a measure of his great nation-wide popularity rather than of the administration's respect for culture.

For the sake of convenience the President's Executive Assistant also had his quarters on the top floor. The perfect assistant, Raoul Novaks contrived to be everyone's friend.

The floor below the Minister's suites housed the centre of government for the whole country. Here the President had his offices, here the Central Committee met in a beautiful oak-panelled chamber looking westwards over the pine forests to the high distant lakes of Novellnyi, and here were the twin administrations of Internal and External Security. The third floor rooms of the building – once the King's private reception chambers – were, on their own smaller scale, probably the most magnificent in the entire Palace. The gilded decorations were heavier, the mirrors were more intricately cut, the marbles darker and rarer, the curtains richer, more fantastically looped and swagged. Much of the furniture in the royal suites was directly Russian in style, showing the natural admiration and awe felt by past kings for their mighty neighbour. Black lacquer predominated, with brass and marble inlays. The total effect was massive and barbaric. The President's private office, the room in which he spent most of his working day, was cluttered with splendour to the point of physical inconvenience. Squat sofas upholstered in white goatskin stood on a central blue and red Persian carpet. There was an ornate grand piano in a domed and mirrored recess. The walls were hung with antique weapons and a tower clock three metres high, carved from a single block of basalt to resemble exactly the mausoleum of Gustav II in the Cathedral of the Blessed Virgin, was positioned between the two main windows. The great stove in one corner was tiled with iridescent blue ceramics from the Beckel clayfields. Beside it a pile of pine logs was always drying, filling the room with a heavy resinous aroma.

D

The ornamentally vaulted ceiling was blue, painted in gold with suns, stars, and signs of the Zodiac, the bases of the arches resting on twisted golden pillars. The President's desk, one he had seen in a minor nobleman's country house, was a vast piece of plain teak, deeply chiselled round the edges and supported on four yellowed ivory elephants. Apart from the oil lamp which the President preferred to use, the only really personal touch in the room was the folding canvas campaign chair that stood in one of the deep window recesses beside the basalt clock. It was in this relic of his service days that he would sit, staring out across the eastern plain, and contemplate the problems of power.

The basalt clock was striking three as the tall figure of the Executive Assistant entered the room from the short corridor leading to the Central Committee Chamber. The unexpected meeting that afternoon had been troublesome. For once the President had come to it with his brief insufficiently prepared, and Novaks had been called on several times to give statistics and other information. This had put him seriously behind in his afternoon's work.

Before the Revolution Raoul Novaks had been a barrister, and therefore in close contact with the working of the King's justice. During the occupation the German courts had operated completely separately. His work took him into both judicial systems and, of the two, he preferred the German. At least it was frank about its oppressive purpose. As a patriot, however, he became – in spite of the dangers of his prominent position – a leading member of the Underground. This in turn led to his active participation in the revolution that came soon after the end of the war. A Party intellectual, the high office that should have been his persistently eluded him. Undoubtedly his upper-middle-class origins worked against him. The President, Marshall Borge, had come up through the ranks, his father a respectable stonemason. In the Palace there were many who said this was how the E.A. preferred to act, removed one step from the public eye. Others said he was simply waiting his moment. It had to be admitted that in the past Raoul Novaks had not shown himself a man to shun the public notice.

The sun was already low over the hills and the President's office was in semi-darkness. The E.A. did not turn on the lights, but made his way quickly across to the windows, weaving his way between the numerous gloomy pieces of furniture. All over the Palace servants came round an hour before sunset to close the shutters and draw the curtains. The President liked to do this job himself — he often chose to sit and stare out at the night, the size of his decisions diminished before the immensity of sky above the darkened plain. The E.A. stood for a moment, looking out not over the Palace walls but down three stories to the courtyard below. As he had expected, he saw the three press cars parked at the end of the row of official vehicles. His appointment with the editors had been for two thirty. He frowned, for he disliked unpunctuality — especially his own.

He went through into his own office, where the shutters had already been closed and the heavy purple curtains drawn. He spoke into the intercom.

"Maria? I've only just got away. You have three gentlemen waiting, I imagine."

"Half an hour, Comrade. They're not very pleased."

"Make my apologies and send them in, will you? Unexpected meeting of the Central Committee — you know what to say."

While he was waiting for the men to be shown in he took out his notes and read through the points agreed with the President. Of the three national newspapers, only the *People's Daily* was the official Party organ. The two weeklies — *Nation* and *People's Progress* — were allowed freedom of comment: freedom, that is, within the aims and ideals of the Party. Set rules within the aims and ideals of the Party. Set rules within which an infinite number of flexible strategies were possible. The E.A. had read his Koestler – it amused him that such a sophisticated intellect should talk disparagingly of 'closed systems of thought' instead of seeing the parallels between 'free' biological evolution and 'free' social evolution. Fixed rules and flexible strategies : the man might have been describing exactly the one party political system. The E.A. had almost decided to put out an essay on the subject. But motives could so easily be misunderstood, and political argument was still regarded with suspicion by too many people ... His line of thought was interrupted by the arrival of his guests.

"Good of you to come, gentlemen. Do please sit down. I expect my secretary has told you why this meeting is a little late in starting."

"State business comes first, Comrade Novaks. Naturally."

The editor of the Party organ spoke stiffly. He disliked being referred to as a gentleman.

"At the same time, my dear Alex, I often wonder if the business of the State is not often better served by you gentlemen than by us here in the rarified atmosphere of the Palace."

The three editors shifted on their chairs and exchanged glances. The E.A. smiled at them, well aware of the falseness of his words.

"Anyway, to business. I'll ask my secretary to bring in the samovar. Unless you would prefer something stronger ... Alex? Victor? Martin?"

Tea was decided upon, brought in on a massive trolley, poured and handed round. Also small circles of bread topped with caviar and pickled cucumber.

"The subject of this meeting, gentlemen, is the Minister of Art and Education, Comrade Korda." The E.A. glanced affably round, met by carefully blank expressions. "The Administration feels that when it has such a universally liked and respected member, it would be a pity to waste him ... Now, I think it was you, Martin, who brought up a few weeks ago the idea of doing Ministerial profiles in your paper. I'll admit we weren't enthusiastic – watchful always against any hint of the personality cult. But events mould decisions just as much as decisions mould events. In the difficult economic period that is ahead of us – mainly due to increased defence commitments on our southern frontier – it has seemed to the Central Committee that a humanisation of certain officials would be a reassuring move. Jolly things along, so to speak."

"And you want us to start with Comrade Korda?"

"Seems a likely opener, don't you think?"

"It would be more logical to begin with the Marshall himself."

"Too logical, my dear Martin. The strictness of the party hierarchy is already greatly exaggerated in the minds of the people. Marshall Borge would rather be placed further down the list, as a gesture of – of basic democracy, if you like."

In government circles all over the world there were certain words that brought an instant, reverential hush. Democracy was one of these. The three pressmen stared at the polished toes of their shoes. Naturally it was the editor of *People's Daily* who spoke first.

"In principle I agree with you, Comrade Novaks. My only reservation concerns the suitability of the Minister of Art and Education to launch the series."

"You may be right, Alex. Whom would you suggest as an alternative?"

Novaks could afford to be generous. Each of the three editors had his own favourite within the government – they were very unlikely to come to any agreement among themselves. He let them argue, and handed the plate of savouries round a second time.

"May I ask you, gentlemen, if any of you has any decided views *against* Comrade Korda's beginning the series?"

Again the toecaps received silent consideration.

"The Central Committee for its part is very strongly in

53

his favour, gentlemen. Journalistic innovations in this country receive a great deal of attention abroad – I'm sure you know that. Such interest is short-lived, like children they will study the first two or three, and then something else will take their fancy. The warmth of Comrade Korda's personality could do a lot to improve relations in many fields – notably in business and cultural exchanges. They have a saying in Britain, for example, that a country gets the rulers it deserves. We're all proud of Comrade Korda, so why not say so?"

To deny being proud of Comrade Korda was out of the question. In the country at large he was known to be the President's favourite, and almost certainly next in succession for the leadership. The three editors agreed to using him with a fair show of enthusiasm.

"Enough material for a dozen stories..."

"The right origins. And of course the Resistance record..."

"And the horse. We may use the horse?"

"Of course." The E.A. smiled. "He's not the Minister of Transport or of Scientific Progress. Be as picturesque as you like. You'll each of you want to angle it in your own way. All right – he's larger than life. But he's also efficient. He gets things done. He may ride round to inspect his schools on a jet-black charger, but remember there are now two hundred more schools for him to inspect than there were before the Revolution. He may write poetry, but remember his Literary Panel has assisted seventy-three writers, eleven of which have subsequently become international figures. He's a young man, and he gets things done, gentlemen. Remember how he started his career as assistant schoolmaster in a mining village near Pol."

The E.A. did not have to pretend to be enthusiastic. Sigmund Korda was one of the most dynamic figures in the government, and a sincere Party man as well. The difficulties ahead of him would enlarge his capacities – nobody gave of their best who had not come up against harsh opposition. The E.A. himself had battled against prejudice of all kinds : against class prejudice, against intellectual prejudice, even against fear of his internationalism – an education in Paris and a period practising in Vienna had been hard to live down. A little adversity harmed nobody. Comrade Korda would emerge a bigger man, just as he, Raoul Novaks, had done.

"Anyway, gentlemen, you must have all the details on your files. Don't hesitate to appeal to me if there's anything more you want to know."

The newspapermen drew in their feet and prepared to stand. The editor of *Nation* cleared his throat.

"One point remains outstanding, Comrade." It was odd how the atmosphere of the Palace forced a formalised jargon on people, no matter how much the E.A. tried to set an example in the other direction. "The question of subsequent profiles, Comrade. Has the Central Committee any views in this respect?"

"Nothing rigid, Martin. Sort it out among yourselves." There would be no subsequent profiles, not if the Korda profile caused all the trouble the President hoped it would. "The Minister for State Building next, perhaps? Or Agriculture, if you like. Somebody fairly uncontroversial. Let us have a list some time. But I'm sure there won't be any difficulty."

The three men had stood up now and were getting ready to go. Novaks judged the moment to be right.

"Just one small thing, gentlemen." Their heads turned. "His country lodge in Paskellnyi – there's no need to make too much of it, I imagine?"

"Country lodge?" It was Martin who first picked it up, as the E.A. had anticipated. "What about his country lodge?"

"Senior Ministers do have an allotment for the purpose." The E.A. temporised, managing to exhibit just a shade of embarrassment. "Surely you knew that?"

"Of course." Martin became pious. "Our leaders have

heavy responsibilities. Nobody should grudge them places for relaxation and recreation."

"Of course not, Martin. Of course not...I should have known not to bother mentioning it."

"Not mentioning what, Comrade Novaks?"

"You must be more explicit, Comrade Novaks."

Victor now had joined the attack. Years of Party directives had not dulled journalistic aggression, merely bottled it up. Signs of official weakness were what they prayed for. Even Alex, a man to whom only obedience and efficiency were possible, showed malicious interest. The E.A. was careful not to capitulate too easily.

"Really, gentlemen, this isn't an interrogation. I think you forget where you are."

"You ask us to be tactful, Comrade. We have to know what it is we are to be tactful about."

The E.A. waved a beautifully relaxed hand. Too relaxed.

"Rumours, my dear Martin. Only rumours..."

"What rumours?"

"If you haven't heard them, then it doesn't matter. Anyway – " taking refuge in jargon – "the spreading of such unfounded slurs would be an action contrary to the best interests of the State."

"Slurs against the Minister of Education? Rumours about his country lodge?"

"You would not force me to be disloyal, would you, Victor? My mistake was to assume you moved in the same bad company as I do and heard the same libels."

"Our associates are often worse, Comrade Novaks, than any you need ever deal with."

"And if even they have heard nothing, then there's obviously nothing for me to worry about."

"But – "

"And nothing for you to worry about either, my dear Martin."

The E.A. left his desk and went smoothly to the door.

He had guarded his actions for so many years that he was by now, when he wished to be, readable on an emotional level of which most other people were not even aware. The over-confidence of his walk spoke insecurity. He opened the door for the three editors.

"Thank you for coming, gentlemen. I suggest that you visit the Central Photograph Agency. They may have some pictures not on your files. And remember – anything else you need to know, please don't hesitate to get in contact."

Each shook hands as he went out. Alex was last, and stayed a moment, pressing Novaks' hand reassuringly.

"Don't worry," he murmured. "I'll talk them out of too much poking around."

"Bless you, dear Alex. Do your best."

He watched them walk away between the yellow watered-silk walls of the corridor, staying to wave just a little longer than usual. Alex's best would not be good enough. Muck would be raked, self-righteousness would blossom, and Sigmund Korda would totter very slightly. Marshall Borge was going to be pleased with the progress made. And the Marshall's wife . . . well, her reaction was better left without comment.

Novaks had a sudden idea, and returned quickly to his desk. He rang down to the office of the Minister for State Building. He was connected with the Minister's Aide.

"Hullo? Boris – how are you, my dear fellow?"

"Very fit, thank you, Comrade Novaks."

"I haven't seen you for ages, Boris. Tell me, is the Minister busy?"

"He's still in conference with the Engineer Colonel. But I could easily – "

"It doesn't matter. I'd rather deal with you, anyway."

"Tell me how I can be of service, Comrade Novaks."

The E.A. sensed the wariness behind the other's words. Always afraid he was going to be taken advantage of, always cautious of committing himself. In the past Novaks had seen him in action at close quarters – it was neither a likeable nor an efficient performance.

"Boris, in a minute or two you're going to receive a visit from some newspapermen – if my guess is right. I want you to tell them nothing. Nothing at all."

"Nothing?" Instantly alarmed. "Nothing about what?"

"The building programme in connection with Ministers' country lodges. Tell them you deal with all accounts personally, and that there have been no irregularities. The Minister would not tolerate any."

"That's quite right, Comrade. The Minister – "

"Tell them what I said, Boris. Nothing else."

"Of course not, Comrade Novaks. There's nothing else to tell."

"Good man." The E.A. paused. "They may be very insistent. But I know you won't let them shake you."

"You can rely on me."

By now the Minister's Aide was in a complete panic. The E.A. listened to several seconds of his silent agony. He gave the other no help, and finally the block was overcome.

"You mentioned irregularities, Comrade Novaks. Surely there are no . . . irregularities?"

"You said you knew of none, my dear Boris."

"Yes, I did. But it's always possible that – "

"Then you're in the clear. You've got nothing to worry about."

"No. No, I suppose not. . ."

The E.A. decided to close the conversation on a comforting note. He did not want to appear to be intentionally spreading anxiety and alarm.

"Anyway, these chaps may not bother you. I've done my best to put them off, short of invoking the Security Clause. And it's never worth doing that for footling little points like this."

"No. No, I suppose not . . . Anyway, thank you for warning me." There was a sudden break. Then, almost in a

58

whisper," My secretary tells me they're here now. I must ring off." And the immediate clatter of a worried man.

The E.A. sat back contented. Poor Boris would give a thoroughly unconvincing performance. Martin and Victor would leave his office convinced that the Administration was attempting to conceal something seriously discreditable. The machine for discrediting Comrade Korda had been assembled and set in motion. From now on it would run its own course.

Abruptly the E.A.'s mood changed. His self-satisfaction left him, was succeeded at once by weary self-distaste so intense that he felt aware of every wrinkle, every patch of dried sweat, every greasy pore on his whole body. And every dishonesty too, every squalid deceit conceived by his mind and uttered by an irretrievable act of conscious will. He knew despair. And in the same moment he knew this despair to be endemic to his nature, irrational, a complaint to be looked at coldly, externally, like stomach ulcers or constipation. Yet he needed protection against it, instant consolation : the mood, once on him, spun him downwards faster than his mind could devise. And the consolation, even as he sought it, was known to be hollow. It rested on judging acts by their outcome, by what they achieved. And achievement was like the shaping of mists . . . His span of life was infinitesimal, its path downwards. So the German was driven out by lying and deceit, so the Revolution came about, so he helped by lying and deceit to create a better life for his people. The lying and deceit did not end, could never end. His span was infinitesimal, its path downwards, his achievement like the shaping of mists. For him to seek consolation was for him to admit being beyond consolation.

A part of his mind saw the false circularity of this. Just as a part of his mind watched himself cover his face with his hands, sob, drag his fingers down, pulling at the grey-skinned eye sockets, bow his head and rock with primeval fear . . . seeing in all this a needless theatricality, a performance put on for his own benefit. Laughable, but doubtless therapeutic. Within another ethos he would have been seeing devils. What he saw instead was futility. Some minds needed devils. For him it was futility, a luxury, an excusable self-indulgence.

This was the part of his mind, the Puritanical part, that pulled him out; also that kept his lapses for the privacy of his office or his bedroom. He had not married – the companionship of a wife would have brought with it more problems than it solved. Once only had his secretary intruded unasked at the wrong moment – thereafter she invariably knocked and tried again five minutes later if there was no answer. She would have liked to be let into his mind, she would have liked to become his mistress, she would have liked to be allowed to love him. The watching part of his mind knew all this, and sealed him away. It felt its hold to be tenuous, the secrets it knew incommunicable.

As he rocked backwards and forwards at his desk under the brilliant chandelier and the blue and gold ceiling, his mind in two parts, allowing itself briefly the sensuous joy/agony of free fall, the fact slowly penetrated his confused consciousness that one of the telephones in front of him was demanding his attention. The white telephone, connected directly to the Central Committee Chamber.

"E.A. speaking." Hand and voice operated automatically.

"File wanted on the revised pension proposals, Raoul. Sorry to bother you."

"At once, Marshall."

How pointless to be depressed by pointlessness. The only necessary point to any one minute was that it succeeded the one before it. Raoul Novaks rose stiffly from his desk, fetched the relevant file and carried it quietly along the short corridor to the Central Committee Chamber. It amused him that his moods really were so easily shaken off, proving them to be no more than self-indulgence. He tried to be less Puritanical, and to argue why not? He smoothed his hair, entered the Committee Chamber without knocking.

"Thank you, E.A. See to the windows while you're here, will you?"

The E.A. went to the first set of narrow, deeply recessed windows. Behind him he could hear the President opening the file and sorting through the papers.

"Five and a quarter million was the figure I was looking for. On a one per cent consumer tax. Not enough to hold present levels, you see."

"We're all agreed that a pension cut is necessary, Comrade President." The Minister for Economic Security sounded peevish. "We agreed that last week, I thought. It's the nature of the cut which was under discussion."

The E.A. closed both shutters and latched them. He drew together the stiff brocade curtains. He turned and glanced briefly round the room. Seven people, five men and two women, at a large horseshoe table. Pools of brightness, drifting cigarette smoke, hands that moved unexpectedly from dark into light and back again, a curiously musty smell, almost of incense. A sensation of weight, of importance. So often false. The E.A. moved the few paces round to the next window and looked out. It was beginning to snow.

". . . review of the entire pension structure. I take it you have all read it?"

"This meeting is too soon, Comrade President. The report was only circulated on Friday. We. . ."

Of course the meeting was too soon. The E.A. smiled to himself. Through thickly falling snowflakes he made out a small convoy of lights clearing the edge of the forest and approaching the Patriot's Gate in the northern wall of the Palace. He knew it must be the skating party on its way back from Novellnyi. He closed the shutters. The snow had held off for them and he was glad.

Four

In the mountains the snow had begun to fall nearly an hour before. Katarin was not sorry. The lakes were beautiful and skating the nearest she ever came in her life to poetry. But even these joys needed to be shared. To skate alone over the hissing ice was only bearable for so long before the dreamlike quality turned to nightmare. The sky and the blank face of the lake joined to make a greyness like the greyness of nothing, the grey nothing that recurred in her dreams, that terrified her so that she woke sweating to lie cold and alone beside the thick imperturbable sleep of her husband. She was a large, practical person : she knew it was foolish to dream of grey nothingness, even more foolish to be afraid of it. She knew also that her dreams would be different if the man she lay beside were Sigmund. Just as the lakes would have been different if there had been Sigmund to share them with. With him she could have skated on and on, far into the night.

That was what the others wanted to do, though for what reason she could not guess, since they only circled staidly, close to the food baskets, four rich women practising their outer and inner edges, thick legs ungraceful, matronly bodies afraid of falling. Matronly – that was the reason. If they skated on after nightfall it would be romantic, it would remind them of other occasions, other companions. Katarin was of an age with the other wives – a year or two younger, perhaps, but no more – yet her total fascination with the

62

present, each successive moment of it, separated her from them as if she had been a child and they her elderly female relatives. Or was it her being Katarin Borge, the President's wife – was what separated her? . . . She had agreed to staying, had ordered the men to fetch a great pile of wood for the fire. She had really had no alternative, being the President's wife. But she had been glad to see the snow start to fall shortly before two. There had been a weighty, determined look about it. "The first real snow this winter," they said, hurrying to unlace their skates.

On the way back she drove the big black Czech Opel herself. The army chauffeur had been reluctant, but what could he say against Katarin Borge, wife of the President? She told him she had driven a six-wheeled truck for the Resistance, which was not quite true. She had been sixteen and skinny, and they had given her a motor bicycle instead. But the six-wheeled truck had been hers a few years later, thundering through the Maria Irene Gate into a Palace only recently taken by General Orrin Borge. The narrow streets inside had been chaotic. Held up in some tiny arcaded square, somebody had shouted to her that she was passing the place where the King had been executed. The place had seem wrong, too prettily Italianate. Then the column of vehicles had moved on, and she had taken a wrought iron lamp bracket away with her tailboard. Her co-driver had laughed, and she had felt ashamed.

She drove the Opel in complete isolation, the chauffeur sitting silently beside her, the rear lights of the outriders glaring in the cleared segment of windscreen in front of her. Snow ran down the heated glass and froze in windblown streaks on the bonnet. She was glad to be shut off from the rest of the car : five rich women undergoing air-conditioned travel in the back of a car with blind windows – it was unnatural, faintly disgusting. She did not like women, squashy women pressed against her, murmuring details of illness and clothes and sex. This segregated

63

skating was ridiculous. As soon as she had heard there was to be a Special Meeting so that the men could not come, she should have called the whole thing off. A group of middle-aged women, too highly-placed to dare to be human, going off together on a skating party – it was ridiculous. On their own they might, in their own way, have enjoyed themselves. But she had to go along with them, it was expected of her. Even though she seldom knew what to say to them, or they to her. They were wary of her, of her strong arms and broad shoulders, and their unspoken questions sickened her. She would never tell them the things they longed to hear. Out of reserve she would not tell them. Out of modesty.

Alone in the front of the Opel, with the army chauffeur a professional blank, not a person, she patiently followed the red lights of the outriders. She allowed herself ecstatic half-dreams. Waking dreams of herself and Sigmund.

As they approached the Palace, lights began to appear through the falling snow. The curved arch of the gate itself, brightly lit, and above the wall a few windows still unshuttered. Katarin identified the Central Committee Chamber, five neat slots in a close group. They went out one by one as somebody closed the shutters. Sigmund was up there. And her husband Orrin. The juxtaposition did not worry her. Sigmund was the man she loved, Orrin was her husband. In the circumstances of their lives divorce was not practicable, so it was for Orrin to be civilised. He was older than she; they had given each other nearly twenty years of mutual fidelity. She never doubted that Orrin would in fact be civilised, that he was capable of it. The last twenty years had shown him capable of being the most civilised man she had ever known. Since by her own definition being civilised implied the ability when necessary to be intelligently unemotional, she herself was probably one of the most uncivilised people in the Palace.

The feel of the car's tyres changed from snow to wet

64

cobbles under the gate. Yellow light poured through the windscreen, illuminating for the first time in more than an hour the lumpish face of the chauffeur. Katarin returned the salute of the guard. She drove through steep, snow-confused streets to the west wing of the Government Building. There she quickly left the driver's seat and hurried into the shelter of the portico. The snow fell steadily, covering her footprints even as she stood and watched.

One of the other women in the car – wife of the Minister for External Security – climbed out and the chauffeur drove away. The remaining three were quartered in the old Queen's Residence by the Gustav basilica. Katarin waited, stamping her feet. She was eager to recreate the illusion of an outing, to go up making plans to recreate the illusion of an outing, to go up in the elevator talking of the fun they had had and making plans for the next time. She felt sorry for her behaviour on the return journey and guilty for having shirked what she saw as her responsibility. She might be Sigmund's lover in private, but in public she was the President's wife. So she waited for the awkward woman to stumble through the snow to her, and laughed, and helped her shake it off her thick fur hood.

"Comrade Katarin Borge – a word with you please?"

She looked out into the falling snow, saw the broad, capable Guard Commandant approaching. He was smiling, his smooth face as incongruous as ever above the stiff grey greatcoat. He always looked rosy and shining, as if he had just come from an over-hot shower.

"Is it likely to take long, Colonel Balenkov?"

"A minute, Comrade. No more."

She let the other woman go up alone. Balenkov interested her. He had a solidarity older than his years. She decided to be haughty. He was an attractive man, and she had at receptions noticed how he made a woman feel interesting and worth talking to. It was strange that he had remained so long unmarried.

"Are you on duty, Colonel? Is this an official conversation?"

"I tell my guards they are always on duty. Sometimes rather more than others, that's all."

"A good answer, Colonel. My curiosity is aroused. Shall we walk?"

"This country is no place for people who mind a little snow. I'll be glad to."

The air was still, snowflakes falling so regularly that they seemed to be part of an illusion, the same flakes falling and rising somewhere behind the scenes to fall again. Katarin went down the steps to where the Colonel was standing, and the two of them turned left, in the direction of the Cathedral. They walked for nearly a minute in complete silence.

"The guard on the Patriot's Gate reported to me that you were driving the presidential car, Comrade."

"That is so. Am I to be reprimanded for it?"

"The chauffeur is a trained man. He has his duty to do."

"And I am a bored woman, Colonel. I gave him an order which he had to obey."

"He receives his orders from me, Comrade Katarin. Orders that are intended for your protection."

"Protection . . ." She shook her head angrily. "Protection from what? Is the man to be punished?"

"He will get into trouble, naturally. I ask you not to place him in such a difficult position again. The roads through the forest are treacherous. Responsibility for the lives of passengers is not to be taken lightly. Besides, it is a simple matter of discipline. As the Marshall's wife I know you will understand what that means."

He spoke calmly and reasonably, doing no more than his job, and she did not resent what he said. She looked away, up at the building they were passing, the brightly painted stucco of its façade hidden behind a thick screen of snowflakes. A structure that had once housed clerks and clerics and bishops in ermine and gold, it was now head-quarters for the Palace Military, the Guards and the Engineers. Behind its carved shutters were orderly rooms, stores, cells, and the quarters of the more senior unmarried officers. Colonel Balenkov would have his rooms somewhere along its marbled corridors.

"Are we really so important?" she said. "Five useless women? Are we really so necessary?"

Colonel Balenkov made no reply. He smiled at her, rosy-faced and innocent.

"I know, Colonel — we are as necessary as we care to make ourselves..." She reverted to the former topic. "I drove a lorry in the Revolution. I can handle a car as well as any of your drivers."

"Better perhaps. Whatever you do, you put all you have into it. Nevertheless..."

He spread his gloved hands in the darkness. His voice had been too level for what he said to be taken as flattery. What he said was true — and what she had was worth more than running her apartment and its small staff of servants, more than organising banquets, more even than providing a conversational foil for the Marshall and sleeping with him on the rare occasions when he could stay awake long enough. Balenkov must have sensed her changing mood, for he paused in the light of a street lamp. Against it the falling snowflakes were black.

"People say that the President is tired," he said. "You should persuade him to take a long rest. The State needs him, but no man is indispensable. You have a country house. For his own good you should persuade him to go there."

"What has this to do with my driving, Colonel?"

"Nothing. Nothing at all."

She walked on slowly, giving him no help. He must come to what he had to say on his own.

"I say what many people think, Comrade Katarin. And

67

I dare to speak because I think you know how much I respect you. And the President."

The last three words were added so flatly as to be significant for that very reason. Katarin brushed away the snow gathering round the inside of her hood. Balenkov was trying to say something he found very difficult. A declaration of personal rather than official regard, perhaps. She would not be angry with him – he was a man she admired and she was glad to be admired in return. She found his fumbled approach endearing and his admiration would always be far too distant to be a source of embarrassment. She paused close to the next street lamp and let him take his time.

"I was in the same Revolutionary Battalion as Sigmund Korda – did you know that?"

"No, I didn't." The apparent switch annoyed her. "Do you come from the same province?"

"Not at all. Drafting was very haphazard in those days. Our different talents were needed, so we were sent. The Battalion stayed in Lorgnyi, down in the south, for more than three months."

"Unusual, for those days."

"During that time, Comrade Katarin, we courted the same girl. We both fell in love with a schoolmaster's daughter called Amélie."

"But that's the name of – of Comrade Korda's wife. You mean to say, Colonel, that you were once in love with little Amélie?"

She thought she understood. He was explaining his unmarried state, the broken heart he had cherished for twenty years, the angel he had been willing to worship from a distance. He would be afraid of anything approaching a real human relationship. His face was the outward sign of his nature – he had never grown up. Katarin turned to him. His shoulders were thick with snow, even the peak of his cap.

68

She could see his face clearly in the light from the street lamp.

"You mean to say you were once in love with little Amélie, Colonel?"

"I was, Comrade Katarin, and in many ways I still am. Which is why I – " He hesitated, removed his cap and brushed the snow from it with his sleeve. "Which is why I cannot bear to see her hurt, Comrade."

"Amélie? Hurt? I'm afraid I don't understand you."

"I think you do."

She had spoken the truth. Not once in the past months had she given a thought to Amélie, to Sigmund's wife. She suffered her migraines. She was of no account. Now Colonel Balenkov's meaning suddenly reached her. And the meaning of his suggestion that she should take Orrin away to their country house for a long rest. She stared at Colonel Balenkov, standing bare-headed in front of her, her anger mounting. He was a brave man, he was telling her to keep off Sigmund Korda. But he was a fool also, and arrogant. It was no business of his how she conducted her life. It was insufferable that he, an outsider, Captain of the Guard, her husband's guard, should dare to speak to her like this. She thought too of how a moment before she had been on the point of –

"You will be angry, Comrade Katarin, but – "

"Tell me, Colonel Balenkov, have you spoken to the Minister of Education on this matter? I would have thought an approach to him the more manly way."

"The Minister laughed, Comrade. He asked me why I was minding this time when there had been so many other – "

Katarin struck him across the face with the back of her gloved hand. She used all her strength, so that he staggered.

"You are a liar as well as a fool, Balenkov. Believe me, you will regret this evening's idiocy."

There was a shout from the steps of the Military Headquarters. The figure of an officer came running through the snow towards them. The officer – he was a major – stopped abruptly as he recognised the bare-headed figure of Colonel Balenkov. The Colonel stared at him. He saluted awkwardly.

"You wanted something, Major Kohler?"

"I'm sorry, Colonel. I thought I saw . . ." He caught sight of Katarin's face deeply framed by her hood. Momentarily he lost the power of speech.

"You thought you saw what, Major?"

"I – I was mistaken, Colonel. Please accept my apologies for intruding."

Katarin smiled as she watched the oaf Balenkov attempting to bluster himself out of an impossible situation. Unless this major was a man of exceptional discretion, the story would be round the Palace within hours. Balenkov was already ruined.

"No doubt you had good reasons, Major."

"No, sir. I was completely mistaken, Colonel."

"You have something you ought to be doing, Major Kohler?"

"I was on my way to see the Engineer Colonel."

"Then do not let us keep you."

"No, Colonel. At once."

The Major saluted, and turned to go.

"And Major – a little more discretion in future, I think. One can make oneself appear foolish, to say the least."

Major Kohler made no reply, but hurried away through the thickening snow. The President's wife cleared her throat.

"Advice for him, or for yourself, Balenkov? Not that he will follow it."

"There are some matters which go beyond questions of discretion, Comrade Katarin." With dignity he brushed the snow from his hair and replaced his cap. "And at least you have given me a frank answer, which I appreciate." He saluted her very formally, then turned and walked quickly away in the direction of the Cathedral. Katarin watched him go. When it came down to it, all some men had left was their dignity.

As she returned to the Government Building the snow on the ground was nearly over the tops of her boots. Even at that early hour the sky was quite dark, its darkness marvellously furnishing endless grains of white. High above her the great Cathedral clock was muted as it struck four thirty. Katarin did not hurry. The gently hypnotic sameness of the falling snow helped her to think.

She had to tell her husband about the incident with Colonel Balenkov before he learned of it from any other source. She wondered what else Orrin might have learned from other sources. Up until then she had blindly assumed her love for Sigmund to be a secret between the two of them : when they were together the outside world ceased to exist, and at other times these moments seemed to have no more substance than dreams. Yet Balenkov knew, and probably the whole Palace knew. And Orrin? What about Orrin – would his need not to know perhaps have kept the information from him?

She was not afraid of his knowing, but the knowledge would demand a change in their relationship. An easing, a disengagement. She would have told him herself weeks ago if she could have found the words. It was necessary now to make certain, to cut somehow through the pretences that had grown onto her life like fungus. She would speak to Orrin at once.

She passed the turning to the entrance in the west wing and went on down the side of the Government Building to Revolution Square. The shutters at the windows of the jewelled reception salons here were seldom closed, and the lights inside shone out brilliantly through the thickly falling snow. The Square was busy with officials coming and going, collars turned up, fur hats pulled well down. Katarin paused to watch a motor cyclist slither away round a corner, buried in the snow nearly up to his axles. Snow falling like this in still air might continue till dawn, then the sky would clear and the temperature drop. Next morning the ploughs would be out, and the motor sleds. When the snow had packed down and frozen it would be really winter, the time for riding out in diamond-sharp mornings, crossing the northern plain to the peopled silence of the forests, or travelling up by motor sled to the ski slopes above Novellnyi before the cold tightened and the snow became dangerous. Sigmund skied like a master. With him she lost her nervousness, drew confidence from him so that she really moved, really felt with him the rhythm and the stride, the curling, creaming hiss as they leaned together, cutting across the cloudlike hillside and down between the flashing trees. On her own the unstoppable headlong descent terrified her. He had once told her she skied like a heron in thick woollen underwear. She was better at skating – it gave her the possibility of second thoughts.

She slowly climbed the steps to the main entrance. Already the guards were out, shovelling the snow away in piles on either side. She stamped her feet to shake off the worst of the snow, and went through the massive oak doors into the Government Building. The guard on the door recognised her and saluted. She responded pleasantly and walked past him into the brilliant Entrance Salon, the heat there striking her face so that for a moment she could not breathe. She made her way quickly across the crowded floor, climbed The Murderer's Staircase, and went on up to the third floor. She looked in on the E.A.'s secretary.

"Snowing hard, Maria. Winter's come at last."

"I hope it didn't spoil the skating, Comrade Katarin."

Katarin frowned. She wondered if there was anything behind Maria's words, the suggestion that she knew more about the skating party to Novellnyi than she was admitting. Katarin checked herself. She liked Maria and had always trusted her. That way of thinking was accumulative,

72

hysterical. You could find hidden motives everywhere, once you started looking.

"We had the whole morning." She unzipped her coat and took it off, throwing it casually onto a chair. "It held off till after lunch, so we had a good three hours . . . Any sign of the Marshall, Maria?"

"The meeting ended about ten minutes ago. I don't know if he's still in the Council Chamber."

Maria got up and crossed to the coat Katarin had thrown on a chair. She picked it up, carried it into the tiny adjoining washroom and shook the snow off it onto the tiled floor. Idly Katarin watched her hang it up on a hanger. The girl was implying no disapproval – she simply disliked to see fine things not properly looked after. It was a sound working class attitude. Katarin herself – of equally proletarian background – had no such delicate feelings. Things were to be used and discarded. Given another position in life and she would have become fat and sluttish and of uncertain temper.

"Shall I ring through and find out?" said Maria, returning from the washroom.

"Don't bother, dear. I'll go and see for myself."

The girl's office oppressed her: it was too small for the amount of furniture stuffed into it. The whole Palace was like that of course. Perhaps it was symbolic of the Administration – too much ancient furniture, valuable only on account of its antiquity. She did not pursue this line of thought, for it was power that interested her, not government. She went into the silk-lined corridor and along to the Council Chamber.

As she approached the door it opened and the Minister for Internal Security came out. Seeing her, he closed the door behind him and advanced quickly. The job he did was that of Chief of Secret Police, but his official title was almost as pretty as his uniform. He wore clothes well, and had a hearty, unsinister manner, with an easy way of purs-

73

ing his lips and tipping his head from side to side as if nothing mattered.

"You're looking very healthy, Katarin. Looking for your husband, eh?"

"I've been for a walk. It's snowing hard."

"That's it, then. I thought something had bucked you up."

"Do I usually look so ghastly, Karl?"

"No fishing for compliments. We all get to look a bit grey, living in this damned central heating."

"I expect you're right. You were going to tell me where to find Orrin."

"Just gone up. It wasn't a very long meeting." He seemed to be edging her away from the Council Chamber. "And you've been skating . . . how's the ice at Novellnyi? I heard it was bumpy."

"It's wearing down nicely. The peasants must get out on it when nobody's looking."

"Ah, a job for my spies. I must send a team over immediately."

Even for him the jocularity was forced. He was handling her badly. Katarin disengaged herself.

"Nonsense, Karl. I'm very grateful to them."

"But I wasn't joking, Katarin. Private property is private property, even in a Communist country."

"You've got that wrong." She needed to prove her own immunity. "In our country it's Palace property that's private property. Anybody knows that."

He shook his head at her sadly, pursing up his lips at the heresy almost as if he wanted to kiss her. But he lived alone and kissed nobody. It was this, she suddenly saw, that disturbed her most about him : his lack of physicality, of sex, she supposed. In other times Karl Tarsu might have been a priest, kissing books and altars . . . She left him and went quickly to the door of the Council Chamber. With her hand on the latch she turned and looked back; he was

74

watching her, but he made no move to stop her. She opened the door and went in.

The large room was in semi-darkness and she entered quietly, thinking at first that it was empty. Then she saw Raoul Novaks seated in the middle of the horse shoe table, in her husband's place. He was looking straight at her down one of the curved sides of the table, and he sat so still that at first she thought he was in some kind of trance.

"You catch me at the schoolboy's game, Comrade Katarin." He remained so still that she jumped slightly at the sound of his voice. "Sitting in his master's seat, in the seat of fear, trying to see the world through his eyes. Trying to get up high enough to be able to look down."

She wondered what this talk hid, what private words had been passing between him and the priestly Marshall Tarsu. At last Novaks moved, smiled, stood up and came towards her.

"Not with longing, I promise you, Katarin. Nor with secret hubris. An attempt, on a superstitious level if you like, to understand the workings of your husband's mind. Only so may I be able to ease his burden."

The room was sound-proofed and totally still. She felt unnerved, for reasons she could not analyse.

"Another one talking to me about the weight of Orrin's responsibilities?" she said, reminded of the outrageous Balenkov. "Is the whole Palace convinced that he's about to pack up altogether?"

"He's tired. Perhaps you're too close to him to notice."

"Of course I notice." His words had hurt. The President's tiredness was new – perhaps it was the tiredness of a civil- ised man. "And where is he now? Upstairs with a pile of work he's got from you, I suppose."

She was tall, as tall as her husband, but the E.A. topped her by half a head or more. He looked down at her now as she strode angrily past him, making her way to where he had sat at the head of the table. Her reply seemed neither to surprise nor upset him. She disliked the way he watched her. She disliked everything about him, his old-fashioned way of talking most of all.

The table in front of her husband's seat was completely clear of papers. There was nothing but a clean note pad. She wondered what the E.A. had really been doing when she came into the room.

"Somebody else has been showing anxiety about the President's health?"

"Just . . . somebody I was talking to. One of the Minister's wives on the way out to Novellnyi this morning."

"Ministers' wives will say anything." The E.A. sat easily on the corner of the table. "They'd each like to see their own man in that seat. Even if it killed him . . . I imply no criticism of you, Comrade Katarin. In many ways you are an unusual woman."

He contrived to make even formality and humbleness expressions of his own inbred superiority. Angered, she took the President's note pad and tore it in two. The unstapled page ends fluttered onto the table and the floor.

"I care *that* for Orrin's position," she said. Raoul Novaks watched, unamused.

"The President has retired to his quarters, Comrade Katarin. And you were right, he has taken papers to look over. I did not give them to him, however. In fact, I removed several from the pile before he got to it."

The other chairs were disordered, three of the ashtrays on the table full, water already forming bubbles in a half-filled glass. Signs of past life which emphasised the present deadness. Katarin felt an almost hysterical desire to get out. She knew also that Novaks would prefer to linger.

"I'll go up to Orrin," she said. "Perhaps I can help."

She walked the length of the room, his eyes on her all the way, expecting him to make some kind of reply. He said nothing, so she left. She felt she had unwillingly told him something he very much wanted to know. How she disliked the man! Orrin disliked him too, but used him. He thought he was close to the leadership: he was no nearer than the man who cleaned the President's shoes. The real successor, the only possible successor, was Sigmund. She made her way upstairs to the Presidential Suite.

Orrin Borge was sitting in the neat upright armchair he preferred, half a tumbler of vodka on the table beside him, a sheaf of papers in his lap. He was asleep. The living room was a soldier's room, with old campaign maps on the walls, books of history on low shelves, volumes of philosophy and illustrated books of travel, especially to Turkey. The Marshall had made a study of Turkey – it was to Turkey that he looked for the next step in the Communisation of Europe. The floor of the room was bare boards, with one peasant rug, and polished as had been the floor of the farmhouse in which the Marshall had grown up. Nowhere in the room, except in its proportions, were there signs of the magnificence that obsessed all other parts of the Palace. Katarin entered quietly, closing the door behind her with hardly a sound, but her husband woke immediately.

"Katarin. So you're back from Novellnyi. I was afraid the weather might have held you up."

"We left early, as soon as the snow started. And your meeting?"

"Scratchy. Active people, they sit and talk only. So they feel wasted. So they take it out on me."

"Poor Orrin. I'm sorry I disturbed you."

"Ridiculous habit, dozing off like an old man at five in the afternoon ... They agreed in the end, though. If I could read through the pension estimates between last Friday and now, why couldn't they?"

"Maybe they think of Sunday as a day of rest."

He gathered the papers on his lap into a neat pile and stood them upright on his knee, leaning his chin on them and staring into space. The attitude, that of a young man starting some new journey in his mind, had long outlived its origins.

"And so should I . . . that's what you mean, isn't it? And you're right, of course." He held out his hand to her and she took it, resenting the need it implied. "I'm frightened to delegate responsibility. I don't want the power I fight for – it's other people's mistakes that terrify me. The only competence I trust is my own. And with so little reason. . ." He shook his head. "It's a new feeling this, Katarin. A new loneliness. I can no longer rest. . ."

Katarin held his hand and stopped listening. Whatever he was trying to say to her she would not hear. Her position with him was impossible. She could accept that he should show weakness in his moments alone with her, and self-pity even. The man she talked about to others, the man she saw asleep in his chair, the man who needed simple comfort, this man she could feel tenderness for, and admiration. But his withdrawal on a deeper level, this she could not tolerate. It represented a failure she found disgusting. Denying himself, he denied her also. All that was left between them was civilised behaviour. So she would test the limits of his civilisation.

"Your Guard Captain, Colonel Balenkov," she said, cutting carelessly across what he was saying, "do you get on with him?"

"I hardly ever see him. He receives his orders from Tarsu."

"He's an odd man. I've seen him once or twice at receptions, but hardly spoken to him." She paused, watching her husband's reaction. "Just now he made a pass at me." His hand tightened on hers. His voice tightened.

"I expect you coped, Katarin."

"Certainly. I hit him. Hard."

The hand round hers remained tense. "Then that's that. He won't be a fool enough to try again."

"It's insulting to you, though. Don't you think – "

"I shall survive. Tarsu says the man's good at his job. If

78

I took official notice it would mean having to lose him."

"You may have to take official notice. The grubby little episode was seen by a junior officer. An engineer major."

"A major will know better than to spread a story like that. But I'll speak to him, Katarin, if you'd rather."

"No, Orrin. Only if *you'd* rather."

He released her hand. He smiled absently up at her, then began to fiddle with the papers. Katarin thought he was going to start reading. Instead he began to speak, each word very slow and careful.

"You know I have always been a jealous man, Katarin. You want to rouse me, telling me of this Balenkov. Very female of you. I ought to be pleased. You make it so that either I speak or I am no longer a man."

Suddenly he was on his feet, his face tight and pale, striking her face angrily, contemptuously with the sheaf of papers. Even the absence of pain was in its way insulting. She retreated, held out her arms to ward him off.

"But I see this the other way, Katarin. I ask how this Balenkov dares even to look at the wife of Marshall Borge. I see that you played with him, Katarin. Hardcocked him and then came running to tell me when you feared I might hear of it from someone else."

The sheaf of papers flew apart in his hand and scattered across the room. He took her shoulders and shook her. She had forgotten his strength. His body stood stiff before her, his arms hardly seeming to move, and she flapped to and fro with wide eyes, as helpless as a lolling rag doll. His rage was disproportionate and still she did not understand.

"You are the wife of Marshall Borge. The major will not dare to speak. But nothing alters my shame, the shame you have brought me."

He released her. She stared at him, still too dazed to reply. But her mind was still closed, shaped by its own smallness. She thought with panic of herself and Sigmund, how Orrin would kill them if he knew. She watched his anger fade, and with it the moment when truth might have been possible.

"We stand too high to be human, Katarin." He turned away. "Collect the papers for me, will you? Every one of them is important."

Still she did not understand what he was saying, for he taxed her with parables. She moved quietly round the room, fearful, gathering the sheets, smoothing them and stacking them neatly. He waited by the big-bellied stove, his face turned away. When she offered him the papers he took them without looking up. He had retired again where she could not reach him, leaving nothing with her but a destructive new fear. His failure belonged to them both.

Five

COMRADE KORDA WAS down in the office of the Aide to the Minister of State Building. He had gone there immediately after the Council Meeting which had taken too long and which had, in his opinion, been totally unnecessary. He was not interested in new pension schemes – the vote of the Council was only formal and could well have been taken in his absence. The President and the Minister of Economic Progress had made all the necessary decisions days ago. Comrade Korda did not mind this way of working : in the President's place he would do exactly the same. It made for efficient government. But to some politicians the games that they played were important, so he had politely followed the rules, listened to the arguments, asked diplomatic questions, smoothed over the pointless difficulties made by the Health Minister. In democratic government one moved at the pace of the slowest, and – once alienated – the slowest could bring the process to a weary standstill. So Comrade Korda was diplomatic. Diplomacy had brought him a long way : with patience it would take him further.

At the back of his mind, however, had been the problems raised by his short telephone conversation with the Minister of State Building just before the meeting began. The Minister and the Engineer Colonel were trying to wriggle out of the schedule set for his library extension. The Palace Library was very important to him. His ultimate intention, not yet disclosed, was to create a library of international importance, famous among scholars of all nations, an intellectual centre of great value to his country's prestige. And to his own.

He was in a hurry. He had been in a hurry all his life. And all his life men like the Minister and the Engineer Colonel had tried to slow him down. They had seldom succeeded.

"How goes it, Boris my lad? Keeping the shareholders happy, I hope?"

"Shareholders, Comrade Korda? I don't – "

"Corruption Incorporated, man. You *are* the chairman, aren't you?"

He watched Kils glance nervously round the room, seeing the hidden microphones, seeing the tape reels turning. He perched on the edge of the Aide's desk and played airily with the buttons of his intercom.

"Man like you, position like yours, little account under an anonymous number at the National Bank in Dorlen – "

"If you have an official complaint to make, Comrade Korda, then the proper channels should be – "

"Don't be so po-faced, man. Of course I haven't got an official complaint. A joke, Boris. J-O-K-E."

"If you press that button you'll disturb the Minister."

Kils spoke surprisingly sharply. Comrade Korda had this running non-joke with all the Aides in the Palace – it helped to keep them jumpy. Not that their jumpiness bore any relation to their guilt, in fact rather the reverse. . . . He looked down at Boris deciding that the little man was probably quite innocent. Otherwise he would have acquired more self control.

"So the Minister's at home, is he?"

"Checking estimates for the new bridge over the Dnetz, Comrade. Shall I tell him you're here?"

"Don't bother." The Minister for State Building was the last person Comrade Korda wanted to see. "No, it's the Engineer Colonel I was looking for really."

"He left about a quarter of an hour ago. You'll find him in Admin. I'll get my secretary to call him."

"No thanks. I could do with the walk. This place would turn us all into blobby parasites sucked onto the ends of telephones if it ever got the chance." He went to the door, opened it, then turned. "By the way, there's a good story going around about the Commissar and the Prostitute."

Boris frowned anxiously. "I'd much rather you didn't, Comrade Korda."

"What a shame. You must have heard it."

He laughed quietly and went out. He caught the eye of the Aide's secretary. She was a tiny person, dwarfed by her typewriter. Her name was Anna. He smiled at her and she dared smile back. All the secretaries knew Sigmund Korda, and not even Marshall Tarsu had yet found a way of eavesdropping on a smile.

"You really shouldn't tease him, Comrade Minister."

"Shit scared. The Palace is full of frightened people, Anna. No wonder we don't get enough done."

The intercom on her desk emitted an unpleasant version of the Aide's unpleasant voice.

"The Poldi file. I finished with it at least half an hour ago. Will you kindly remove it?"

"Poor Anna. Now I suppose he'll give you hell." She shrugged her shoulders. "Never mind – it'll all be changed come the Revolution."

She looked at him without smiling. "But we've already had the Revolution," she said.

"You should mug up some theory, my pet. Revolution is a continuous process."

He patted her bottom and turned away. As she opened the door behind him he heard the Aide's voice raised in a querulous stream of complaint. He shuddered, wondering what the hell her life was like there at the Palace. One of the clerical grade dormitories, clerical grade messing, and an occasional bunk-up behind the Gustav Basilica. Not surprising that she was disenchanted with revolution.

He hurried down the stairs and across the gigantic cedar-panelled foyer. The glare from the four towering chandeliers caused him to narrow his eyes .The foyer was empty except for one tiny messenger approaching from the Department of Agriculture. As they passed, Comrade Korda realised that the man was of normal stature, perhaps even an inch or two taller than himself. The sheer size of the Palace had this effect on people, explaining the platform shoes and tall head-dresses of the old Royal Family, and the competitive magnificence of their robes. He went down the brown marble staircase and across the Entrance Salon. One of the guards saluted.

"It's snowing hard, Comrade Minister."

"I'm only going as far as Admin, thank you."

"The paths aren't cleared yet. I'd use the passages if I was you, Comrade Minister."

Sigmund looked down at his thin Palace shoes and his elegant grey worsted trousers.

"Perhaps you're right, Corporal. Thank you for warning me."

He turned left into the Grand Salon exhibition hall. Monday was not a tourist day, and the huge gilded and mirrored ballroom was lighted only by dim working lights, the illuminated area tapering off into unfathomable darkness all around. Korda walked close to one wall, passing more than sixty of the silver-tapestried chairs that lined it before he came to the unobtrusive doorway that led into a small lobby giving access to one of the many catacomb staircases. He ran lightly down into a tunnel so narrow that he had to turn sideways in order to avoid brushing its flaking walls. A further, rougher flight of steps led him down into a large vaulted chamber with many other tunnels leading from it, each clearly signposted. In bad weather the upper levels of the catacombs were used more frequently than the streets above. The passages were well-lighted, but in many cases this brilliance only served to emphasise their tiny, burrow-like nature. Some people were worried by this and preferred the open air, whatever the weather was doing. Comrade Korda himself experienced only a mild unease, which he easily overcame.

He made his way unhesitatingly through the warren, up and down many steep little staircases, stooping through slimey green archways and turning numerous corners before he came to the final long incline that led up into the base-ment of the Admin building. The bare walls of the dungeons here were still set with the iron rings and chains used by the torturers once employed by the bishops in the marble halls above. Sigmund knew too much about the present Palace administration for the sight of these to make him feel self-righteous, but at least the methods used by Marshall Tarsu were less physically degrading. He ascended to the ground floor and the offices of the Engineer Colonel.

For a second the long mirror by the door delayed him – in his service days an adequate military turnout had never come easily to him. Instinctively he paused and examined himself. His suit was neat enough, but the shirt and tie were far too florid. The Engineer Colonel could not possibly approve. He knocked on the door and went in without waiting for a reply. With some people it was necessary to establish the relationship crudely at the very outset.

"Colonel – don't get up." The old man had not even had time to start. "I just thought I'd come and have a short word with you about the revised schedule on this library project."

"Sit down, Minister," said the Engineer Colonel. "Seen the snow?"

"Pretty thick, so they tell me."

"A metre in the last two hours, and there's more to come."

Obviously the snow was a great comfort to the Engineer

Colonel. Not even the Minister of Education could expect his men to work on the outside of a building in two metres of snow. Sigmund played along.

"Trust our damned weather, Colonel. I was hoping it might have held off at least until the scaffolding was up. It's a great disappointment."

"I'm sorry too, Minister. Believe me, if this hadn't happened we could have been well up to schedule."

Korda gazed at the Engineer Colonel's veined and pouchy face. Like hell you would, he thought. And you've been bashing the Minister of State Building's brandy by the look of it.

"I appreciate your concern, Colonel. I was wondering if you might have any bright ideas."

"Bright ideas?" The old man's mind struggled to cope. "I don't follow."

"Difficulties are made to be overcome, Colonel." Very brisk. "This project is of great national importance."

"The country is no longer a monarchy, Minister. In those days if workmen got killed nobody cared a monkey's."

The brandy was making the Engineer Colonel brave. And the knowledge that he had the Minister of State Building behind him. His reply was very near to being openly offensive. Comrade Korda decided to give him one more chance.

"Then you've no suggestions?"

"Nothing to be done till the spring, Minister. Till then there's enough vital work inside the Palace to keep my men busy twice over."

There was too much emphasis on the word 'vital'. Korda lost his temper.

"That's a very great pity, Colonel. Myself, I thought it was the Central Committee that decided what was vital and what wasn't."

"If your Central Committee makes the snow go away I'll start on your library immediately. Till then there's nothing more to be said."

"I'm afraid there is, Colonel. You've a good record. We might almost have considered your long service in the Royalist army to be successfully purged."

"What precisely are you suggesting?"

Korda allowed a long pause, observing how the sudden pallor on the old man's cheeks threw the veins and distended blood vessels into ugly relief, and how the bloodshot eyes flickered, keeping only spasmodic hold on their focus. There was no opponent here, and therefore no victory. He dulled the edge to his voice, speaking almost sadly.

"I only suggest, Colonel, that to other people your present attitude might seem uncooperative ... Surely a man like you, a senior officer respected and near to retirement, would want to avoid such an impression? I myself, of course, would never dream of questioning your loyalty to the Party. All the same – "

"Loyalty?" The word roused a last flicker of resistance in the old man. "You say I should feel loyalty to the Party. I tell you I also have a loyalty to the service, to my men. I cannot believe that the Party would have me betray – "

"Cooperation, Colonel – all the Party expects is your cooperation. Your best efforts to find a way round this temporary difficulty."

"What way is there round two metres of snow? You tell me and I'll take it."

"Good man. I knew you would."

The Engineer Colonel leaned his elbows on his desk and covered his face with his hands. They were shaking, and brown stains showed in the skin on their backs. Sigmund felt sorry for him. So worried for his pension and so little time left in which to enjoy it.

"The promptings of duty force unpleasant tasks on us, Colonel. You know that as well as I do. I'm sorry." The Colonel did not move. "Mind if I use your phone?"

The Engineer Colonel made a small gesture of agreement. Sigmund felt ashamed even of his gentleness, for that

87

too was less than the man deserved. He lifted the receiver and asked to be put through to the Minister of State Building.

"Oscar? Sigmund here. I'm down in the Engineer Colonel's office. We've been discussing the library project and he's come up with this really great idea." There was silence in the office while Oscar told him that snow was snow, and that there was nothing anybody could do about it. "I know all that, Oscar. But the Colonel tells me he's thought of another way. Put the floor in first, light the upper story artificially, and knock the windows through from the inside. No scaffolding, no risks. Simple, isn't it? Makes me angry, not having thought of it myself."

The conversation continued. Sigmund began to realise that the snow had been no more than an excuse, that the Minister of State Building had reasons of his own for postponing the library extension. He hoped the Minister would not be hard on the Engineer Colonel: standing where he did the Minister ought to be sympathetic about the pressures available against the frightened old man.

In the end it was agreed that the work should go on and that, with the labour saved from the erection of scaffolding, the schedule might even be improved upon. Oscar rang off with expressions of the most cordial regard. The Engineer Colonel now had the palms of his hands flat on the desk in front of him.

"It can't be done," he said.

"Of course it can. You're going to do it."

"What about lintels? What about exterior flashing?"

"The lintels can be cast *in situ* and the flashing you can leave until the spring."

"Seepage. The frost will crack the whole thing wide open."

"It'll mean a lot to your record, Colonel, an achievement like this. It's enterprise that is rewarded nowadays, not like in the old days when it was how much you spent on

Mess Nights that counted, how much vodka you bought the General."

The Engineer Colonel did not reply. To him this super-erogation of his authority seemed like ruin. Sigmund patted him on the shoulder, then left him and went to the door. When did the wish to comfort merely look like condescension?

"This project will give you a valuable boost, Colonel. I'm relying on you."

He left the Colonel fussing with his fingers, beginning to come to life. Once out in the wide, echoing corridor he hesitated, uncertain what he should do next. Amélie would be waiting for him, needing the solid comfort he could not give. Their marriage had always been so, seeking radically different ends. His mind ran like fire – he pitied her for the security that Balenkov would have been so happy to provide. He created turmoil and she demanded peace. The only peace she had been able to make for herself was in the tortured shadows of a curtained room, migraine driving all other life away. Yet every day she waited for his return, and every day she hoped. He did not feel ready to face the demands he could never meet.

Remembering that it was snowing, he opened the shutters on one of the high corridor windows. Flakes were piled against the glass, and grey shapes whirled in the blackness beyond. For him each year the coming of the snow was a great event. He wanted to be out in it, chal-lenging it, galloping on Kerrill between the lashed, fantastic drifts. But his soft Palace clothes were useless: to go out in the weather entailed hat and coat and boots, and explaining to Amélie the inexplicable. For her such weather was another cause for complaint. At her home down in the south such winters were the exception rather than the rule...

He heard the approach of quick footsteps and closed the shutters wearily. There were times when the Palace snapped shut and held even him fast. An army officer came down the long straight corridor towards him, starting hardly a finger high. Outside the Engineer Colonel's door the officer paused, looking from Sigmund to the door and then back again.

"Is the Engineer Colonel back from his meeting yet, Comrade Minister?" The officer was out of breath.

Sigmund nodded. "I've just left him," he said.

The officer moved to the mirror, drew himself up in front of it. He appeared to be gathering courage. Then he knocked on the Engineer Colonel's door, waited some seconds before he received a reply, and went in. Round the edge of the door Sigmund saw the Colonel set down an empty glass.

"Six hours late, Kohler. God, you're an officer in the Engineers, not a shambling, pox-shot civil servant. When you receive an order, Kohler, you're supposed to obey it. Or didn't you know that? Or perhaps you thought my orders not worth obeying, Kohler. Did you? Is that what you thought...?'

The door swung shut. The purple face of the Engineer Colonel disappeared, but the sound of his voice continued to be faintly audible through the door panels, rising in short bursts and growing louder. Sigmund Korda walked back down the corridor the way he had come, unconsciously trying to make as little sound with his feet as possible on the marble floor. He became aware of himself, of the air he displaced. The Moorish arches over the windows that lined one side of the corridor were deeply notched and carved with intricate tracery picked out in black and yellow, the shutters over the windows themselves covered with brittle red lacquer that threw back at Sigmund even the soft slither of his shoes as he passed. Behind the closed doors on his right everything was silent. He might have been totally alone, the labyrinths around him inescapable, endlessly void. Irrationally he had an impulse to return to the Engineer Colonel's door and the hysterical rasping voice within . . . Then footsteps approached, a group of soldiers appeared from a side corridor, and the grip of the Palace loosened. Sigmund hurried forward, nodded to the soldiers as he passed them, noticed that they recognised him, every one, and made his way quickly back to the basement entrance to the catacombs.

For some reason the smallness of the underground passages made them more bearable, more easily contained in his mind. He needed to be able to contain things, to stretch his understanding in an almost tangible net over events and ideas, people and places. He remembered the snow piled against the window panes and, smiling, broke into a run as he made for the Mantua Gate, the nearest contact with open country and the only gate to have direct access from the catacombs. During the journey there his path crossed with that of an official messenger, and he greeted the man noisily, his voice battering between the stone walls and floor and vaulting as he gripped the man's arm and then hurried by. The messenger was disturbed by his animal excitement and stared after him.

The Mantua Gate was a square tower designed by Alberto and Allesandro Bertoli, father and son, who had been invited to the Palace by Georg II and had stayed nearly seven years. In this time they supervised the construction of three towers, a spectacular shrine to Our Lady of the Annunciation, and a new north front to the King's Residence which was unfinished at the time of their sudden return to Italy. The Palace archives were reticent about the reason for their return, and it is likely that they were murdered. For foreigners (by nature seditious and unreliable) to have lasted in the Court of that time as long as did the two Bertolis was very unusual. It can only be surmised that their persons were as charming as their architecture.

All of this that now remained was the Mantua Gate, an elegant yet massive structure spanning the roadway from the Palace that led eastwards towards Dorlen. The other two Bertoli gates, the shrine, and the west front of the King's Residence had all succumbed during the intervening three hundred years either to fire or to the demolition gangs of modern-minded Royalty. The Mantua Gate housed a troop of Guards, a chapel now used to store works of art, and two pairs of ancient cannon. The Sergeant-in-Command was a huge one-armed man, a Legionnaire who had returned to his country at the time of the Revolution and had fought in both the major revolutionary battles. In the second of these he had been in command of one of the platoons in Lieutenant Korda's company, and a mutual respect had grown up between them. He stood now with the Comrade Minister under the high round arch of the gate and watched the snow outside falling vertically in the still air. Sigmund wore a stiff grey overcoat borrowed from one of the guard.

"Plenty of work for the men when this stops, Sergeant."

"Bloody good job. Tire the sods out. They've been sitting round on their arses too flaming long."

"I hear they won the Troop Award, though."

"See the opposition, did you? Shower of weak piss, the lot of them."

"At least nobody could call your men that, Sergeant."

"I chase 'em, Comrade Minister. They know I'm a bastard. Let 'em once get bored and that's your number."

On the outer side of the gate the snow was drifting gently in, and two guards were collecting it almost as it fell, shovelling it up and putting it into bins for disposal later. Their breath lingered in the still air and their bodies steamed visibly as they worked. The lights up under the arch of the gate glared down, glinting sharply on the fire-fighting equipment in racks along one wall and on the big brass bell rung each morning and evening before the opening and closing of the gates. As Sigmund watched, the falling snow thinned and then ceased altogether. Buildings inside the Palace became dimly visible, the open square inside the gate, the narrow streets leading from it, the traffic signs and directions on the wall of the small Palace hospital straight ahead. The Sergeant-in-Command left his side and went into the guard room. Sigmund heard him shouting up the stairs to the relief watch, ordering them down with shovels and brooms.

From the street to the left, leading to the vehicle pool, came the characteristic clatter of a tracked snow plough. The M.T. sergeant was on his toes as well. Four guards came down the stairs and began clearing the foot approaches to the gate. Another two started scraping the path down to the river for quick disposal of the snow spoil. Sigmund paced the bare cobbles under the archway, cursing his pansy Palace shoes. The Sergeant-in-Command stood motionless in the guard room door, watching his men and abusing them obscenely in four languages. The snow plough appeared in the square. The shining vee of the blade below its head-lights peeled the snow apart like foam that tumbled in slow motion and then set, ragged ridges hard against the white surrounding sea. It approached, clanking and jerking, and burst deafeningly onto the bare cobbles, toppling waves of snow two metres high against the stone walls. There it stopped, throttled back, shed white compacted wedges from the teeth of its tracks and tainted the contained air with heavy blue diesel fumes.

The Sergeant-in-Command shouted up, ascertaining that it was going on out across the bridge and along the road between the marshes to clear a basic route if necessary as far as Dorlen. Sigmund watched and listened, his blood pounding like a little boy's with the excitement of the monstrous noise, the stink, the huge power. The tracks of the plough stood above his waist, its bonnet and radiator like a vast metal tomb, its vertical exhaust pipe as thick as a seven-year fir tree. He found he was shaking all over. He went to the sergeant and spoke loudly in his ear. The sergeant nodded, climbed up onto the track, opened the cab door and conducted a short argument. Then he closed the cab door and climbed down.

"He says there's no room inside. But you can sit on the bloody toolbox behind if you care to. And if you freeze and fall off it's no sodding business of his, he says." The sergeant winked. "I've not said who you are, see? Just that you're a friend of mine."

"I won't freeze. A few hundred yards, that's all. Thanks."

He climbed up onto the track, and thence to a long metal box fixed to the bodywork behind the rear window of the cab. The ironwork he gripped was surprisingly, painfully cold, and he made gestures till the sergeant sent for a pair of gloves and handed them up. He found that by bracing his feet against a handgrip below the toolbox and his back against the cab he could make himself reasonably secure. He tapped on the cab window and showed his raised thumb. The juddering of the engine smoothed into an unbelievable roar and the vehicle moved forward under the quivering arch of the tower. For a moment Sigmund lost his grip, nearly fell. Then the blade of the plough entered the snow on the other side and steadied. He found handholds and clung to them. The bright lights passed close overhead and were replaced by darkness, tearing ranges of cloud and behind them a pale moon with two haloes. The wind could be seen screaming high above, while out on the snow plains beyond the river a candle flame would have burnt with hardly a flicker.

The thickness of the snow on the road increased, and the front of the plough developed an uneven up and down motion, easing in and lifting and cutting open. The pace was that of a slow walk, four or five kilometres an hour. The ripped path behind them grew almost imperceptibly, till the yellow-lit gateway was suddenly smaller and their track could be seen tapering in towards it. Growing used to the movement, Sigmund was able to relax, to feel the total hardness of the metal, its sheer unstoppable weight beneath him, its noise that beat along the barren walls of the Palace. Utter mechanical confidence, ugly and crude, raping the tense skein of surrounding stillness.

Larger than himself, and at the same time nothing, he clung to the grey steel-studded plates. He crossed the bridge, the sound of his progress changing, and lumbered eternally on down the road. Behind him sections of the ripped walls of snow fell silently. The patterns of the tracks repeated themselves, the exhaust pounded monotonously on above his head. Suddenly, for no reason he could afterwards remember, his trance broke and he found himself falling, slipping helplessly down over the sloped plating. He fell on his side in the roadway, unnoticed. The snow plough moved on and away, its size and noise dwindling with distressing ease.

He picked himself up. The snow was crushed hard underfoot, scattered with the tight little leavings from the caterpillar tracks. He dusted dry powdered snow from his great-coat and looked back at the Palace. As big as he had been before, now he was tiny. Already the plough was almost out of earshot, two distant points of red light, only its exhaust fumes lingering as a presence in the still air. The moon was clear of the clouds now, its two haloes pale and precise as silver filigree. Sigmund took a few paces back towards the bridge, then paused and looked out over the sliced-back snow at the marshes, their few spikes of vegetation black and desolate. And beyond the marshes the dark rambling hulk of the Palace. He stood, arrested, unable to drag his eyes away, defensively reshaping its image around the safe internal sequence of rooms and staircases and corridors with which he was so familiar. Size, situation, architecture, the accumulated human passions of five hundred years . . .He particularised, examining the two great gilded domes over the Government Building black now with the moon behind them. Under the southern one was the lavish apartment of Marshall Tarsu, under the other was the Radio Communications Centre. The twisted spire further north –

near to the base of that were the Palace stables, Kerrill restless, feeling his oats no doubt. And the flat block of the Arsenal, double-guarded day and night, a central elevator, remote controlled, to its five sealed floors. He tried to see the Palace as a complex territory, capable of being walked over, encompassed. Yet even as he did so he was aware that the whole was greater than the sum of its parts. Or if not greater, then qualitatively different...

Particularly it dominated those who thought they could harness its power, its dark symbolism, to their own fleeting human purposes.

Making a great effort, he turned away. He shrugged his coat closer about him and started back along the road. At least he knew, had always known, the real enemy against which he must set his strength. Perhaps he could manage to hold it off, manage to survive. As he walked back over the patterns left by the tracks of the plough the snow under the thin soles of his shoes was blunt like fine velvet. He was very tired, and needed to rest.

Part Two

DECEMBER

Six

IN DECEMBER THE cold gripped the walls of the Palace so that they creaked, and bloomed with frozen tears. The willows along the frozen river grew brittle enough to snap in the ancient wind that blew indifferently across the eastern plain. The days of autumn had never been, when the sun had slanted down the shallow slopes of pine forest to light obliquely the domes and towers, fining them down to shimmering pinnacles of glass in the uncertain, misty air. What sunlight there was in the short December days came white and cold through the ice-dry air, bringing a relentless clarity to the conflicting and monstrous symmetries of the Palace, draining the scarlet spires and green-coppered gables of everything but the gigantic human arrogance that had raised them.

Inside the Palace, however, little was changed. For most people the machinery of life and government brought a reassuring continuity, a knowledge that this too would pass. For most people, but not for Major Kohler. For him the weeks that followed his first inspection of the Paul VII Passage were a continuous nightmare. Of the incident he had witnessed between Colonel Balenkov and the wife of the President he thought nothing. His mind was obsessed with the wall of indifference and wilful obstructiveness that stood between him and what he now knew to be the saving of the Palace.

The nightmare had begun with the grotesque interview

that evening with the Engineer Colonel. He had missed his superior officer's return from the Government Building and had waited by the entrance to Admin for nearly an hour before a passing orderly had told him that the other was already in his office. In the corridor he passed Comrade Korda apparently coming from the Engineer Colonel. Whatever the subject of their meeting had been, it had put the old man in a particularly ugly mood. Kohler had expected the man to be angry, but he was quite unprepared for the stream of disconnected abuse that began the moment he appeared in the doorway. At the time, however, he excused the Engineer Colonel, seeing that the man was old, and drunk, and a senior officer. It was only later that the dangerous injustice of his treatment began to oppress him.

Standing erect against the full flood of the Engineer Colonel's invective, he tried desperately to divert it, to break off the conversation and perhaps carry it on the next day when the old man would be ... more himself. He failed completely.

"I need more facts, Colonel. I need time. Perhaps I could – "

"Time? Time for still more incompetence? I expect orders to be obeyed, Kohler. I have to have men around me I can rely on. If the Minister is dissatisfied, it isn't you he blames. It isn't your incompetence. I have forty-three bloody years of service behind me, Kohler, and I'm not having them all put to nothing while you sit back on your bloody arse dreaming up pretty little stories till the bloody cows come home. Incompetence, Kohler. You're not fit to be shovelling shit, Kohler. You ought to be – "

"I made a thorough investigation, Colonel. It took a long time. I've laid out the results for you there."

"Results? What sort of bloody results are these, Kohler? You expect me to pass on to the Minister this load of shit, do you? He's a busy man, he expects a certain level of competence. As I do too, Kohler. A certain minimum, piss-brained level of competence. And what do you give me, Kohler? I asked you for a negative bloody follow-up report, and what the bloody hell do you have the face to give me?"

"I've kept it unofficial, Colonel. Naturally you would need to give your approval before – "

"Tell me, Kohler, what did I bloody ask you for? Can you tell me that? Or has your week-end of sexual excess weakened your brain? Is that it? Have you really forgotten my orders, Kohler?"

"Of course not, sir. But a thorough on site investigation showed that – "

"What was my order then, Kohler? You still haven't bloody told me."

"I was to make out a negative follow-up report, Colonel."

"And what is this, Kohler? What is this pretty bloody little piece of paper?"

"On site examination showed that areas of – "

"It's not a negative bloody follow-up report, is it? It's not what I asked for at all. When I give you orders, you bastard, I expect them to be obeyed."

Major Kohler dared all.

"I thought you were interested in the true facts of the case, Colonel."

"True facts?" The Engineer Colonel crumpled the page of closely-written notes into a ball and flung them away. He rose carefully from his chair and leaned across the desk. "True facts? How dare you ... So you're suddenly God, Kohler. Suddenly you know what is true and what is not. But you're not bloody paid to be God, Kohler. You can safely leave that to others. You're paid to obey orders, simple orders that even your piss-brain can understand. You're – "

"Colonel, the Paul VII Passage is in danger of collapsing, sir."

"Let me tell you something, Kohler." He splattered the Major's face with saliva. "You're a good man, but you lack experience. For twenty years I've had men running to me

- sir, the bridge is collapsing, sir, the trench is collapsing, sir, the whole bloody world is collapsing . . . . And you lack bloody discipline, Kohler. You treat the army as if it was a whore's teaparty. It's not good enough. It's not bloody good enough. . ."

The Engineer Colonel began to subside. Major Kohler tried to see where the scrumpled ball of his precious notes had fallen. He wondered how he could dare retrieve them. The Engineer Colonel returned to his seat, covered his face with his hands, spoke with difficulty.

"You force my hand, Kohler. You force me to take notice of your incompetence. In the morning I shall write a survey of the case. Being incompetent, your opinions of course are worthless. So you force my hand again . . . You force me to make out the negative follow-up report myself."

"Colonel, if mud continues to enter the Palace sewers, then – "

"I'll tell you what enters sewers, Kohler. Shit. And that's what you are, Kohler. Shit." He opened his eyes wide. An idea had just come to him. "And I'll tell you another thing, Kohler. If mud *is* entering the Palace sewers then we both know where it's coming from. It's coming from the embankment you're supposed to be mending, Kohler, and all this talk of collapsing tunnels is nothing but flannel. It's that bloody fancy shuttering of yours – it's letting the stuff through like a sieve."

"The nearest sewer inlet to the embankment is three hundred metres, Colonel. River mud couldn't poss – "

"You're full of talk, Kohler. But all the bloody talk in the world won't get you out of this one. You have two possible alternatives, Kohler – if there's mud in the sewers it's coming from your embankment. And if there's no mud, then you've invented the whole thing because you – "

"You've only got to send a man down, Colonel. Inspect the sewers, and – "

"Listen, Kohler, I haven't *got* to do a bloody thing. The

Minister *trusts* me – your mischief-making won't do a bloody bit of good. You'd like to see me down in the shit, but you're in too much of a bloody hurry. I'm not down yet, and by God, I'll fight you every inch of the way. Now get out."

"But, Colonel – "

"Get out. And stay out. Or I'll have you for insubordination. Your fancy friends won't help you then, Kohler. Nobody likes insubordination – it's a nasty word. So get out. You'll find your orders in the Orderly Room in the morning. You're shit, Major bloody Kohler. Shit."

Major Kohler had got out. And he had stayed out.

Reporting to the Orderly Room next morning he had been detailed to take over Kitchen Duty Officer from Lieutenant Kritz for an indefinite period. From the insulting nature of this assignment his fellow officers quickly realised that he was out of favour with the Engineer Colonel. A withdrawn man, never very popular, he received little sympathy. His closest friend, an M.T. Captain called Farkas, was a man as inarticulate as himself. No doubt they were attracted to each other for this reason, making no demands on each other, playing chess or walking the Palace walls in companionable silence. To confide in Captain Farkas would have been pointless. A degree of mute sympathy might have resulted, followed by a period of tactful disengagement.

For Major Kohler the matter rapidly shifted from the field of reasonable behaviour into that of pride and injured dignity. He performed his kitchen duties with unnecessary zeal, suffering tight-lipped the greasy steam and endless clangour, living up to a private standard of behaviour aimed at humiliating his superior but inevitably harming nobody but himself. During this time he was able to obtain the file copy of the Engineer Colonel's follow-up report on Lieutenant Mandaraks' memo. It was an ingenious document, detailing a sufficient number of his own findings to make it seem thorough and then arriving at radically different conclusions. In winding up, the Engineer Colonel had written — *Since the investigating officer comes to us with the highest recommendation from the Mining School at Pol, I see no reason to doubt his conclusions.* The signature of the Engineer Colonel at the bottom of the page was neat and soldierly.

Major Kohler soon knew the report by heart. Night after night he lay sleepless, experiencing the sensation of separation, almost of exaltation, that came from impending martyrdom. Whatever happened, the Engineer Colonel had himself covered. Obviously the old man's basic strategy was to rely on the ancient masonry holding out the nine months or so till his retirement. This was a reasonable hope. In engineering matters the Colonel was no fool — the catacombs had been there so long that their structure was almost an organic whole. If gradually applied, external pressures of incredible magnitude could be withstood. But what the situation needed more than anything else was constant vigilance. Without this — and to Major Kohler's knowledge nobody had been near the passage since the morning of his inspection — the subsidence when it came might be so sudden and disastrous as to bring about the destruction of a large part of the Palace structure.

His room in the Officers' Block was medieval and spartan. As a Major, he had a bedroom to himself — Captains and below doubled up — and often when he could not sleep he would get up and sit at the simple army-pattern table, doing calculations with no answers. He knew the Palace was seriously threatened. Any underground shock could be transmitted through the entire complex, finding out weaknesses and provoking an incalulable chain reaction . . . Sometimes it was as if cracks were already creeping beneath the whitewash of his stone cell walls, insinuating up the deep embrazure of his window, slyly warping its heavy iron grill. In these moods the smallest noise would make him start and break out into a sweat. The tick of a cooling radiator would have him braced, ready for the floor to split and drop him into a raging yellow torrent below. He took to leaving his door ajar, so that it would be less likely to jam in the event of a subsidence.

To occupy his mind he composed a statement, rewriting it over many dead hours of sleeplessness, that reconstructed the notes he had given to the Engineer Colonel and made his own situation absolutely clear. It was a statement that could never be used: short of entering an official impeachment of his superior officer, which demanded a quorum and laid its initiators open to a counter charge of mutiny, he was powerless. But the statement comforted him. After reading it through and reshaping some paragraph, he would be able to sleep. Kitchen Duties started early. He had to be up before five to supervise the firing of the bakery ovens.

Fasch was the only man who had any idea of his secret, and the demands of discipline and loyalty to his superiors made discussion between them impossible. Lieutenant Mandaraks had received a copy of the Engineer Colonel's follow-up report, so for him the matter was naturally closed. Major Kohler knew himself to be quite alone, and took to courting sleep via the dulling effects of alcohol.

On a Saturday morning well on into December, the day of the President's official visit to Nass, Major Kohler was on duty as usual at precisely five o'clock. The sun would not rise for another four hours. This early part of his day, however, was the most pleasant, for he was able to keep away from the kitchens, either in the bakery or supervising the collection of litter from the Palace Stables. This last was a job over which he would linger – although he was not a riding man he liked horses, their size and muscularity, and the warm smells of straw and hay and dung and saddle soap that filled the huge slate-floored stables. He liked the kicked wooden partitions between which they were tethered, the muffled rasp of their chewing, the steam that rose from them into the blurred darkness of the high vaulting. They were alive in a way that was unfamiliar and exciting.

And he liked the efficiency of the men who looked after them. It was gentle and well-judged and somehow totally sympathetic. In the early mornings the stables were noisy with buckets and rushing water and the conversation of the men with the animals. But the noise was never excessive, always suitable to the job on hand. The work had been done in very much the same way for the last two hundred and fifty years, ever since the stables had first been built to house the crack Palace Cavalry of Gustav I. Continuity was reassuring.

When the straw cart was loaded he walked with it over to the bakery. The noises there were more mechanical and the lights brighter, but the smells had the same timeless quality and the bakers' floury hands performed traditional patterns of kneading and pulling and knocking back. Two furnacemen took charge of the cart and wheeled it round to the furnace room where they began placing the damp straw carefully on the white-hot bed of coke they had prepared. Major Kohler had a technician's appreciation of the skill needed: fired too slowly, the straw dried out and flared away to dust in a matter of minutes. Fired too quickly, it formed a damp cake that might smoulder all day, giving out no useable heat at all. He watched the furnacemen for some time, and then wandered back into the rising room. At that moment the paper van from Dorlen came into the floodlit yard, its chains clattering on the swept cobbles. In spite of steady falls of snow the roads to and from the Palace were kept clear for wheeled traffic – the vehicle pool had six tracked ploughs permanently on call. The van stopped alongside the loading platform and the aged driver blew his familiar three blasts on the little brass hunting horn that was his trademark. He threw out the kitchen staff's bundle of papers. Then he reversed out and was gone. One of the apprentices took the papers in and began sorting them.

Major Kohler followed the boy into the rising room. The bakers had just finished the day's mixing and were standing talking and drinking tea. They stiffened slightly at his approach. He was a difficult man, fair-minded but with a disconcerting habit of retiring behind protocol and formula pronouncements. Perhaps he had once been caught out by the secret police, they thought. Once that had happened it was said you never trusted anybody. They longed for the more convivial days of Lieutenant Kritz.

He wandered round the room, idly tapping his cane on his boot-top, watching the dough working in the big stainless steel vats. The smell of the burning straw still lingered about him, mingling pleasantly with the yeast in the bakehouse. The newspapers seldom interested him. In the Officers' Mess a few days before, Captain Farkas had drawn his attention to the *People's Daily*, which was starting a series of profiles on prominent government figures. The first one was about the Minister of Art and Education, but the paragraph headings were unpromising — *Barefoot childhood, Just a village schoolmaster, Revolutionary zeal* ... How flattening and meaningless were those last two words. He had handed the paper back to Farkas unread. Somewhere the official writers had forgotten what revolution was like, had forgotten the ecstasy and left out the pain. The ecstasy of hope for the future and the pain of denying the traditional structure that was by definition right. They had forgotten everything, and invented instead the code words *Revolutionary Zeal*.

On Saturdays the bundle of newspapers was extra large, for it contained the non-party weeklies as well as the *People's Daily*. Major Kohler noticed that these were causing excitement among the men. They were arguing angrily, passing the papers from hand to hand. Mildly interested, he moved closer.

"...a Hero of the Revolution. Why shouldn't he have something a bit better than the rest of us?"

"I've an uncle who's a Hero of the Revolution and they won't even grant him a flaming bicycle. 'Cause he's tried. And I'll tell you why. 'Cause my uncle's only a – "

"Doctors, lawyers, men with college education, you don't expect them to get only the same as us, do you?"

"One law for the rich and one for the poor. That's the way it's always been."

"There's a rate for the job, though. That's what I say. And if he's stepping over the rate, then someone's working a fiddle, see? And that's not right."

"Of course he's stepping over the rate. Don't it say so? Good luck to him, anyway."

"Not in so many words, it don't. You got to read between the lines, like."

"One law for the rich and one for the poor. Don't you think?"

"Anyway, flaming good luck to him. Brightens the place up a bit."

"There's a rate for the job, I say."

"And flaming good luck to anyone who diddles the system, I say. Anyone who gets a bit more than this lot thinks he should, I reckon he deserves a flaming medal."

The last speaker checked himself, ending in mid-inflection. He had become aware of Major Kohler standing close behind him. Kohler decided not to have heard.

"What's the *People's Progress* found to complain about this week? Hm?"

"If you ask me, they're given too much rope, Major." The same man, seeking to reinstate himself. "Some little cooperative manager, that's all right. But when they start on at Ministers, well, what's it going to look like to foreigners, that's what I say."

"I'll agree that *Progress* isn't always as tactful as it might be. But that's the democratic way." Major Kohler considered the silver head of his cane, "The state and the people are one. Nobody is so high as to be above criticism."

"It's the Minister of Education, Major. They're trying to say he's living it up like a flaming nobleman."

"You get knotted. They don't say nothing of the sort."

"You just got to read between the lines, that's all."

"I shouldn't take anything the *Progress* says too seriously, Comrade. The Minister does fine work and enjoys great popularity. There'll always be people wanting to knock down men like him. It's an easy way of getting noticed."

"It's in the *Nation* too, Major. Fancy bits about all his good work, and then a dirty little sting in the tail. Here, Major, down at the bottom of the page."

Major Kohler avoided the paper that was being thrust at him. Frankly he did not understand why the gutter press was allowed to persist. Most of the articles it printed – aping the decadent West – did little but bring out the libidinous worst in people. And even when it attempted to cover a serious subject, as in this profile of Sigmund Korda, it could not resist the snide comment, the cheap and ill-informed attack. Major Kohler edged away, almost as if the paper were physically unclean.

"No doubt the Comrade Minister will survive," he said. Then he raised his voice slightly. "A few brooms now, I think. And there's a sack of flour split half way down the right hand pile. Get it re-bagged, will you? Otherwise it'll be all over the floor."

He moved away a few paces, suddenly borne down by the weight of his secret knowledge. He went outside and looked up at the sky, at the great uneven bulk of the Palace buildings white-rimmed against the stars, seeming falsely to partake of their eternity. That such permanence should be so impermanent, and the crass fools behind him arguing over gutter journalism. What would they do if they had to bear the weight of his knowledge? They would shout among themselves and accomplish nothing. And he was no better...

Heroism came in many disguises. Though many would have thought it nothing, for himself he would rather have built a dozen bridges under the guns of a dozen enemy batteries than faced again Comrade Boris Kils or the Engineer Colonel. But as long as he shirked the ordeal he was no more than the harmless fools bickering over their newspapers. He returned to the warm bakery, to the heady smell of the dough. He had decided to make one more effort.

After the newspaper van had delivered to the bakery, the generating station and the hospital, it turned into the tiny parade ground outside the Guard Orderly Room and drew up by the long verandah. The driver blew his hunting horn and then got out of the cab and trotted briskly in with the Guard Room papers. He was on good terms with the duty sergeants and was in the habit of receiving a glass of tea generously reinforced with rough local brandy. An elderly, pansified little man with slipping false teeth, he maintained good relations with his service customers by allowing himself to be a complete figure of fun. As the years passed he came to caricature himself more and more.

"Morning, boys..." His lisp was a piercing whistle. "Today's free gift is a big fat cigar for the boy with the prettiest bum." He sensed an unfamiliar tension in the air and did a little dance. "No need to be shy, boys. Not with Uncle."

A very particular little person, the actuality of a bum would have shocked him deeply. But he went through the routines his customers liked, the routines that had come to be expected of him.

"What the hell's going on out there?" The voice came through the half-open door to the inner office. The duty sergeant closed his eyes, as if in prayer. The off-guard sat rigid, their faces carefully expressionless.

"It's the man from Dorlen with the newspapers, Marshall."

"Tell him to get out. This is a guard room, not a common drinking house."

The duty sergeant made an urgent shooing gesture and the old man took the hint. He tiptoed exaggeratedly to the door, turned, and raised two fingers in the direction of the inner office.

"I said get him out, sergeant. Has he gone?"

There was the sound of a chair being pushed back. The old man registered theatrical horror, opened the door, and scuttled through. His two raised fingers were visible for a moment on the other side of the glass panel before he retreated down the steps. The duty sergeant cleared his throat.

"He's just gone, Marshall."

"Some of these civilians are impossible. He should be replaced."

The hunting horn sounded – rather more prolonged than usual – and the paper van was heard to drive away.

"He's been on the job for a long time, Marshall. It wouldn't be easy, finding another man to make the long drive out from Dorlen."

"There must be a fat profit in it, otherwise he wouldn't bother."

Privately the duty sergeant doubted this : he suspected that the old man's daily glass of tea and a chat was his only social contact. Marshall Tarsu appeared in the office doorway, holding three different sets of papers.

"The President's departure schedule, Sergeant. Copies to go immediately to M.T., to the E.A., and to Colonel Balenkov. Balenkov also needs this personnel requirements detail. We discussed it yesterday, but he'll need this in confirmation. And here's a requisition for the extra firearms to be carried by the guard accompanying the President. I'd like you to draw those in person, sergeant. And check each one thoroughly. Remember the Marinel fiasco."

One of the guards on the bridge-opening ceremony at Marinel the previous summer had been accidentally issued with a dress pistol, its firing pin filed down. Threatened by agitators, he had attempted to fire on them. His failure to check his own weapon had resulted in his being overwhelmed and the life of the President seriously endangered. The guard had been court-martialed, and with him the Sergeant-in-Command, the storeman, the armourer and the guard's Commander. All five men were dismissed the service, the guard and his sergeant given heavy prison sentences in addition. It was a mistake that nobody was likely to repeat for a very long time.

The duty sergeant took the various sheets of paper and looked them over.

"Colonel Balenkov sent down a roster of personal guards last night, Marshall. He knew you were coming in early and he thought you might like to check it. They've all had fifth-grade screening, he says."

"Tell Balenkov it's his job to choose the guards and that I trust his judgment." Marshall Tarsu stretched and yawned, for he was unused to such early rising. "The secret of proper command is delegation, sergeant. I know that, you know that, and so does Colonel Balenkov."

He also knows, thought the sergeant, that he'd much rather you carried the can should anyone make a ballsup. Only you're not having any. Marshall Tarsu turned back to his office, then appeared to notice the bundle of newspapers for the first time. The duty sergeant formed the opinion, however, that it was they that he had come out for in the first place.

"Distribute those to the men, sergeant. And bring me one of each. There's twenty minutes before we need think about guard inspection. I'll just have a look at what's happening in the outside world."

Back in the privacy of the inner office he disregarded completely the happenings in the outside world and turned at once to the profiles of Sigmund Korda contained both in the *Nation* and the *People's Progress*. Scanning down these reports he quickly found the passages he was looking for. These he read several times, with satisfaction. Then he picked up the telephone and asked for a number in the Government Building.

Comrade Novaks had no reason, that particular Saturday, to rise early. The President was not scheduled to leave for Nass till nine o'clock, half an hour behind the advance guard that cleared the road and tested for mines along the secret route. This was late enough to be comfortable, and early enough to make it hardly worth his starting work before the President's departure. The E.A. was not accompanying Marshall Borge on this particular factory visit – the party was to be made up of the Minister for State Building and the Minister for Scientific Progress who was to be attended by his Aide. All very workmanlike and suitable to such a technical occasion. Thus the E.A.'s only duties before nine o'clock that morning would be to make sure the President was carrying a copy of his speech, and to go downstairs with him to the door of his waiting car.

Comrade Novaks had a telephone extension by his bed. When it rang he woke instantly.

"Raoul Novaks? You're quick off the mark. Tarsu here. Just confirming that everything's ready for the President's little outing."

Oh, God, thought Novaks, surely the only telephone monitoring in this place is done by him? Has it simply become a habit? Does he really have to go through all this rigmarole? And at five thirty in the morning?

"Perfectly ready, Marshall. He'll be in the Entrance Salon nine o'clock sharp."

"Good man. Good man . . . I was just thinking, Novaks,

perhaps we ought to lay on an official photographer for the departure. The papers will be handling the Nass end of things, but the people love these Palace pictures. Good for morale, national pride, that sort of thing."

"I'm sure you're right, Marshall. I'll see the official agency man is there."

"Talking of the papers, Novaks, I've got a couple of the weeklies here in front of me. There's an interesting article in them both. Differently worded, but it's obviously from the same source. I'd like your opinion on whether we should take official action. Get them sent up to you, shall I?"

"Don't worry, Marshall. My own copies will be arriving soon." So the Korda affair was out in the open. They were all in for a busy day. "Thank you for getting in touch, Marshall. I'll be ringing you later."

He rang off and lay back in the bed that had once accommodated a Crown Prince. The canopy above him was of tea-coloured Spanish lace. It was a strange choice of bed for a man with such spare tastes, but Comrade Novaks, who did not always sleep alone, found its opulence amusing and a useful conversation piece for the – to him – crucially embarrassing moment when the girl and the bed first came into unmistakable conjunction. The ugly translucent glass bedposts had tided him over many awkward buttons and straps. He lay now and stared up into the shadowy folds. As it happened, the timing for the Korda affair had worked out very well: with the President away from the Palace all day and therefore not available for comment the story had the best possible chance of building up beyond its real worth.

On his return the President would of course crush it – for Sigmund Korda was a great personal friend – but controversy within the Palace would not die easily. And the nation at large would have a further entire day in which to speculate, since the President's rebuttal would not reach

114

them until the Monday edition of the *People's Daily*. The matter would not be readily forgotten. The President's statement would turn out to have been provisional – later he would reluctantly agree to institute an enquiry. And this in its turn would reveal just enough to damage Sigmund Korda without destroying him. For another year or two the Presidency would be safe.

Novaks turned off his light and listened in the darkness to the gigantic silence of the Palace. He savoured its power : beneath him and around him was the essence of an entire nation, its past and present and future. To control even obliquely such an organism was an inestimable private pleasure. He preferred his pleasures to be private, secret even. The open wielding of power would be a lesser joy to him, yet he knew that his whole life was unavoidably dedicated to its achievement. If orgasm was a little death, then power was personal annihilation. In their different ways both brought sadness and disgust . . . With a great mental effort he changed the direction of his thoughts, for he knew where the former line would lead him.

He considered instead the nature of Orrin Borge, with particular reference to his strange friendship with Korda. Try as he might, Novaks had been able to detect no sign that the President was aware of what the rest of the Palace treated as common knowledge : the fact that Korda and Katarin Borge were lovers. It was possible to remain wilfully ignorant, of course, but Raoul respected the President too much to believe him capable of such self-indulgent deceit. The only alternative was to believe that Marshall Borge was too occupied with the machinery of power to be concerned any more with reality on a personal, individual level. To Sigmund Korda the little death in the arms of Katarin; to Orrin Borge his Presidency. As a threat to this Presidency Comrade Korda existed – witness this plan inaugurated by Borge himself to clip the Minister's wings. But as a threat to the President's private life Korda was nothing, this being an area of existence for which there was no longer any room. As men they liked each other, as rivals for power they hated each other, and as rivals for Katarin they disregarded each other.

The distinctions were fine, but Novaks found them completely satisfactory. They were just the distinctions he would make. He turned over on his side and immediately fell asleep.

Seven

MARSHALL BORGE was by long habit an early riser. He was always awake when he and his wife were brought their early morning breakfast of fruit juice and cinnamon toast at six o'clock, and usually he was up and dressed. He had a precise internal clock that never failed; on the morning of his visit to Nass it woke him at five thirty-five exactly, and he got out of bed at once. He was looking forward to his factory visit – contacts with other people and other places stimulated him and he had been confined to the Palace for too long.

His movements disturbed Katarin. Her sleep that night had been restless, plagued with dreams of conflicting anxiety and bravado. Now she lay very awake and watched him dress. Soon he would go and not be back until late on Sunday morning. She felt as if she were being left alone in the Palace, alone with Sigmund. The plans she had made terrified her. She loved Orrin – the other thing was madness, external to her, inexplicable.

"Let me come with you, Orrin. I'd like to see Nass again after all these years."

"Not possible." He was pulling on his boots. He despised men who had valets to help them dress. "The party was made up weeks ago."

"But I wouldn't be in the way. Please take me."

"You know what these official tours are like, Katarin. The factory authorities will have organised a companion for each of us. The research into our interests, our likes and dislikes, will have been very thorough. We can't suddenly throw you at them. We have to be considerate, Katarin. We can't upset people just because we feel like it."

"I could give the tour a miss, Orrin. It's the evening I'd like. The evening with you."

"These official banquets. I won't have a spare moment. And there's a meeting with local commune leaders afterwards. You know how you hate being parked somewhere. No. No, it's quite impossible."

He straightened his back and looked at her. She knew how she must seem, puddled with sleep, her hair a mess, and she turned away, pulling the duvet high up on her shoulders. He walked round the bed and sat down beside her. He was in his shirt sleeves, the collar open at the neck, his face still unshaven. She felt his enormous reality, the rarity of his presence actually within her grasp.

"What's the matter, Katyi?" Her concern pleased him. "You're not afraid of something happening, are you?"

"Yes. Yes, I am afraid." He had given her a valid excuse. "These journeys are dangerous. Let me come with you."

"If I know Tarsu he'll have screened everyone within a hundred miles of the place. There's really no need to worry."

She reached out and pulled his head down, feeling his stubble against her naked shoulder. He made a movement, perhaps habitual, to nuzzle the upper softness of her breast. It would be so easy to love him again. The other was self-torture, insanity.

"You're all I have, Orrin – don't go. Tell them you're ill. Even a president can be ill, can't he? Let's have just two quiet days. No documents, no meetings, no speeches. Just us."

"Katarin . . . Katarin my dear, I know. I do understand. I'll see what can be done. Another week-end perhaps. In the new year things will be easier. I'll tell Raoul to keep a couple of days clear some time in January."

She stilled her hand that had been stroking his head.

"January, Orrin? Am I really so unimportant to you?"

"So many demands, Katyi. Don't cry. Don't make it more difficult for me. It's the price we pay for shaping history."

"The price *I* pay, Orrin." But she would not quarrel with him. She held him closer. "I know that's not fair. I know you pay too — "

There was a knock on the door.

"You never cry, Katarin. I've never seen you cry, not in twenty years. Don't make it so difficult for me, my dear. I have to go." He spoke very gently. "You know I do."

"Also I know that I can't come with you. That it would embarrass some bloody little factory manager."

The knock was repeated. Her hold had eased and he roughly twisted his head sideways.

"What is it?"

"Marshall Tarsu's compliments, Comrade President, and would you care to take breakfast with him."

"No, I would not care to take breakfast with him. Tell Marshall Tarsu I'm breakfasting with my wife."

There was a silence from the other side of the door, then an apologetic cough.

"Marshall Tarsu has matters to discuss with you, Comrade President. Important matters regarding today's security arrangements."

The President disengaged himself from Katarin's arms. She made no further effort: it was a battle that had been lost years before.

"You see how things are, Katyi. Not even breakfast is free to me any more." He raised his voice. "Please tell Marshall Tarsu I'll be with him in about ten minutes."

"At once, Comrade President."

Orrin Borge stood up, looked down at Katarin and rested his hand lightly on her head. He seemed to be on the point of saying something. Then he changed his mind and went quickly away into the adjoining bathroom. She listened to him stropping his razor and running water. The hot water always took a long time to arrive.

"What are you going to do with yourself, Katarin, while I'm away?"

She could imagine him tucking the towel carefully into his collar. This shaving with his shirt on was a relic of the years spent under canvas.

"I haven't really thought." She hunted half-heartedly for a handkerchief, then blew her nose on the corner of the sheet and tucked it out of sight. "Novaks' secretary is down with shingles. She's a nice girl – I might go down to the hospital. Take some books."

"You spend too much time indoors, Katarin. Why not go out for a ride? The forecast's good. Omar needs exercising. The stablemen have enough on their hands in the winter without that."

He spoke jerkily as he concentrated on working up a fine lather. She tried to look seriously at the day ahead of her, at the hours that needed filling till the night. The man in the bathroom was thrusting her away. Even if Sigmund did only use her, at least he did so out of need. Orrin tried to put her off with promises like a child.

"I'll ride seven times round the Palace, Orrin, blowing a horn. Then when you get back from Nass there'll be nothing for you to be king of."

"What the hell are you talking about?"

"Jericho, my dear. And the walls came tumbling down. My mother was a keen Christian – did you know that, Orrin?"

"You know I never met your mother." Shaving now, the rasp clearly audible through into the bedroom. Sigmund had never lived under canvas : he used an electric razor.

"One day, Orrin, I shall go and visit the hovel where I was born. The official photographer can be there to take a snap of my tears."

"If you're getting into one of your clever moods," scrape,

scrape, "you'll make me glad I'm having breakfast with Tarsu."

You are glad, she thought. You're delighted. No more demands on you, no more having to think of things to say to me ... Suddenly he appeared in the bathroom doorway, his face lathered, a cleared oblong down one cheek.

"I'm sorry about today," he said. "If you can wait I'll make it up to you. I really will."

She stared at him incredulously, his soapy face, the towel round his neck like a child's bib, his immaculate breeches and boots. It was something he could not do to her, insult her, reject her, then palm her off with cheating appeals to her loyalty. Loyalty was different from love: it had to be earned. He thought her a commodity to be put into cold storage until some more convenient moment. She wanted to tell him no, no, it was too late for waiting. She wanted to tell him she had waited for ten years, now it was far too late ... But she said nothing. Foolish as he looked, he frightened her.

His eyes narrowed and he turned back into the bathroom, having observed enough no longer to expect her to answer. There was a long silence broken only by the sound of his shaving. Then he ran water and began shaking his bottle of hair oil.

"By the way," he said, "we never did hear any more about that idiotic business with Colonel Balenkov, did we?"

She turned on her side and covered her head with the duvet. By now his only victories were with words. Hers would come that night in his bed. She had not cried for twenty years, he said. She wondered why she should be crying again now, so soon.

During the men's breakfast, from seven to eight, it was Major Kohler's duty to go round the Mess Hall with the Orderly Officer of the day, hearing complaints and making a note of any that needed following up. The relationship between him and the various Orderly Officers was always difficult, since he was occupying a position usually held by a junior subaltern and thus subordinate to the full Lieutenants he accompanied. Neither side quite knew how to handle the situation. By chance the Orderly Officer that day was Lieutenant Mandaraks.

"Boiled liver this morning, Major? I thought so. Smelled it over by the Company Office."

"Wholesome enough food." Major Kohler forced a wry smile. "Full of iron, so the dieticians tell us."

They walked in single file between the noisy tables, trying not to look at the speckled brown lumps of liver on the men's plates. At the end they turned and paused.

"How may oxen are needed to supply this little lot, I wonder," said Lieutenant Mandaraks. "Frozen after the autumn killings, I suppose."

"The peasants would give a lot for a breakfast like that, Lieutenant." Kohler felt compelled to be sententious. "They'd make it last all day too."

"Which is why we never have any shortage of private soldiers."

And back they went between the next two rows of tables. A man stood up and complained about pipes. Pipes in his piece of meat. Not wishing to argue, Major Kohler sent him back to the counter for another helping. The pipes could go back into the pan for the next sitting. At the end of the following row Major Kohler detained the Lieutenant with a hand on his arm.

"I don't suppose you've been doing any more conduit work, Lieutenant, since the snow came?"

"As a matter of fact I have. Why do you ask?"

"Even after the heavy frosts of last week?"

"That surprised me too. I'd have expected the cold to cut the flow down almost to nothing."

"But the water still comes?"

122

"And the mud. Must have shifted thousands of kilos by now. Why do you ask? Have you a theory?"

"The Kitchen Duty man? My dear Mandaraks, what right has the kitchen boss to theories?"

This was the first show of bitterness Kohler had ever allowed himself. Ashamed, he moved away between the tables before Mandaraks could question him further. But the Lieutenant's information was worrying. Since the river was now frozen, this seepage must be occurring well below the surface. Once in the sewers there would be sufficient organic life present to raise its temperature high enough to keep it flowing even in the shallow exterior overflow conduits. This organic heat was all that prevented it from blocking the storm outlets, freezing solid and gradually flooding the entire drainage system. Already the ground was frozen to a depth of over a metre. A few more degrees of frost and the organic heat might prove insufficient to keep things moving. It was more necessary than ever that he should get to see the Minister of State Building as soon as possible.

At the end of the men's breakfast Major Kohler returned to the Officers' Mess. His batman, mutely sympathetic about his unfair treatment at the hands of the Engineer Colonel, had brandy and hot lemon waiting for him. The following two hours, until ten when preparations for lunch began, were free. Often tired out, he had formed the habit of lying down fully dressed and dozing till the batman called him at nine forty-five. During duty hours, when the barracks were noisy with boots and shouting and slamming doors, he found it easier to sleep. The tiny noises of the Palace were drowned and it was therefore safer.

On this particular morning, however, he refused the drink and asked the batman instead for his best uniform. While it was being made ready he washed and shaved himself again – entirely for his own benefit, since the Minister for State Building was a civilian and notoriously ill turned-out. The Ministerial day began at eight thirty, and promptly at that hour Major Kohler presented himself to Anna, the Aide's secretary. He was careful in his dealings with Anna. He did not know many of Tarsu's people, but he was certain that she was one of them. Two years before, when she had been new to the job, he had entered her office and interrupted a muttered telephone conversation. Everybody in the Palace knew that the telephones were monitored as a matter of official policy, so her secretive manner could have meant only one thing – that she was in communication with Tarsu himself. Major Kohler hoped that the Aide was careful. He would need to be.

"Good morning, Comrade Anna. I do not have an appointment, but I would very much appreciate a word with the Minister. It's very urgent."

"It was urgent three weeks ago, Major." She was a tiny person, unsure of herself. But the military were easy to deal with, out of their depth in civil matters and uncertain of their rights. "So urgent that you forced your way into Comrade Kils' office."

"You have a good memory, Comrade." It was necessary to humble himself, even before her. "I was hoping my bad manners might have been forgotten."

"Last time you wanted to see the Engineer Colonel. This time it's the Minister himself."

"If it's at all possible."

He stood silently in front of her, relying on his total acceptance of her power over him to make her generous. It was a fact of command that the seated human being gained in authority over the standing. She looked up at him for some seconds, then leant forward and pressed the intercom switch.

"There's an Engineer Major to see you, Comrade Kils. He wants an interview with the Minister."

"And so do half a hundred other people."

"The Major says it's very important."

"Tell me when it isn't very important."

A small man, loud with his small power.

"If you saw him yourself, Comrade Kils, you could probably deal with whatever it is without troubling the Minister."

"I too have a full diary, Anna." But the flattery worked from within, like heaven. "All right. Tell him to come in."

She released the switch and smiled up at Major Kohler, her influence over the mighty made clear. Much of this, he thought, and I should go mad.

"I didn't tell him your name, Major, or he would certainly never have seen you. It *is* Kohler, isn't it?"

"Again the excellent memory. I must congratulate you." He gave a slight bow. "May I go in now?"

"You know the way."

He knew the way. All dignity discarded, on hands and knees.

Comrade Boris was at the window, watching the day lighten as the sun, still out of sight behind the Palace walls, rose in a motionless sky of dirty clouds streaked with green. Below him on the tiny floodlit parade ground a troop of guards was just marching off after inspection. Getting ready for the President's departure, no doubt. He tensed his stomach muscles and winced. A day or two away from it all would be just the thing. Over breakfast that morning his wife had told him he would be getting an ulcer if he did not relax more. But he did not dare leave his desk, even for a day. He was worried about Poldi. So far he had been able to delay Ministerial discussion of the contract renewal, but he knew his time was running out. And he had made no progress with Poldi, none at all. Gulping his coffee, he had told his wife it was she who needed the ulcer – then perhaps she would get off some of all that fat.

He heard the door behind him open and close. He stayed at the window, looking out. His hands were clasped behind his back, his shoulders hunched like folded wings. He was waiting for the stomach pain that came every morning now, twenty minutes after breakfast. Behind him his visitor fidgetted, one boot squeaking against the other.

"Well, Major?"

"I'm very worried, Comrade Kils. I wouldn't come bothering you if I wasn't so worried."

He recognised the voice. Major Kohler. He swung round and hurried to the desk, his head jerking slightly as he walked. Kohler knew that his moment of greatest trial had come.

"Is our appointments system too difficult for you, Major Kohler? I would have expected even a child to be able to understand it."

"Last time I came the circumstances were different. Last time I came the – "

"Last time you came you were most offensive. I remember it distinctly. Hardly a hopeful basis for appearing now and asking favours."

"It's not for myself, Comrade." Already savaged almost to the limits of his endurance, Major Kohler battled on.

"Not for yourself? Is this the beginning of some sob-story, Major?"

"It concerns the safety of the Palace, the safety of every one of us."

"Come now, come now..." The Aide allowed himself a dry little smile. "From your look-out in the tower you've seen the enemy hordes approaching – is that what you've come to tell me?"

"I'm an engineer, Comrade." Kohler's self control was ebbing fast. "I'm talking about the structure of the Palace. The bricks and mortar."

The Aide to the Minister of State Building sat down very slowly, pulling up the knees of his trousers before he did so. He had forgotten his pain. With an army man who had clearly lost his reason this was going to be better than a picture show.

"Correct me if I'm wrong, Major – service procedure being

126

rather out of my competence – but should not any information you have regarding the structure of the Palace be addressed in memorandum form to your immediate superior? To the Engineer Colonel?"

"That is so."

"Well?"

Major Kohler braced himself for the final step, the lie that was going to place him beyond all help.

"The Engineer Colonel," he said, "is on a week-end pass."

The Aide accepted this without comment. He was, as Kohler had hoped, ignorant of the military's leave arrangements.

"And in your opinion the matter is far too urgent to be left till Monday?"

"Far too urgent."

Boris Kils considered the situation, and took his time. It was just possible that this Major was not mad after all. Was that a risk that he, the Minister's Aide, was entitled to take, indeed dared to take? Of course, the whole idea was ridiculous. The Palace was as solid as a rock. After seven hundred years it was hardly likely to fall to pieces, just like that. Nevertheless. . .

"Perhaps you could tell me a little more, Major. Have you found a death-watch beetle? Or perhaps – "

"It's no laughing matter, Comrade."

"I'm waiting to be convinced, Major. Why not convince me?"

"But time is so short. If I could just see the Minister – "

"I have the Minister's ear in these matters. Believe me, there is a great deal I could do for you if you would only explain yourself."

Major Kohler hesitated, trying to decide if he was being played with. A moment before he had thought he was near to winning. Perhaps this jumped-up little bastard really did have the power to get something done.

"The danger is one of flooding. Flooding and general subsidence."

"Flooding? At this time of year? With the river frozen and fifteen degrees of frost?"

Briefly Major Kohler had a picture of how mad the situation must seem to the other man. Perhaps he *was* mad. Would a madman go over the same set of figures and always get the same non-answer? Perhaps so. He tried desperately to sound sensible and practical, conversant with technicalities.

"It's underground flooding that is possible, Comrade. Perhaps we could just have some heavy equipment standing by. Pumps in particular. Two large capacity centrifugals, at least a thousand litres per minute."

This was the worst thing he could possibly have said. A shutter closed abruptly in the Aide's mind. Pumps meant Poldi and Poldi represented all that he had decided not to think about. So pumps were out of the question. All indecision disappeared. The Major was clearly mad.

"Well, well, well . . . Heavy equipment, eh? You know, Major, Saturday is a very bad day to come asking for contract indents. Why don't you wait till Monday, see the Engineer Colonel, and then – "

"My God – rivers don't look at calendars, Comrade. You can't just – "

"I'm sorry. I have no authority over the ordering of contract equipment. There is absolutely no way in which I can help you. I'm sorry, but there it is."

He stood up, suddenly irritated again. The man was wasting his time. If he had said he wanted heavy equipment at the beginning that would have been an end of it. It was not precisely true that he did not have the authority for contract indents – in an emergency his powers of discretion were very wide – but what sort of an emergency was this? The unsupported word of an hysterical army Major? It would be totally irresponsible for him to take

128

any action at all. And as for breaking his three-week silence with Poldi and ordering expensive pumping equipment, the whole thing was quite out of the question.

"So there it is, Major. May I suggest that you go back to your quarters, and have a rest, and try to forget about the whole thing? I'm sure that in the morning you will – "

"Then if you can't help me I must see the Minister. Please will you ask him if – "

"The Minister is not available."

"But this is a matter of extreme importance."

"I'm sorry, Major." Boris glanced down at the clock on his desk. "The Minister is accompanying the President on his official visit to Nass. He should be leaving the Palace at this very moment."

In the high gaudy office silence descended, broken only by the tick of the clock and a rasping noise as the Aide scratched the inside of his thigh. Very distantly the clatter of Anna's typewriter began. Major Kohler found himself aware of these tiny sounds to the total exclusion of any cognitive process. Presented with an insuperable obstacle, his mind shifted onto another level. A faint noise from the floor above was studied and finally identified as that of a vacuum cleaner. Or perhaps the obstacle was not totally insuperable after all.

"They'll be leaving by the Entrance Salon?"

"Already gone by now, unless something's seriously wrong with the schedule."

"Then I might be lucky." He was already at the door. "Thank you, Comrade. I might just be lucky."

"He won't see you, Major. You can't possibly break in on him when he's with the President – "

But the Major was already gone. Boris sat down and stared at the closed door. It was papered in a shiny marbled design that exactly matched the black marble dado . . . The Major was mad. He was the original Mad Major. Breaking in on the Minister was just the sort of thing he would do.

And get away with it. Fill the Minister up with some nonsense and have him ringing through from the foyer ordering centrifugal pumps and all sorts. Then off to Nass leaving a shambles. And Poldi fairly crowing... He tapped his desk for a few seconds, then got up. He fetched his coat and went into the outer office pulling it on. He was in a hurry.

"Just going out, Anna. If anybody rings, I'll be back in about an hour."

"Where shall I say you are, Comrade?"

"Out, Anna. Just out. It's not as if you were my nursemaid."

He closed the office door behind him. He had not yet made up his mind where to go. But if he were not available, then the Minister would have to leave without giving any orders. And by Monday the Mad Major would probably have thought better of the whole thing... He decided to visit the reference library for the next hour. There must be something he could be looking up, were he questioned.

Eight

THE E.A. HAD risen and breakfasted in a pleasantly leisurely manner. Being unmarried, he shared domestic staff with the other bachelor on that floor – Marshall Tarsu. But he ran his life completely differently from the Marshall, breakfasting as late as possible, taking a very light luncheon and then dining heavily, usually alone, at seven thirty. Marshall Tarsu on the other hand, whether on duty or not, ate massively four times a day, at seven, twelve, five and nine. So the two men rarely met over meals, a fact they both considered to their mutual advantage. Too much of the rest of the time they spent almost in each other's pockets.

His late breakfast this morning was particularly fortunate, since it gave the staff time to recover from the extra strain of entertaining the President. Raoul discovered that the the two men had been deep in conversation, hardly noticing their food at all. He wondered if their subject had been the Korda profile. He thought not: Tarsu had received all his instructions through Novaks himself and so would have no way of telling if the President were a party to the plan or not. In such circumstances Marshall Tarsu's discretion was – unless designedly otherwise – absolute. Raoul wondered if he should himself pass the news on to Marshall Borge before he left for Nass, but quickly decided against the idea. There would be plenty of time for that when the President returned on Sunday morning. With luck there might be other things to report to the President by then.

He read the two newspapers. Between them, he and the editors concerned had done a fine job.

Hard-working and hard-playing Sigmund Korda enjoys getting away from it all as much as do any of us, remarked Nation. *And of course, unlike lesser citizens, the services of our popular Minister of Education seem to be rewarded equally by the Paymaster and by the Tax Collector. Nobody grudges him his Paskellnyi mansion, containing, it is rumoured, many fittings made from pure gold. But we do wonder, in common with the humble citizens of Paskellnyi, how he manages it. By money or by love? Tell us, Comrade Korda, what is your secret?*

The People's Progress was more dignified, but no less savage.

Our reporter visited his country residence to try to discover how Comrade Korda spent his leisure hours. The old retainer was reserved: the Master took holidays only when the affairs of State let him. Loyal servants kept his place always ready for him. Yes, of course he was popular in the surrounding district ... Obviously our progressive Minister of Art is as well served in his recreations as he is in his work.

The old retainer ... loyal servants ... Raoul Novaks smiled. Emotive words indeed – to describe an old housekeeper put in by the Government and a part-time ex-serviceman gardener. Even the crude *Nation* invention of the gold fittings was sound: to the peasantry gold was a symbol of the former Church, and that was a symbol of oppression. Taken together, especially with the odious love or money insinuation, implying gross favouritism, these two paragraphs would be very hard for the President's office either to answer or ignore. Sooner or later an enquiry would have to be instituted, under the fatherly and impartial eye of Marshall Tarsu.

Raoul Novaks folded the two papers till they would go in his inside pocket. It was time he waited on the President before the departure to Nass. Out in the corridor the rising sun was just clear of the section of Palace wall visible through the narrow window at the far end. It reached feebly a few metres across the carpet, leaving the rest of the passage, like a deep well, lost in shadows beyond shadows. Novaks paused, fascinated by the tiny distant oblong of mullioned light, by the cushioned silence, the slightly breathless air-conditioned warmth. As a lawyer he had grown accustomed to richness, to the velvet hangings of Judges' Chambers, even to the priceless carpets and overdone furniture plundered by the German occupation forces, but he had never, not in nearly twenty years, grown accustomed to the laboured yet oddly unconsidered magnificence of the Palace. It still gave him a despicable thrill occasionally to remember where he was and what he had at his disposal.

Marshall Borge was in his private office, standing by the elephant-legged desk, shuffling papers into a briefcase. He had a single oil lamp lighted on his desk, and behind him the windows were obliquely greenish with the dawn. Pine logs hissed and whistled in the newly made-up stove. In the darkness the crowding shapes of the furniture might have been anything: boulders, animals, distant groups of huddled soldiers waiting for daylight. Novaks watched from the door into his own office as the President continued to shuffle the papers meaninglessly, his mind far away.

"Your speech, Comrade President. I have it here. Your speech for the factory combine at Nass."

"Tarsu's worried, Raoul." Marshall Borge did not look up. "He reports an awkward mood in some of the cities. Even in Dorlen."

"It's Marshall Tarsu's job to worry, sir. Besides, if his agents go more than a month without reporting anything he begins to accuse them of incompetence."

"Then you think there's nothing in it?"

"There's always something in it. If people aren't dissatisfied they aren't alive. I think this visit of yours to Nass comes at an ideal time. You're a people's leader, sir – they should see you more often."

"If I had the time young Korda has . . ."

"Besides, your reception in Nass could be quite revealing." The E.A. wished to avoid any discussion of Comrade Korda who was, as it were, *sub judice*. "It's a representative industrial town. Industrial workers are the ones the agitators go for."

"Official receptions, Raoul. What the hell good are official receptions?"

"You've been an army commander, sir. You know when your men are with you."

Marshall Borge nodded absently. The E.A. had the strong feeling that instead of humouring he was the one who was being humoured. He offered the text of the speech again, and it was taken. The President looked round at the huge basalt clock, the hands of which showed five to nine.

"Balenkov is always very punctual. I must go down to the car."

He snapped the briefcase shut. There were sections of his life, however, that could not be sealed away so easily.

"See to Katarin for me if anything happens, Raoul. Her life's enough of a mess as it is."

Before Novaks could reply the President had leaned forward, quickly blown out the oil lamp, and hurried away between the dim outlines of the furniture to the door. Suppressing a moment's anguish at the commission he had been given and the way in which he would carry it out, the E.A. followed him and together they silently made their way down past offices and ante-rooms, along velvetted corridors to the big first floor foyer. There the double line of Colonel Balenkov's guards began, sombre grey uniforms strangely impressive against the shimmering splendour. His instincts as a commander caused the President to slow, to give the men the respect they deserved. He paused here and there for a few words with soldiers he recognised. The

E.A. followed now at a formal distance. This was a ritual the President never forgot, was never too busy to give due time to. The loyalty of the army, so easily won, was Marshall Borge's most precious single asset. The E.A. found himself wondering to whom he would turn for loyalty when the time came. If it ever did.

At the head of the Murderer's Staircase Colonel Balenkov was waiting, and behind him the men who were to accompany the President on his official visit: the Minister for Scientific Progress and his Aide, and the Minister for State Building. At the sight of them Marshall Borge suffered a moment's brusque depression. Separated from him by far more than the differences between his officer's and their burocrat's uniforms, they were not companions he would have chosen for a three-hour car journey through bleak and uninteresting countryside. They were men of cheerful expediency, pragmatists, concerned always with the attainable – in politics, in their whole lives ... But Colonel Balenkov was waiting at the salute. It was time to go down to the car.

The E.A. had seen this tiny hesitation and guessed its probable cause. The most that could be said for the Minister of Scientific Progress was that he had an unsympathetic nature. Possessed of a large family, he ran them on a roster system, with strict rates of increased yearly consumption, and he feared them deeply. The Minister for State Building, on the other hand, was an amiable enough man but that worst of all social liabilities, a thoroughly bad but enthusiastic raconteur. The E.A. moved forward quickly, in order at least to be able to help the President over the initial civilities.

The party moved slowly down the staircase and across the blue tiled floor of the Entrance Salon. Beyond the two rigid lines of guards the vast salon was totally deserted, its floor set about with dozens of glass showcases gleaming blackly in the light from the six great chandeliers. In these cases were exhibits detailing the brutal and oppressive rule of seven hundred years of hereditary kings. The footsteps of the President's party echoed in the huge stillness of contained air. Through the open doors at the end the jumble of buildings round Revolution Square was drab and streaked with frozen snow. Three flagged cars were waiting and a dozen motor cycle guards. It was too early for any Saturday busloads of tourists to have arrived, but a small crowd of spectators, mainly the families of Palace servants, had gathered on the steps outside to stare at the President and perhaps cheer. The official agency photographer was on his haunches, the camera held in thickly gloved hands, waiting for the impressive shot up the guard-lined staircase as Marshall Borge and his companions emerged through the Grand Entrance. The Cathedral clock began ponderously to affirm the punctuality of responsible government, and on the fifth stroke the President came quickly down the steps, nodded to the crowd and ducked into his waiting car. The Ministers and the Aide were close behind, and Colonel Balenkov, with the air of a hotel *patron,* brought up the rear. Marshall Tarsu's presence a little to one side of the Grand Entrance was so discreet that few people other than the E.A. noticed him. Raoul Novaks, his duty to the President performed, waited while Colonel Balenkov stooped in at the door of the car making sure that its passengers were comfortable, and then turned away. Behind him he heard the car door slam and the guard present arms. Then the roar of motor cycle engines as the motorcade departed. The Cathedral clock arrived at its ninth stroke and stopped.

He was about to wander over to Marshall Tarsu – ostensibly to congratulate him on the efficiency of the arrangements – when he noticed the solitary figure of an army officer hurrying down the Murderer's Staircase between the waiting guards. The officer stumbled, recovered himself, and obviously became suddenly aware of his extremely prominent situation. He came on, however, walking briskly at the embarrassed half-march of a junior officer not quite off the parade ground and not quite on it. He traversed the entire length of the Entrance Salon, caught sight of Marshall Tarsu, and saluted. Then he paused, looked uncertainly down the steps at the empty roadway and at the outside guard being marched away under the Guard Sergeant. Raoul Novaks was intrigued.

"Can I help you, Major?"

"I'm afraid not." Major Kohler had an uneasy feeling that he ought to know the civilian who was addressing him, at least by reputation. "The President's party has gone, I see."

"I am the President's Executive Assistant. If it's something important, perhaps – "

"No. No, thank you, Comrade. It was the Minister for State Building I was hoping to catch. But I'm obviously too late."

"The motorcade left at nine o'clock, Major. We're nothing if not punctual, here at the Palace."

Major Kohler's mind was in a turmoil. He distrusted the E.A.'s slightly mocking tone, yet at the same time he desperately needed someone in whom to confide. In many ways the President's Executive Assistant might be the ideal person – a man who had the confidence of the highest authority in the land and yet was himself approachable, without authority, hardly more than a glorified secretary. He hesitated, terribly aware of the hundreds of pairs of eyes upon him. Raoul, on the other hand, had lost interest and was turning away.

"Perhaps . . . perhaps a moment of your time, Comrade? A matter effecting the safety of us all?"

"A security matter, Major? Then Marshall Tarsu is – "

"An engineering matter, Comrade. Certain faults in the structure of the Palace . . ."

He suddenly saw the folly of it, going round begging,

telling his same drab, improbable little story . . . A very strange heroism.

"If the matter is urgent, Major, you know who to see as well as I do. In the absence of the Minister for State Building his Aide has full authority."

"That's what I thought, Comrade." Kohler allowed himself vengeance. "But he denies it. Protecting himself, I think. He seems to be afraid of something."

The E.A. had been on the point of dismissing the whole affair: junior officers came up with cranky ideas from time to time and the system filtered these out before they caused too much trouble. But this remark about Boris Kils was worth further investigation. Only the E.A. himself and perhaps two other people knew just how right Major Kohler was.

"You interest me, Major. If you wouldn't mind waiting a moment . . . Then we can go up to my office."

Major Kohler watched his tall companion walk away to where Marshall Tarsu was standing. He watched him stop and speak urgently. Neither man looked in his direction. The E.A. tapped the inside pocket of his jacket meaningfully several times. The conversation was obviously important. Major Kohler looked away.

All round him the Entrance Salon was busy with guards forming up and marching away, shouted commands, the muted stamping of soldiers in their unstudded Palace boots. Two men came and closed the huge entrance door and the chandeliers were switched off. The Salon returned to its gloomy, working-day appearance. Suddenly Major Kohler looked at the implications of his latest action and was appalled. If to go above the head of the Engineer Colonel was dangerous, then to bypass both the Minister for State Building and his Aide was professional suicide. To the E.A., a civilian, the fact of being right in the end might be sufficient justification : to the President, a soldier, it would be irrelevant. Comrade Novaks finished his conversation and returned. His opening remark showed him to be quite as aware of the situation as Major Kohler himself.

"Speaking to me like this, Major, makes you either a brave man or a fool. And I believe I can spot the latter at a hundred metres. We'll go on up to my office."

They went upstairs without speaking. Apart from a group of cleaners dealing with the extra dirt brought in by the soldiers to the upper foyer, the Government Building had settled back at once into the routine of a normal working day. In working a full Saturday the Palace set an example to the whole country, an example only indifferently followed. In the copper mining areas, for example, the men had recently gone on strike – illegally, of course – for a bourgeois free Saturday afternoon. They were still out on strike, starving, while the mines were being run, rather more efficiently, by army engineers and immigrant labour. The forty-four hour week was an invention of the decadent West, emasculated by centuries of soft living on the blood of the proletariat.

It was the first time Major Kohler had been up onto the third floor of the Government Building. The magnificence to which he was accustomed, and which he respected, was more rugged, more national. To his uninformed eye the passages he was led along might have existed in any of the reactionary stately homes of the West. He disapproved.

Once in his office the E.A. sat Major Kohler down and listened carefully to what he had to say. The Major assembled his facts neatly, and spoke well. During his discourse the E.A. took notes, and asked occasional questions.

"Your observations have been spread over three weeks, Major. Presumably this subsidence has been going on for some time. Why is it suddenly so urgent?"

"This morning's measurement was dramatically different, Comrade," Major Kohler lied. He could not admit that the urgency might only exist within himself. "The floor of the

Passage is twisting and rising. It might break at any moment."

"Exactly how serious would that be?"

"The immediate effects are hard to guess. Certainly there would be sudden inundation. How far that would rise I cannot say. But it's the secondary effects that are worrying. Rapid erosion of the Passage walls so that the barrel vaulting gives way. A major earth movement of that nature could easily set up a chain reaction."

"I see . . ." The E.A. was concerned with a private speculation of his own. "Tell me, Major, this pressure of water – where is it coming from?"

"From the river, almost certainly. Exactly how I'm not quite certain."

Comrade Novaks was silent. More than anything else, it was essential to avoid any precipitate action. There was a great deal more involved than the Major knew about. He was glad that the matter was now in his own hands, rather than in those of someone less responsible.

"Now, Major, I must get this absolutely straight. You told the Minister's Aide all this – " a vital point – "and you asked him for emergency equipment, pumps and so on. These he refused?"

"I didn't tell him as much as I've told you, Comrade. There . . . wasn't time. Frankly, he didn't seem to be particularly interested."

"Comrade Kils is a busy man." Meaningless formulae. The time for drawing in Comrade Kils had not yet come. "I'm sure he acted properly – especially since the machinery you require demands a special indent to the contractor in Dorlen." He smiled secretly. "So what do you suggest I do, Major?"

"A word from you, Comrade, would be enough. If the Minister's Aide could quote your authority, then – "

"Yes, I see . . . And the water is coming from the river, you say?"

"I've studied the maps very carefully. There used to be a tunnel leading out under the river, but it was demolished and sealed five years ago. So the only other possibility is that there's been a movement of rock strata somewhere, causing. . ."

But the E.A. was no longer listening. The problem had always been how to maintain the escape tunnel and at the same time preserve its secrecy. Now that it had collapsed the situation was extremely delicate. He had always considered the Central Committee's insistence on keeping the route open to be melodramatic and hopelessly unrealistic. For the secret to become known at that particular moment would be untimely. No administration, but especially not one ruling by the will of the people, should have its need for a bolt hole made public . . . Novaks decided to gain himself time in which to think.

"Major Kohler, I agree that emergency equipment should be obtained. I shall see to it at once."

"I'm very grateful for your faith in my judgment, Comrade Novaks."

His judgement fitted only too well with what Comrade Novaks already knew. The E.A. nodded wisely.

"At the same time, Major, you must see that this is not an easy situation. The last thing we want to do is to start a panic among the Palace staff, many of whom are very simple people. Also there is your own position to consider, Major. While I myself appreciate your having come to me, there are others who won't see it that way at all."

The threat was extremely politely put. Major Kohler had been too long at the Palace, however, not to recognise it. He waited for the ultimatum.

"Discretion, Major. Nothing more. Keep this between ourselves for the moment. I shall tell the Aide that the pumping equipment is needed for draining the fire fighting reservoirs."

"He'll think it a strange coincidence, Comrade. First me wanting pumps and then you."

"Ministers' Aides are not there to see coincidences, Major. They obey orders. Just as you do."

Comrade Novaks possessed a power not immediately apparent. Tall, thin, frequently stooping, he might at first glance have been mistaken for a slightly condescending lecturer on political philosophy. This judgement would have ignored the assurance of his movements, the incisive quality of his voice, the keen intelligence of his eyes, above all the calmness that came from reasoned application of his own strength. No matter how quietly he spoke, when he told a person to do something they did it. Major Kohler stood up.

"Then I shall do nothing further, Comrade Novaks."

"Just keep an eye on conditions, Major. And Major . . . you may never be mentioned in despatches, but, believe me, the Administration's very grateful to you." He knew how these little remarks mattered. Major Kohler bowed slightly, then went to the door. "I'll see that the pumps are here first thing tomorrow, Major, Sunday or not."

Major Kohler left the office. Closing the door behind him, he took out his handkerchief and wiped his hands, finger by finger. An interview that had begun as a last desperate cast had ended in glory. He replaced his handkerchief in his pocket and set off down the corridor, contained in a golden aura. The E.A.'s words would stay with him for the rest of his life, the tone of voice, the warm smile; even the setting, the blue and gold ceiling, the purple curtains, the ebony desk with brass inlays, the gilded plaster cherubs supporting the many lights that burned against the slow December dawn. Major Kohler's mind held the entire scene exact down to the smallest detail. It compensated him magnificently for the past weeks of sleeplessness and squalid work in the kitchens.

If a thought niggled at the back of his mind, the thought that with all this secrecy nothing constructive, such as strengthening the Paul VII Passage, could ever get done, he kept that thought firmly out of sight. He had his pumping equipment, and he had the gratitude of the Administration. A loyal officer, he asked for nothing more.

The E.A., meanwhile, had encountered a minor difficulty: the Aide to the Minister of State Building could not be found. All that his secretary would say was that he was unavailable. Out. The E.A. asked her politely to ring him back the moment the Aide returned. A Minister's Aide had no right simply to be unavailable during working hours. The score against poor Boris was mounting.

Poor Boris . . . For a blinding moment the chasm opened in front of Novaks. Means and ends were one, two aspects of the only reality. Ignoble ends begat ignoble means. Furthermore, ignoble ends begat ignoble means begat ignoble men. To use a pathetic little schemer like Boris was despicable . . . Raoul snatched the newspapers out of his pocket and flung them on the desk. To use unprincipled newspapermen was despicable. To use people at all, use their weaknesses, push them around without dignity left on either side, was this leadership? And if it was, then what was the man attracted to leadership but a cheap manipulator, selling himself for no more than the chance to sell himself again?

Seeing the edge of the pit, he was able at the last moment to draw back from its fascinations. Leaders were ecologically necessary: to judge them was irrelevant. He turned away, shuddering, and fixed his thoughts on the existential moment, on the papers in front of him on the desk. They reminded him of Sigmund Korda. A man who would embrace leadership like a child embracing an enormous puppy. Sometimes one would be on top, and sometimes the other.

Comrade Korda had gone that morning to the library to inspect progress on the new annexe. He was not pleased with what he found. The floor joists were not yet in, and the work was seriously behind schedule. The officer in charge, a Captain Felsen, was not a very enterprising man and he had also had bad luck. One workman had been taken to hospital with his eyeball lacerated from a chip of flying stone, and another had fallen from the interior staging and broken both his legs. Sigmund had little patience – he knew from experience that some officers were more accident-prone than others. The date for the opening ceremony of the extension had been fixed, academics from many European countries invited. Still to be struggling with floor joists at this late stage was ludicrous. He listened to the Captain's long explanations with unconcealed anger.

On leaving the annexe he paused in the unfinished doorway to dust himself down. Looking round the reading room he caught sight of Boris Kils hunched over the morning's papers at a side table. Amused to have caught the man out – such ascendancies as this were always useful – he wandered quietly over to where the Aide was sitting.

"What's this, Boris? Has Corruption Inc. made so much that you're now on the retired list?"

The other man started visibly. He fumbled with the paper he was reading and tried furtively to push it away under some Party magazines. Sigmund leaned on the reading desk, one hand accidentally pinning the corner of something called *Nation*.

"Certainly not, Comrade Minister. I was in the Reference Library on business, and I simply paused on my way back to the office to see what the gutter press is up to."

"I see. And what *are* they up to? It seems to make good reading, whatever it is."

"Not really, Comrade Minister. Only ... only some trumped-up grievance among the steel workers. They're always complaining about something."

He tried to turn over the page, but Korda stopped him.

"Hold on, there. Isn't that a photograph of me?"

Boris capitulated.

"They didn't get it from me, Comrade Minister. Not one word. They tried, mind. They came, three of them. and asked all sorts of questions. But I – "

"The French have a saying, Comrade. He who excuses himself accuses himself. In the circumstances a dignified silence would be far more becoming."

"It's not that at all, Comrade Minister. I assure you, there's nothing I – "

"Hold your tongue, man. At least let me read what you're making all this fuss about."

The Minister's Aide sat in edgy silence, his stomach giving him hell. Sigmund read the article from beginning to end, maintaining his slightly amused frown through to the bitter end. When he had finished reading he closed the paper, folded it, and replaced it with the others on the reading desk.

"I can't think why you're so worried, Comrade. You'd hardly tell them I've got gold fittings when you know damn well I haven't. And anyway, what the hell are gold fittings?"

"But they must have got the information from somewhere."

"There's no need. The thing is a complete fabrication – that's why they cover themselves by admitting it's only a rumour. We could get them for spreading irresponsible rumours, I suppose. If it's worth it."

"But why should anyone want to make up rumours about you, Comrade Minister?"

"It's lies that sell papers, my dear Boris. The truth is usually so dull."

Comrade Boris silently contemplated the enormity of newspapermen. He was relieved to have somebody other than himself at fault. The Minister's calm impressed him. Lesser men would have been furious: Comrade Korda appeared to be, if anything, saddened.

"Well, Boris, there's a grindstone waiting for both of us, I expect. About time we got back to it, don't you think?"

"Of course, Comrade Minister. I was only – "

"I know you were, Boris. I know you were."

This flash of irritation was all that showed of the turmoil behind Sigmund's careful affability. Boris got to his feet, offered a half-bow, the legacy of pre-Revolutionary days, and hurried away. Sigmund waited till the door had closed behind him, then found the day's copy of *People's Progress* and glanced through it. Clearly a campaign had been started by someone seeking to destroy him. The source must be within the Palace – Boris's account of the three reporters made that obvious. They had been advised where to go and what questions to ask. He tried to calculate who would be likely to benefit most from an attack of this nature. Finding this impossible, he turned to a count of his friends instead. The first to come into his mind was the President himself.

Politically he and Marshall Borge were very close. On a personal level they were also very friendly. He wondered for a moment if the Marshall might have found out about his relationship with Katarin, but dismissed the idea. If Marshall Borge knew that he was Katarin's lover then the President would have no interest in political disgrace : he would want Sigmund dead. Korda had no doubts about this – the conflict between the two men was ultimately one which both could not survive. Indeed, he recognised now that this was the issue he had subconsciously chosen, for only on such terms could the Presidency be contested. Until this challenge was recognised and accepted, political considerations would outweigh all others. So the President was his friend.

Of the others he was less sure. About the E.A. he had no illusions at all : Raoul Novaks was nobody's friend, not even at root his own. Marshall Tarsu put the Party above all personal considerations : surely from that basis he would not contrive the discredit of such an active and politically orthodox Party member as himself? The Minister of Economic Security would stay uninvolved whatever happened, absorbed in the intricacies of international accountancy. The Minister for Scientific Progress, would not he benefit from educational advances and therefore be friendly? Or would he conversely be resentful of the money apportioned to the Arts and therefore have to be counted an enemy. . .?

Korda abandoned his survey. There were too many imponderables. He decided to concentrate on the known, on Marshall Tarsu and the President. And the President, as Sigmund knew very well, was away in Nass till the following day.

Nine

MARSHALL TARSU HAD as his office a small room leading off the wireless and communications centre in the squat, golden-domed tower at one end of the Government Building. He liked its atmosphere of continual activity. "In some parts of this holy morgue," he would say, "you feel you ought to apologise to the rooms even for breathing in them." He liked to be at the centre of things, and since the term 'communications' was in the main a euphemism for telephone monitoring and desk bugging, his office was in a very real sense the centre of everything that went on in the Palace. At any time of the day or night he could go to the duty operator and ask for a live hearing on any one of more than five hundred outlets. Alternatively, he could ask for a playback from one of the twelve recorders that ran continually, taping samples from every corner of the Palace. The principle behind his system of surveillance was preventative. Everybody knew it existed, so the temptation to utter disloyal thoughts was reduced. "I can't control people's thoughts – at least not yet," he would say, "but damn me, I can prevent them spreading the seditious nonsense around."

This open surveillance, coupled with an unnumbered band of agents, worked very well. There had not been a seditious thought uttered within range of his all-hearing ears in fifteen years. When plotting did occur, then it took place far away from the seat of government and was bound to make itself known before it achieved dangerous momentum. It was this factor more than any other that had decided the President – on advice from Marshall Tarsu – to resist the urging of many of his associates and not to decentralise the moment he came to power. He had never regretted his decision.

Korda knocked on Marshall Tarsu's office door and entered without waiting for a reply. The room had been stripped of all the Palace furnishings and decorations that were so ideal for the concealment of microphones or more lethal devices. In their place Marshall Tarsu had chosen bare colour-washed walls, a plain fitted carpet, and office furniture on thin metal legs. The chairs relied for comfort on loose foam-plastic cushions. The Marshall was a man who took few chances.

"Aha – Sigmund. I was wondering how long it would take you to get here."

"Then you've seen the papers?"

"Naturally."

"And you knew I'd come to you?"

"The obvious choice. With the President away I'm probably the only man you can trust in the Palace. Sit down, my dear Sigmund. We must think this thing out."

Sigmund went to the window. The shadow of the Palace from the sun still low behind it lay, elongated and precise, across the snowbound marshes. He identified the outline of the dome above his head, distorted into the black flame of a huge black candle.

"What do you think the Central Committee will do?" he said.

"No need to make a drama, Sigmund. What should they do?"

"For God's sake, Karl," he swung round, "I'm accused in the public press of misappropriating Party funds. They'll have to do something."

"You have no very active enemies. They'll do what the President tells them to."

"That's what I can't understand. You say I have no active enemies. But a story like this – it didn't just spring out of thin air."

Marshall Tarsu pursed his lips and tipped his head sideways.

"I was talking about the Central Committee, Sigmund. Farther down, who can say? A civil servant somewhere whom one has slighted? I don't have to tell you how easily that can happen."

"We all tread on people's toes, Karl. Surely the man who started this must be getting rid of more than just a petty grievance?"

"You talk as if it were going to do you any harm. You underestimate your popularity, Sigmund. A simple statement from the President denying the allegations and that'll be the end of it. After all," he added innocently, "everybody knows what good friends you and the President are."

Which was exactly why a simple statement from the President would do more harm than good. Korda turned away to hide his sudden doubts. Such a snide comment – would a friend really have offered it in the guise of consolation . . .? Perhaps sensing his mistake, Tarsu joined Sigmund and put his arm round his shoulders.

"A bad joke," he said. "Please forgive me . . . You came here wanting my help. Anything I can do, you've only to ask. You know that."

"I wondered . . ." Sigmund was wary. "I wondered if you might have picked up anything, anything suspicious, any clues as to who might be at the back of this."

Tarsu spread his arms.

"Not a word. Not a word. And you know my coverage. The President himself is only safe within his quarters and his own private office."

"But your agents – would they think something like this worth reporting?"

"Insinuations against a member of the Central Committee? Of course they wouldn't. Besides, who would dare? Knowing the coverage, who would dare risk it?'

Korda was silent. Somebody had dared. And it had to be somebody knowledgeable, somebody the newspapers would listen to, somebody within the Palace. Unless of course. . .

"Do you have a tap on Ministers' country lodges, Karl?"

"Only when the Minister is in residence. Manpower isn't unlimited – we have to draw the line somewhere." Marshall Tarsu gave his shoulders a little cuddle. "Pecker up, old boy. Dirt sticks, we all know that. But not for long. The peasants are fickle – they'll find another victim soon enough."

Victim. Karl seldom used words carelessly – he was having his situation explained to him. He was a political victim, able to do nothing but sit tight and wait till everybody lost interest. And sitting tight was completely foreign to his nature.

"I shall go to Paskellnyi this afternoon," he said suddenly. "I must see old Sorelle. Perhaps she will know something about all this."

"All that way, Sigmund? Why not use the telephone?"

"No, I must speak to her face to face." What would she say, knowing the telephones might be tapped? Besides, he needed action. "Besides, Kerrill needs the exercise. It's the perfect day for a ride."

"Forty-five kilometres? Going it a bit, don't you think?"

"Two and a half hours. I shall enjoy being extended for once. Don't you ever find the Palace stifles you, Karl?"

"The way I look at it, old boy, it's the other way round. It's I who stifles the Palace."

This answer pleased the Marshall very much. He laughed extravagantly, watching Sigmund till he too managed, as an admission of temporary defeat, overt laughter. And as he laughed Sigmund received a sudden shattering revelation. He realised the childishly simple fact that he must regard the Marshall as a rival, the Marshall and probably every other member of the Central Committee. He realised that his planning up to that moment had been simple-minded, that in his cheerful egoism he had made the conflict dangerously one-dimensional, that he was engaged in a race in which there were other runners. And that in consequence he was himself totally alone, with the Palace as sole referee and judge. He stopped laughing.

"My dear Karl, if you think that about the Palace then you're a doomed man. If you set yourself up against it you'll lose every time." He went to the door. "I tell you, the man who gets these old stones on his side will be invincible."

The Marshall's sudden uneasiness showed. It was a triumph for irrationality.

"The poet Minister," he said, still laughing strenuously. "Personally I put my faith in electronics."

Sigmund would have been amused by Katarin's image of the Marshall as a priest. New times, new religions. He allowed himself, this time from strength, to join the pretence that they were both joking.

"I must go now," he said, "before this conversation gets too metaphysical. Thanks for the advice, Karl. I'll do my best to take it."

And he went out.

He had told himself that he was totally alone, but that was not true. Surely in Katarin he had someone with whom he did not have to compete? Somebody who envied him nothing and sought from him nothing but a satisfaction it was in his power to give? He believed that she loved him. As for his feelings towards her, they were too complex for him to dare to analyse. If love were among them that was enough ... He remembered their coming evening and night together which was impossible now that he had to go to Paskellnyi. He went slowly away from Marshall Tarsu's office, choosing a route through the maze of corridors that led him to the long gallery lined with the official portraits, uniformly flattering, of twenty-seven kings and princes that formed the approach to the President's private quarters.

Katarin Borge had stayed in bed until after her husband had returned from breakfast, collected his cap and overcoat and gone through into his private office. He had paused on the way out to say goodbye in precisely the same dutifully affectionate way as ever, just as if nothing had happened. Perhaps for him nothing *had* happened. Then he had gone out and she had lain rigid, listening to his footsteps on the bare floorboards of the sitting room. The door into the far office had opened and closed. Only then had she been certain that he was not coming back, that her face – her name even – was for the moment safely forgotten. She had collapsed like a puppet with cut strings, the sudden release of tension leaving her limbs unbelievably heavy, the current of her strength flowing out into the indifferent bedding. She had lain like this for perhaps half an hour. Then abruptly she had sat up, rung the bell, ordered her breakfast, cheerfully restarted her day. She told herself that her husband had made the decision for her.

When Sigmund knocked at the door to the Presidential apartment, she opened it herself for she was expecting him.

"Good morning, Comrade Katarin. May I come in?" For the benefit of microphones in the gallery. "I have some papers for the President's attention as soon as he returns."

"If they're so important, Comrade Korda", mocking him, "don't you think you should show them to the E.A.?"

"Comrade Novaks is not in his office. Besides, these are for the President's personal attention."

"Then I suppose you'll have to come in. Though it's an awful nuisance."

She closed the door firmly behind him. They kissed, playing fishlike games with their tongues, laughing softly, bodies very close. Her legs weakened till he was supporting her completely and she was hardly able to breathe. She wrenched away.

"How dare you." She was suddenly angry. "You'd like me helpless like that before you always. How dare you."

"Comrade Katarin will now give her famous exhibition of taming three Siberian bears single-handed."

"It's not funny. I ride as well as you. I drive a lorry, work a chainsaw – "

"Two kisses and you're just a helpless little jellybaby. Which is only right and proper."

She picked up a chair, fully meaning to hit him with it.

"Talk to me like that ever again, Sigmund, and I'll – "

"I'm sorry, Katarin. I shouldn't talk to anybody like that. I'm sorry."

He was completely serious. Always she dazzled him with alternating tenderness and anger, ferocity and submission. With understanding and patience he could bring the extremes of her sexuality together and make them one. He believed it was for this ability that she loved him. She lowered the chair warily.

"You mustn't tease me, Sigmund. It's worse even than being ignored."

"Katarin my dear, I came to tell you something." He had to lower the pitch of the conversation. He took the chair from her and made a long pause while he replaced it in its former position. "Something you won't like. I have to leave the Palace immediately after lunch. I shan't be back till tomorrow at the latest."

"Leave the Palace?" Not him too. Not Sigmund. "Where must you go?"

154

"To Paskellnyi." He told her why. "You see how urgent it is. How vital to my, to our whole future."

She noticed his slip but did not resent it. He would think of his future just as she would think of hers. They were separate, and equal.

"I shall come with you," she said. "I would love to see Paskellnyi. It's the obvious answer."

"But Katarin, how can we possibly just ride off and – "

"You mean Orrin? He doesn't care a damn."

She knew this at once to be only a partial truth. As long as he had her, Orrin might not care. But the moment he knew he had lost her . . . she remembered how that morning he had frightened her just by being. Sigmund's anxious face gave her a way out.

"Don't look so worried, Sigmund. I'm not going to plead with you. Either you want me to come with you or you don't."

"Of course I do." And he did. The thought of the two of them in Paskellnyi was intoxicating. "But it's too dangerous. You know it is."

"I know a man like you can arrange anything if he wants it badly enough."

It was a child-like dare, one Katarin should have disdained, one he would all the same try to meet. It was just possible . . . He knew he could trust old Sorelle, the woman who looked after the Paskellnyi house for him. She had been headmistress of his village school and in the Revolution she had been wounded, her left leg amputated below the knee. Too old to learn to manage a false limb, she had been drafted to a home for incurables down in the south. Sigmund had heard of this, taken pity on her and asked her to accept work as his housekeeper. A small flat went with the job, room for her books and a few remnants of her life. In Paskellnyi she had found a small group of children the State considered ineducable, and to these she gave lessons each day when her light household work was done. She was possibly the one person in the whole world that Sigmund could count on to be utterly loyal. If he was able to protect her by not letting her know Katarin's real identity, so much the better.

"Supposing I did arrange it, Katarin . . . Do you stick to what you said about Orrin not caring?"

"Well. . ."

"Because you're wrong, Katarin. The day Orrin finds out the truth he'll be driven to destroy us both, himself even, if necessary. It's a risk we daren't take."

"He'll be bound to find out one day, Sigmund."

"Not till we're ready. Not till my position is prepared."

Katarin recognised too much of Orrin's objectivity. She lowered her head. She had been eager for the grand gesture, riding with Sigmund out of the Palace, bestriding the same horse, the wind streaming her hair out behind her, challenging everything that marred the innocence and inevitability of love. Consequences, she told herself, were nothing to her. His parsimony disappointed her.

"Prepared, Sigmund? You're not always so cautious. In what way prepared? And what position?"

His eyes went momentarily blank and she knew he was not going to tell her.

"Katarin. This afternoon I ride to Paskellnyi. There's a little car there – I keep it for my housekeeper who's crippled. I'll drive back at once, reaching the Mantua Gate around seven. We'll be in Paskellnyi by nine. I'll get you back here in plenty of time for the return of the official party on Sunday."

"Do I wear a false beard? Is that what you expect of me?"

"It won't always be like this, Katarin. Just for the moment my political standing is very shaky . . . The moment has to be right. My enemies would – "

She had to stop his excuses, stop him destroying himself. Besides, what she had she should be grateful for.

"I'll be there, Sigmund, with my hood buckled tight.

I'll be there at seven – try not to keep me waiting. It would be so . . . noticeable."

Her irony was wasted, his mind racing on, accomplishing the entire night in a moment.

"The guard on the gate is an old war comrade – he'll look after you . . . The Paskellnyi house is so beautiful, Katarin. Down by the lake, its verandah leading down to a boat-house and a little wooden pier. If the sky is clear we can skate in the moonlight, then go back in to baked vinegar potatoes and hot ginger . . . I'd like you to try my housekeeper's recipe."

Katarin was silent, pictures slowly growing, an atmosphere establishing itself, mysterious, sharpened a little by danger, romantic, attractively unreal. Sigmund sensed her mood. He described the drive out, the wooden house, the pine forests, white owls floating in the clear dry air. He described the bare interior of the house, the simple carved staircase, the bedroom under the eaves, the sills of its low windows level with the floor, sheets that smelled of lavender and the ancient oaken press in which they were stored. He told her about Sorelle on her stumping crutches. He so enchanted her with images that she gave up trying to resist. He had the soul of a poet, she thought. Politics lessened him.

"You'll come, Katarin?"

"I'll come."

Already he had stayed longer than was discreet. He kissed her very gently and went. After the door had closed on him she leaned with her back against it, smiling foolishly. She lacked the objectivity to see herself, a woman of nearly forty, with thick arms, a Hero of the Revolution, pathetically in love. Her pleasure, she told herself, was at the prospect of getting away from the Palace for a few hours. It had lowered over her for too long. Afterwards could look after itself. There was always an afterwards – until you were dead.

Sigmund Korda was on the telephone to the Engineer Colonel. There was the question of the library extension to be dealt with.

"Minister of Education here, Colonel. I've just been inspecting our library extension. Getting a bit behind schedule, aren't you?"

There was a short pause.

"Not far behind, Minister. Making good progress, I'd say."

"I'm afraid I wouldn't. Your Captain Felsen tells me the floor won't be in before next Wednesday. That's four days late, Colonel. I – "

"A – er – very tricky operation, Minister. Felsen's a good man."

"He struck me as being an utter fool. I thought you understood the importance of the work. Have you no-one better?"

Another pause as the Engineer Colonel struggled with the conflicting forces of his pride and fear.

"Captain Felsen is a very conscientious officer."

"What about the new classrooms we built for the Palace primary school – you had someone else in charge then, didn't you? He seemed much more enterprising."

"You mean Major Kohler."

The hatred behind these words could be felt even down the telephone wires. Sigmund ignored it – he had no time for the Engineer Colonel's likes and dislikes.

"Kohler – that's the name. Put him on it. He'll get things moving."

"Major Kohler is on Kitchen Duty, Minister."

"Then take him off Kitchen Duty. Tell the kitchens they'll have to do without him for a bit."

"There's a rota for these jobs, Minister."

"Then change it. Once the library's done you can leave him on Kitchen Duty all summer for all I care."

The Engineer Colonel's silence managed to convey deep misgivings. Sigmund decided to lose his temper.

"Look, Colonel – that extension must be finished on time. I don't give a damn about rotas or anything else. I'm frankly surprised at your dilatory manner, Colonel. I thought we understood each other."

"Captain Felsen has equally high qualifications, Minister. I really – "

"Is he capable of Kitchen Duty?"

"That's not the point."

"Is he?"

"Of course he is."

"Then swap them round, Colonel. I shall be on site first thing Monday morning to discuss the plans. I shall expect Kohler to be in charge." There was no further protest. "After all, we're both thinking of your record, Colonel. The successful completion of a job like this will look well. Very well indeed."

"Just as you say."

The Engineer Colonel rang off sharply. Sigmund had no objection to allowing him his little rudenesses, as long as he got what he wanted. If any man could catch up on the schedule, then Kohler would. Sigmund called his secretary. With only three hours till lunch there was a great deal of work to be done, and very little time in which to do it. He started checking staff appropriations for secondary schools in the administrative district of Beckel.

The part of his day in the kitchens that Major Kohler detested most of all was the period from ten o'clock until lunch was served. He found the coarseness of army catering very distasteful, the huge sheets of yellow fat on the horse-flesh, the smell of pastry made with slightly rancid margarine, the grey froth on the cauldrons of boiling potatoes. He had acquired the habit of slipping away during the cooks' break at eleven thirty when the cooking was well under way, and of spinning out his absence until twelve or after. This was the time when he usually visited the Paul VII Passage.

During the previous week all distortion to the floor had ceased. Major Kohler was inclined to interpret this as a bad sign. If a state of full compression had been reached, then the danger of sudden collapse was very much increased. In the face of this he had developed a heightened awareness, an almost hysterical sympathy with the structure seemed to act directly on his body, on his nervous system. He stood in the narrow tunnel and shared its slow disintegration. He walked down it, his skin pricking with the effort of concentration. At one point he kneeled and placed his ear against the stone. The whispering was louder. And above him the cracks in the vaulting had spread, an earthquake of crevices travelling across the worn masonry, seeming to move even as he watched. He ran his hands delicately along them, feeling them, hearing them, knowing them.

He walked to the far end, to the blank wall where work had ended when the king had died. The vibration there was violent, quivering under his feet. He returned to the foot of the metal ladder, suddenly afraid. Even here in the ladder well distortion had taken place. On the way down he noticed that the ladder was slightly loose on its mounting. The well was unlighted, so he took out his torch and examined the iron trunnions. He saw for the first time that the lower section of the ladder was demountable, held in place on each side by bright steel pins. The stonework behind the ladder, although dirtied, was new also, where an ancient archway had been filled. He swung the ladder back out of place and examined the masonry behind it more closely – its carefully aged appearance seemed to him curious. The stones were fitted so closely that he could see no sign of mortar between them. He prised at one and found it loose. Starting at the top, he soon removed enough to make a hole sufficiently large for his head and shoulders. The sound of running water was very loud.

The first thing he saw through the opening was another wall some two metres away, but when he shone his torch downwards he disclosed a vertical well descending some six metres before it ended in a thick yellow river streaming angrily past. Down the side of the shaft bright new steel rungs gleamed in the light from his torch.

He replaced the stones one by one and fixed the ladder back in position. He knew quite well what he had discovered. He remembered the E.A.'s anxiety and understood his real reasons for urging discretion. He understood in what a difficult position his information had placed Comrade Novaks, and also how hopeless it now was to plan any major reconstruction work in the area of the Paul VII Passage. He thought of the workmen who must have made the secret entrance – who were they, and where were they now? In former times they would have died as soon as the job was completed. Had the Administration any more reason to trust its servants today?

Back in the kitchens he found a messenger waiting for him with orders that he should go immediately to see the Engineer Colonel. He went, resigned to whatever might happen, convinced that one or all of his transgressions had come to light. He learned instead that he was being put in charge of work on the library extension. Brusque beyond the point of incivility, the Engineer Colonel informed him that he was to take over on Monday morning. In case he might think this was a sign of returning favour, he was to do a full day's Kitchen Duty on the intervening Sunday. To simplify administration, the Engineer Colonel said.

For Major Kohler's part, he would willingly have worked the full thirty-six hours non-stop, if he could have been free of the kitchens at the end.

Ten

UNLESS TRAGEDY CAN be seen in drab resignation too easily accepted, Amélie Korda was not a tragic figure. All that she had ever expected of life was that it should treat her in a manner about which she could feel justifiably aggrieved. Her childhood was aggrieved, and so were her schooldays. Her striking appearance coupled with her arrogant stupidity had made her generally disliked. When her poor academic performance led to her not gaining university entrance she told everybody that this was on account of the examiners' prejudice against female students. Her father was a schoolmaster: she blamed him for not being able to use his influence. And when the hated office job she had been forced to take suddenly ended as a result of the Revolution, it quickly became the only chance she had ever been given, the one thing in her life that had ever been really worth doing.

Revolutionary soldiers had come to her town, behaving – as she had expected – like pigs. The lower ranks whistled and shouted after her because she so obviously despised them, and conversations with the officers never progressed beyond a few cold words in the post office or the lending library. She assumed that the pattern of her life was fixed, that she would go lonely and unappreciated to her grave.

Then one evening her schoolmaster father brought two young officers home to dinner. One had been training to be a teacher himself before the Revolution, and the other

– slightly older – had been at medical school. Under the eye of her father she was obliged to be polite to Lieutenants Korda and Balenkov, indeed, more than polite. Almost charming, in fact. She felt a great sympathy for the two young men, their lives – like hers – ruined by the coming of the Revolution. They were intelligent people, with the seeds of greatness even, and now – like her – they must resign themselves to lives of total insignificance. She offered them tea from her own pre-Revolutionary hoard. And they responded next day with army supplies, a dozen eggs and some very hard black chocolate. She treated them as equals, comrades in misfortune.

The next few months of her life were the most happy and normal she would ever know. She fell in love, or thought she did, first with one and then with the other and finally with both. She took secret dancing lessons and permed her hair. They were both very attentive, and both asked her repeatedly to marry them. She had a lace dress of her mother's that she wore whenever she thought a proposal was in the wind. She always refused the proposals because she could never make up her mind. And anyway, there was plenty of time. . .

The summer was very hot, the two young officers had little to interest them. All over the country Revolutionary troops were being disbanded – Balenkov said he was going to transfer to regular service and Korda tried to talk him out of it. Both of them were completely dedicated to the Revolution. They allowed Amélie to tease them about their Communist principles since she was a charming girl, and to do otherwise would have been to deprive them of the comforts of her father's home. Her heart was in the right place, they told each other. All that was needed was a little education of the right sort.

Then suddenly the regiment was to be moved to the Palace and the dream was shattered. Seeking safety in numbers, the two young men called together to say goodbye.

It would be very hard to blame Amélie for what she did. With the officers gone her life would end, her youth, her love, her happiness. So she prised them apart, intending to send first one and then if necessary the other down to the bottom of the garden on a fruitless errand while she reminded the remaining officer of his proposal and told him that she had now decided to accept. The order in which the young men went to the bottom of the garden she left entirely to chance. It seemed a romantic notion.

As things turned out, it was Balenkov who went first, and Korda who stayed. Lieutenant Korda was too humane at that time to do anything but express joy at this sudden change in his fortunes. Lieutenant Balenkov accepted his defeat like a hero. And so Amélie, making – as she was willing to admit three weeks later – the greatest mistake of her life, went to live in the Palace as the wife of Lieutenant Korda. Secretary Korda, private secretary Korda, Minister's Aide Korda, Junior Minister Korda, Central Committee Member Korda, it was all the same to her ... The Palace was a mausoleum. In her father's house there had at least been conversation. And laughter. Besides, somebody should have told her what men were like. Her father had always seemed so delicate-minded. At least *he* – she told anybody who would listen – would never have expected of her mother what Sigmund expected of *her*. Had expected at first. But not latterly. Thank God.

Her place in the life of her husband and of the Palace was very small. Mostly she was a resigned background presence, thin and faded, pitiable only to the lover lucky enough to be sent down the garden first. She was to have her moment later, but on the afternoon when Sigmund was getting ready for his ride to Paskellnyi she was, although in the next room to him, almost non-existent. The Kordas' apartment was one of the most magnificent sets of private rooms in the Palace. Retaining all their original fittings, their grandiloquence amused Sigmund and flattered him, and provided Amélie with almost the only consolation left to her. She lay now behind drawn curtains on a green velvet chaise longue in her bedroom, trying to assuage one of her migraines with green velvet dusk. In his bedroom next door Sigmund was changing into his warmest clothes – by the time he reached Paskellnyi the sun would be down and the temperature far below freezing. He knew her headaches to be very real, whatever their cause, and usually he respected them by preserving total silence. On this occasion, however, he felt a sad need to make her understand.

"One day I shall be President." He spoke the thought for the first time. "One day Orrin's distance from people will make him miscalculate. His enemies are influential. The man he trusts most of all, Novaks – even he would down Orrin if the chance presented itself. Novaks sees himself as President, they all do. When the moment comes there'll be a scramble for the top. And for a man to come out of that on top he needs two things: the support of the people and the support of the army."

He pulled on thick woollen socks reaching to above his knees. From his wife's bedroom he heard a faint sigh. He presumed he was boring her.

"Until yesterday," he went on, "I had both. Today both are in danger. This lie about Paskellnyi must be refuted utterly. I intend to organise a reception there immediately, a meeting of artists and writers from all over the country, men known for their outspokenness. The ostensible reason will be to discuss extensions of State patronage. The house will be open to all. These men, whom the people trust, must come and see for themselves how their Minister lives."

He zipped up his breeches and stamped to settle them around his calves. He put on a second knitted jersey and then his long leather riding jacket. His words were frank – nothing he said would be news to anybody with political sophistication, certainly not to Karl Tarsu or the President.

"This is why I must go to Paskellnyi. First to speak to old Sorelle, find out if anybody has been spying there. And second, I must make preliminary arrangements for the reception. You see how important this is, Amélie. If this lie is not refuted it could mean the end of my political career." The continuing silence irritated him. "It could mean us having to leave the Palace, it could even end in my death. Do you understand now, Amélie, how important it is?"

The silence in the next room prolonged itself painfully. Sigmund sighed, and began to tug on his boots. Suddenly he stopped, recognising the distant barely audible sibilants as the sound of his wife's voice. He concentrated his attention.

". . . and if the shops are open when you get to Paskellnyi you might see if they have any tapestry canvas. I have a new design to trace. The servants don't go to Dorlen till Tuesday. . ."

He fetched his long white fur-lined cloak and flung it about his shoulders. He had a white bearskin hat with ear-flaps and the collar of his cloak stood up in front almost to his eyes.

"I'll do my best, Amélie," he said. "But you know the village – a couple of shops and a post office. I doubt if they'll have what you need."

"Of course," said the distant reed beds, "if it's too much trouble. . ." and the wind among them died, leaving them silently grieving.

Sigmund took no notice. He put his head round the door, whispered his goodbye into the green gloom and hurried away unanswered. With no time to waste he took the lift down, and then went quickly through the swept streets to the nobly-proportioned west front of the Palace stables. A contemporary archbishop had complained to Gustav I that he housed his horses more nobly than his God. A shrewd criticism this, it had resulted in two new chapels and an enlarged nave to the Cathedral of the

Blessed Virgin . . . Sigmund's cloak billowed out behind him as he walked; a wind was getting up, its direction hard to judge in the narrow streets of the Palace. He frowned – a head wind could add half an hour to his journey, scorching his cheeks and bruising his eyes in their sockets. Goggles were available, but he disliked to be blinkered. As he entered the stables an orderly was bringing Kerrill from his stall. The Stable Sergeant came running to check the saddlery. Sigmund stood at his horse's head, making himself known, his familiar smell and the apple he always offered. The animal jerked and danced sideways, clattering on the ancient embossed tiles.

At that time of day many of the stalls were empty, the horses being exercised in the old market place outside the Palace walls. The huge barn-like building was unusually quiet, and Kerrill's noisy fuss made Sigmund slightly ashamed. He took the horse away from the sergeant and out into the open. The old soldier was wasting his time – he would have to check each item for himself before mounting. The sergeant stood in the doorway watching, and clucking to himself and wiping his hands on the soft yellow cloth he used for rubbing up the horses' flanks and the flat hard sides of their necks. Kerrill was a black gelding, probably the finest horse in the stable. The sergeant's eyes, that had seen so many, never tired of looking.

At last Sigmund was mounted and away. He rode through the echoing intricate streets and out under the Maria Irene Gate. From the roadway beyond there was a glimpse of the top floor of the Palace and the windows of the Presidential suite. The sun shining on the windows made it impossible for him to tell if Katarin were watching for him or not. He reined back, Kerrill rearing heraldically as he removed his white fur hat and waved. His white cloak snapped in the wind and his shadow, even at two in the afternoon, was long on the chain-patterned snow. Kerrill pranced, his hooves throwing showers of chips like bright steel filings. Then he got his head down and was off over the bridge and away.

The wind was behind them and a little to one side, so that for most of the time Sigmund seemed to be travelling in still air. He let his horse gallop off the first excess of energy, then settled to an easy canter. The road wound across the plain for about three kilometres between snow-covered banks, passing two low farmhouses with their windbreaks of black, steeply-leaning trees, and a constantly changing geometry of angled fences that receded seemingly without end into the haze of distance. They met a tractor towing a trailer piled high with steaming manure, and later a solitary child carrying a basket and scuffing the toes of its red rubber boots in the snow. At the edge of the forest Sigmund rested his horse briefly before beginning the long ascent through the trees.

He looked back at the Palace, the fantasticated tip of a black mountain steep against the surrounding plain. Even as he watched, he half-expected it to slide quietly beneath the surface, the fields moving in as if it had never been. What were his aspirations in the face of such transience? The thought amused him. He turned away and urged Kerrill on up the road, smiling to himself, thinking of the Emperor Aurelius who from the summit of power had philosophised on its insignificance. Perhaps when he got there he too would pretend to disregard it.

Among the trees the snow had fallen unevenly, leaving some places bare and piling huge drifts in others. The plough had sliced these away. Sigmund rode, now at a trot, through surging canyons where the noise of his progress died at once against the blunt sheer walls. Kerrill's ears were forward, picking tiny sounds out of the forest silence, jumpy perhaps from ancestral memories of the wolf packs. Sigmund rose to the trot easily, staring round, sniffing the scentless cold, enjoying his horse's perfection of movement. Kerrill was right at any pace, graceful and in complete control, with the quiet stability of a fine, deep-keeled ship. They came to a junction, where the road to Novellnyi led off down to the left. They went on up through the woods to the top of the ridge. Sigmund paused again. Kerrill stood, shifting his hooves on the beaten snow, waiting patiently.

And so down the other side and along the bank of the river, now frozen, that fed the Novellnyi lakes. There were marks where a small herd of deer had crossed the ice, and further up a frozen waterfall where a new bridge carried the road across. The water had piled down the side of the rock like wax down a candle, thick and ugly. Not even the setting sun struck any sparks in its diseased opacity. The place was uneasy, faintly malignant. Sigmund rode round the side of the hill into night, pushing his horse harder now for the way was level and they would soon come to the second river that meant they were nearing Paskellnyi. There was a side lane here that avoided the village and approached his house along the shore of the lake. He was tempted to take it in order to discover if it had yet been cleared, for it afforded the best view of his house, the one he would have liked for Katarin. But he remembered his promise to visit the shops in Paskellnyi, so he kept to the main road and finally arrived in the little steep village square.

Paskellnyi was a typical lakeside mountain village, with a way of life that had hardly changed in five hundred years. In the summer the villagers fished and farmed in the bottoms of the valleys around, and in the winter they tended their few wintering stock, collected firewood, and stayed indoors making lace and carving traditional figures, dolls and bears, and representations of their ancient local god, Paska. They fashioned their god in the image of those they had down the centuries feared most, a perfect low-browed Mongol with slit eyes and high cheekbones. Their village was built in the shadow of his hill, and their lake was watered by streams that sprang from his mouth.

The village comprised about thirty houses, a thatched church, built under protest at the express command of Paul VII, who was very zealous in the faith, and hardly entered since, a school, two shops — one of which sold petrol and did motor repairs — and a post office. The main street that Sigmund rode down from the square was unlighted, for the village had neither electricity nor gas. A hydro-electric scheme at one end of the lake had met with continual setbacks. To officials the people laughingly said that Paska must be angry. How they spoke among themselves no outsider would ever know.

The houses that Sigmund passed were two-storied, and from their lower floors came the comfortable sounds and smells of animals being bedded down for the night. He stopped at the first of the two shops, tethered Kerrill to the hitching rail, and went in. After the darkness of the night outside the single oil lamp on the table was painfully bright. There was no formal counter, indeed, no formality of any kind at all — certainly there was no formal price structure. Life was hard for the villagers and correspondingly hard for the two shopkeepers who supplied their meagre needs.

The combine that had been set up after the Revolution had made as much impact on their lives as had that earlier imported ethic, the church. Without constant surveillance, the State manager had quickly succumbed to village hostility, and the old ways crept back. Poverty was an unanswerable counter to political solutions. As far as the shopkeepers were concerned, what was lost on the villagers had to be made up on the visitors, on the rich outsiders who had foolishly built houses down on the dangerous shores of the lake. Dangerous for reasons that were never explained. A few years ago the visitors had been aristocrats, now they were high Party officials. The change made little difference to business: there had been generous aristocrats just as there were mean Party officials.

Sigmund looked round for the shopkeeper, finally distinguishing him with difficulty from the pile of old potato sacks on which he sat.

"Old man – " it was a term of respect – "old man, I want to buy some tapestry canvas for my wife. Also a bottle of pickled sheep's eyes for the old housekeeper."

The villagers liked to be given reasons for things. They liked proof that the outsiders were real. Sigmund had been in the shop several times before; the old man must surely recognise him. The shopkeeper did not move from where he was sitting.

"Nobody in Paskellnyi makes tapestry," he said. "Our women are lace makers. They leave tapestry to others."

Having but five teeth, and these more trouble than use, his speech was obscure. But his tone of voice left no doubt as to his opinion of tapestry makers. Sigmund controlled himself: they were after all a very poor and backward people.

"Then I am to tell my wife you have no tapestry canvas?"

"Now if she were to make lace. . ." The old man woke to the possibilities of making a sale. "For lace, honoured sir, I have all materials. Bobbins, weights, frames, cotton of the highest quality imported from – "

"Sadly I must refuse, Comrade. My wife is an excellent woman, but she has not learned the great skills of lace making."

This statement saddened and at the same time comforted the old man, confirming all his worst suspicions about the women of other villages. He rose from his heap of sacks and came forward into the lamplight, bringing with him a strong smell of goats. He made out for the first time Sigmund's white cloak and hat. With deep misgivings he recognised his caller as a government official. So the visit had nothing to do with tapestry canvas or with pickled sheep's eyes.

"I have permits, Excellency." He rummaged in a heap of pre-Revolution magazines. "My shop has been inspected and approved, Excellency. I have permits of every kind. We're lawful people here in Paskellnyi."

"Keep your permits, old man. All I want is – "

"My slaughterer's licence, Excellency . . . I have it somewhere. All who see me say I am a true artist. Pigs may squeal, but they feel nothing, so neatly the knife enters. And no blood is wasted. I have witnesses, Excellency, who will tell you."

"All I came to your shop for was a – "

"My potato wine is to government specification." The knuckles of his clasped hands glistened with sincerity. "Those who tell you otherwise are – "

"Enough, old man. Now be quiet. I have no interest in your shop, none at all. Just sell me the sheep's eyes and I'll be on my way."

"If your Excellency is sure. . .?" The shopkeeper had heard of traps like this before.

"And I'm not your Excellency. If you must call me something, I'm Comrade Korda." He looked in vain for signs that his name meant anything. "Perhaps you know my housekeeper, old Sorelle, her with the one leg."

"That one?" The old man scratched his beard agitatedly, convinced at last. "You go to see her now? She is a bad one. You tell her from me, Excellency, that the meat she returns is not bad at all. You tell her I eat it myself, cooked with no more than a thimble of paprika. Delicious. You tell her it is a crime to blacken my name. You tell her. . ."

Finally Sigmund was able to buy his jar of pickle, beating the shopkeeper down to a figure not quite twice its price in a Dorlen supermarket. He also obtained the assurance that tapestry canvas was to be bought nowhere in Paskellnyi. There was no demand, the old man said, and Sigmund believed him. Lace could be sold in the cities, but tapestry – tapestry was the pastime of the idle rich. And the mindless idle rich at that. He went out into the street.

The moon was rising in a clear sky, and he found Kerrill's reins stiffly frozen where he had knotted them over the rail. He eased the leather carefully and mounted. Villagers who passed him as he made his way on down the street said not a word, turning perhaps understandably away from the tall white figure on the tall black horse. He rode at a walk, keeping himself motionless. Individuals he could not contact depressed him. In Paskellnyi his slightly satirical theatricality was unsuitable and separated him from precisely those whom – on a certain level – he had an emotional need to reach. They were, he reminded himself, a very backward people.

He went slowly down between the jumbled, stone-slated houses, and out along the road to the lake. As he left the village behind he became more cheerful. His secretary had telephoned Sorelle to say he was coming, and he knew she would have made ready a warm welcome. His parents were long dead, she was unmarried and childless – it was not surprising that a close relationship had grown between them.

Kerrill sat back on his haunches for the last steep descent to the lakeside. The house was among the trees immediately below them, and Sigmund smelt sharp pine-wood smoke from its chimneys. Then they were down in the shadow of the hillside, in front of them the lake gleaming like fine pewter between the narrow tree trunks. The snow was softer here, and muted the sound of Kerrill's slithering hooves. A lighted window came into sight, and then the whole ground floor of the house, lamps in every room. Sigmund shouted, and urged his horse forward, turning in at the short drive that led to the wide wooden verandah. Sorelle was on her crutches in the doorway. And an owl, alarmed, dropped from the top of a telegraph pole and flew silently away across the open space in front of the house like a huge pale moth.

"You're bloody late, Comrade Minister. Only yourself to blame if the borsch has boiled too long and tastes of dishclouts."

"I think of my horse first, and your soup second, Sorelle. Anyway, it always tastes of dishclouts."

"In your mouth the old words don't sound right. With all your art and education you'll be bringing us television next. The days of the old words are numbered. And the language of literature. Soon we'll be using Newspeak, and writing it too."

He dismounted and began to lead his horse round to the stable. Sorelle followed him, hopping with great agility through the snow.

"I can remember when we tried to speak as the great ones had written. Today books are written as the fools speak. It's the death of language, I tell you."

"Sorelle, you old fool, at least let me get into the house, can't you? I'm cold, I've ridden forty-five kilometres, and your soup is spoiling."

"Your fault, Comrade Minister. All your bloody fault, burying me here with nobody to talk to. Sometimes I think the grunts of the villagers will kill me. Kill me. And they do it all day long, just grunt, grunt, grunt. . ."

"And what sort of talk would you have got from the incurables, eh, Sorelle? Tell me that."

He was unsaddling Kerrill and drying him down. A storm lantern, ready lighted, hung from the low central beam of the stable.

"I know I'm ungrateful. I know I could be worse off. But here you are, like meat thrown to a starving wolf. Can you blame me that I eat you up?"

"You have the children, Sorelle. Surely things aren't so bad?"

"Hopeless. Impossible. You might as well talk with

174

maniacs. Now the accumulator in my wireless has gone, and nobody in the village to replace it."

He was squatting down to examine his horse's feet.

"Silly old fool. D'you hear me, Sorelle? You're a silly old fool. Worse than that, you like to suffer. A word to my secretary while she was ringing you, and I could easily have brought you a dozen new accumulators. But now . . . you'd rather suffer."

"Me? Ask that toffee-nosed little whore? She wouldn't know what I was bloody talking about. 'Hai'm so sorry, Comrade. Could you spell that please?' Secretary — I know another word for that sort."

Laughing, he straightened and fetched the horse blanket. "Dear Sorelle . . . I'll send you out an accumulator first thing Monday morning. And that's a promise."

"Which brings me to another thing, Comrade Minister. This coming alone and staying but the one night — what's that for? 'Business,' her ladyship says. Trouble, I say."

"Trouble indeed, old woman." He hunted inside his cloak and brought out the two newspaper cuttings. "Take these into the kitchen and read them while you're stirring up your witch's brew. And if they make you spit venom, see you do it in the fire else you'll have me poisoned for certain. Go along now."

She propped herself up to take the cuttings. Then she hop-thumped away round the side of the house to the kitchen porch. Sigmund finished dealing with his horse, then looked into the garage next door. The car had been out that afternoon, probably for supplies, its engine still slightly warm. He would have no trouble getting away for the return journey to pick up Katarin.

In the kitchen his soup was already on the table. The room was furnished with his high-backed wooden chairs, a dresser, and a samovar big enough for the entire Royal Guard. The stove hissed with heat, and the room was filled with the powerful smell of red borsch. Sorelle sat at the table reading the cuttings. Sigmund sat down where his place was laid and began breaking his bread into pieces which he dropped into his soup. When the old woman looked up he knew all the fooling was over.

"This is serious, Sigmund. What are you going to do?"

"I've made my plans. But I must know where the papers got their information. Has anybody been to see you?"

"Not a strange face in three months. This is Paskellnyi, not Lyck or Dorlen."

"Are you sure? They can be very cunning."

"They'd have to be cunning indeed to dress up as the moronic goatsmilk man or the squint-eyed post mistress. They and the shopkeepers have provided my only conversation in three months. And you wonder I talk you into the ground."

Sigmund remembered the shopkeeper's message but decided it would have to wait. The first few mouthsful of soup were making him sweat. The refinements of Palace cuisine had lowered his resistance.

"These gold fittings, Sorelle — I know the villagers are simple people. Could they really make up a thing like that to tell a reporter?"

"The gold fittings are nothing. Anybody could have made them up, even the villagers. What I don't like is the suggestion that your work, your reputation, is built on the talents of others. It's a subtle attack, very hard to counter." She looked at him sharply. "Any idea who's at the bottom of it?"

He had no idea at all. Instead, he told Sorelle of his plan for a reception. She nodded, making no mention of the back-breaking extra work it would mean for her. He said he would go round the next morning and try to talk to the villagers, to the man who cut wood for all the government houses. One of them might know something. Then he told her he had to leave almost at once, taking the car. He did not say where he would be going.

"You're cold and you're tired, and you've ridden forty-five kilometres. Now you're going off again somewhere. Either you're mad or you've got a woman."

"Which is, dear Sorelle, just another form of madness."

"You said it, Comrade Minister, not I. So you've got another woman. Do I know her?"

"I think not." For the old woman's sake he hoped not. The President's wife was seldom photographed, there was a fair chance Sorelle would not recognise her. "But she's very nice. I think you'll like her."

"I never liked that first one, with the French name. It was too late, though – you'd married her before I met you. Are you going to marry this new one?"

"And commit bigamy?" He laughed. "How would that look at the next elections?"

"Trust you to bloody know that bigamy's a crime and adultery is not." She pointed an arthritic finger. "And don't tell me I split my infinitives because I know it. Some of our best poets have split their bloody infinitives."

Which was a way of closing the discussion. She did not ask who his woman was, or where he was driving to fetch her. She watched him finish his soup. Then she held his cloak for him as best she could, and went with him to the garage. She saw him drive away back up the way he had come. She was filled with a deep fear for him. Leaving the garage doors open for his return, she swung herself back into the house and began heating a second brick for the big double bed. It had been a long day and her shoulders ached from the crutches.

Eleven

MAJOR KOHLER WAS drunk. This was for him a rare condition. It was usual for soldiers in the Palace, officers and other ranks, to get drunk on Saturday nights, but Major Kohler usually preferred to keep himself apart, to go to bed early in fact. The reason he gave his friend Farkas was that once drunk he might possibly make a fool of himself. Was that not the point of getting drunk? said Farkas. To make a fool of oneself and not care a damn either way? At this point Major Kohler always moved out of the discussion, feeling his incomprehension of this attitude to be unmanly and even shameful.

Therefore, although on this occasion emotional pressures had prompted him to drink heavily – the Mess Special was a port and vodka concoction dashed with tabasco to aid the digestion – his inner censor remained cloudily watchful, repeatedly warning him to mind how he walked, to be careful how he talked, and above all to resist the temptations of the follies indulged in by his fellow officers. There was, for example, the game of Romanian Football: in this the younger officers got down on their knees and shuffled backwards, wildly kicking at some suitable object, usually the youngest officer's hat. No goals were ever scored at this game, the real interest being in whether or not the object's owner got away from his captors in time to rescue it before it was totally ruined. Another game – of necessity played less frequently and called simply the Table Game – involved two spurred officers squatting Cossack fashion on one end of the long polished dining table and hopping in this position to the far end. The winner of this was awarded a bottle of champagne and the loser paid for the table to be repolished.

Major Kohler found himself encouraging the latter contest with disturbing fervour. While one small part of him was remembering his previous disapproval of this game, the rest of him was cheering itself hoarse. Indeed, he would have taken part himself if Captain Farkas had not forcibly restrained him. Captain Farkas, a veteran of many Mess Nights, knew just what a large part of even a Major's pay went into the simple work of stripping, sanding and repolishing. So he held Kohler back, and interested him instead in the less expensive sport of putting out a candle blindfolded, at six feet, with a soda syphon.

The noise in the Mess was appalling. After Major Kohler had discharged his syphon into the lap of a Lieutenant Colonel and the Lieutenant Colonel, without apparently noticing, had continued to toss olives into the Regimental Fencing Trophy on the self-rewarding basis of one eaten for every two that went in, there seemed little more to be done except to retire to the bar for further Mess Specials. He and Captain Farkas sat and drank, and watched a musical junior officer pour beer into the body of his guitar, and they laughed until sticky tears ran down their cheeks. Most of Major Kohler had not enjoyed itself so much since his very first party at the Palace, eight years before, when he had . . . But the laughing part of Major Kohler blanked that memory out and went on laughing.

Then somebody produced a piano accordion. At its first chord the entire Mess fell silent. Colonel Balenkov had a few words with the player, then stepped forward and sang. He sang a folk song of the Northern Province. His voice was huge, the song very simple and sentimental, and it seemed to Major Kohler the most beautiful sound he had ever heard. Other songs followed, fierce, gay, mournful, occasionally obscene, all the officers joining in with parts and descants and noble rallentandi ... till Major Kohler's heart grew so full and his censor so bemused that he gave in to an overpowering desire to confide in his dear, his only, his most beloved friend, Captain Farkas.

"D'you know what he said, Farkas? I can ... see him now, just as if he was here in front of me." The voices surged around him. Farkas seemed half asleep. "He said – Farkas, are you listening? He said, 'Major Kohler,' he said, 'you may not be mentioned in despatches, Major Kohler, but believe me, the Administration is very grateful to you. Eternally grateful.' He said that. 'Eternally grateful...' Are you listening, Farkas? What d'you think of that?"

"I think it's bloody marvellous, old man."

"You do?"

"I said I do. I think it's bloody marvellous."

The guitarist got up to play his beer-filled guitar, taking an untidy drink from it first. As the cheering died down he started to sing, accompanying himself with great charm and precision. The song told of spring evenings in the forest, of young love, of death. All this the officers knew and understood. They listened in clammy silence, eased their swollen necks in their collars, nodded with emotion. Captain Farkas, who had dozed off again, suddenly awoke.

"Bloody marvellous," he said loudly. "But you haven't told me why. You haven't told me why the Admini ... why the E.A. was so bloody grateful."

Men were turning in their seats and glaring. Major Kohler nudged his friend.

"It's a secret, old man. The Central Committee's little secret."

"I don't like that. I don't like secrets." Captain Farkas screwed up his face, trying to think. "I don't like a man

who keeps secrets from his friends. It shows a lack of ...
of confidence."

"But where goes discretion, Farkas? An officer without
discretion is like a whore without. . ." The simile escaped
him. "An officer without discretion is no more use to the
service than a — "

The Lieutenant Colonel of the olives leaned forward and
tapped Kohler's shoulder.

"Would you mind, Major?"

"Mind? Mind what?"

"Some of us are trying to listen to the singing."

"Oh, I see." Kohler turned back to his friend. "There,
Farkas, you're spoiling people's enjoyment of the singing."

"Wouldn't have happened, Kohler, if you hadn't got so
... so peremptory with your secrets. A flagrant act of
provocation. A breach of the — "

"All right, Farkas, supposing I tell you. In front of all
these people, supposing I tell you — what then?"

"Won't be the same. Not the same at all."

The singer had stopped singing, and was taking a last
drink from his guitar which had begun to leak. It is hard
to believe that Farkas and Kohler did not on some level
of consciousness know what they were doing, and therefore
deserve the rough handling they received. With a great deal
of shouting and jostling they were carried out one by one
and dumped in the snow. The door was slammed behind
them.

The Officers' Mess was on the first floor, built over store
rooms, and a wide cobbled walk circled three sides of it,
communicating by means of ramps with the ground at one
end and the top of the Palace Wall at the other. In times
of seige these ramps were used for ammunition trucks going
up and stretcher bearers coming down. Major Kohler and
Captain Farkas sat on a pile of snow and stared around
at the roof-tops glistening under a brilliant crescent moon.
In the Mess behind them the guitarist had begun to sing

again, his song rendered even more beautiful by the thick oak doors between. Captain Farkas spoke the thoughts of them both.

"It's like a bloody fairy tale," he said.

It was so magical it made them want to weep. Then the snow began to penetrate their trousers and they stood up, lending each other unobtrusive support. They wavered for some minutes, overcome by the sorrowful beauties of the scene. The song ended, and the officers in the warm Mess under the glittering chandeliers applauded distantly. Major Kohler began to walk away, and Captain Farkas followed him, to look after him. They made their way together up the ramp onto the battlemented wall. The air was quite still, the sounds of the Palace weaving gently round them. A motor bicycle revved and drove away to silence. A bucket clanked as it was emptied. A dog howled and then was stopped by shouted abuse. Above them against the tingling stars the great Cathedral clock began to strike seven. It made them jump. The night was very young, the revelry hardly started. In a minute they would go back down, sneak in and find their old places by the bar. Though not quite right, no longer in keeping with their mood, it was all that remained to be done. Till then they walked a little, leaned on the wall, looked out across the fields at the distant forest. The cold pricked them like needles.

"You were going to tell me a secret."

"Was I?"

"You were."

They leaned side by side and absently watched a tiny black shape moving far out among the fields.

"You said it was the Central Committee's secret. You were going to tell me it."

"Oh, *that* secret . . . But I was asked to to be discreet."

"Quite right. All officers have to be discreet. That's why it's safe to tell me."

182

"Good old Farkas, of course it's safe . . . I say, isn't that a car out there?"

Now that it had been made a specific object, they watched the shape with real interest and even a degree of possessive pride. It was *their* car coming to *their* Palace. Soon they were able to see its headlights.

"It's Emil coming back off leave."

"On Saturday night? Use your head, Farkas."

"I'll bet it's Emil. Let's go down to the gate and meet him."

But Major Kohler did not move, so they stayed where they were. The car approached till they could make out the up and down movement as it bounced over the uneven snow on the road. It crossed the bridge and came on. Then, about a hundred yards from the gate, it stopped and its headlights were turned off. The watchers waited for somebody to get out. The car stayed motionless in the roadway. They could see its make, so close it was.

"It's not Emil. He drives an army Opel."

"Saturday night. Nobody comes back from leave on Saturday night."

"It's a Skoda Octavia." Captain Farkas prided himself on his car lore. "About four years old."

"Whoever it is, he's crazy. What's he doing out there — admiring the view?"

A dark figure emerged from the shadow of the wall, hurried the few remaining yards, the passenger's door was opened from the inside, and the figure climbed in. The car reversed back across the bridge, turned in the road where it widened, and then drove away.

"Well I'm damned. D'you think we should tell somebody?"

"It was a woman. See that from the way she walked."

"A spy, maybe. I think we should tell somebody."

Major Kohler watched the car's tiny rear lights. They vanished round a bend in the road.

"I'm freezing," he said.

"So am I."

"The sergeant on the gate's a good fellow. He knows what he's doing."

"Of course he does. What we need is another drink."

They lifted their numbed forearms off the rough stone of the parapet and tucked their hands under their armpits. They stood strait-jacketed for a moment longer, staring at the car now tiny again among the silvered fields, then turned away and trudged back to the Officers' Mess. The guitarist was still singing as they crept in. They ordered Mess Specials, what they had seen out in the frozen moonlight already no more than a dream.

For the first half-kilometre or so neither Sigmund nor Katarin spoke. They sat and watched the road spin itself out in front of them. The car's engine was quiet, nearly drowned by the harsh whining of the heater. Sigmund reached forward and tapped its casing.

"I'll have to get a new one sent out," he said. "It's run a bearing by the sound of it."

Katarin did not reply. The romantic clandestine escape, there should have been laughter, passionate kisses, a hundred tender endearments. Instead Sigmund had fiddled with the gears, nearly stalled the engine, and cursed. She had seen his strained face twisted over his shoulder as he had reversed back across the bridge. In the green light from the dashboard he had looked terrible, and a little mad. She had corrected herself – it was she who was mad, risking everything like this, and for what? For a career politician, a vain man who must have some secret reason even for this journey, otherwise he would never have undertaken it.

So now when he let his hand slip away from the heater and rest on her knee it was far too late. She moved her leg irritably.

"What's the matter, Katarin?"

184

"I hate being pawed like a pick-up, that's all."

He was silent for some minutes, driving a little faster.

"No trouble at the gate, I hope? The Guard Sergeant looked after you all right?"

"The President's wife? Of course he looked after me."

Sigmund raised his eyebrows and stared straight ahead. If she was going to behave like this he ought to turn round at once and take her straight back. Did she think he had driven all that way just in order to have a row? Waiting there by the bridge in the full view of a hundred Palace windows – did she think he took that risk just so that she could be sarcastic with him? He drove faster, seeing out of the corner of his eye that she was nervous.

"You're going too fast."

"You know all about cars."

"I know you're driving too fast for safety."

"Shall I stop? Would you rather I turned round and took you back?"

He was cheating, making the decision hers. She accepted it.

"Yes, I would. Much rather."

He braked savagely. The car skidded, spun sideways lifting its offside wheels, regained stability and settled nose down in the ditch. Stillness came so suddenly as to be improbable, ludicrous even. And darkness, the headlights buried in the snow. The moonlight slowly established itself.

"Are you all right, Katarin?"

"He asks that now. Yes thank you, Sigmund. I'm perfectly all right. Perfectly."

"Even the very best drivers have been known to skid on occasion, Katarin."

She did not consider this worth answering. She sat quite still, staring at the snow heaped on the bonnet and waiting for him to do something. He restarted the engine and tried to back out. She listened without comment to the snow flailed up against the underside of the car by its spinning back wheels. He climbed out, secretly relieved that his door still opened. He walked round the car – the bank of snow into which they had slithered was deep and soft. Katarin wound down her window, called to him as if he were an uncivil policeman.

"Well, what are you going to do about it? You must do something."

"It's a shallow ditch, Katarin." His voice was tiny in the vast open plain. "Nothing seems damaged. We ought to be able to get out fairly easily."

"That *is* good news."

She smiled at him charmingly and wound the window up again. He had expected her to get out and help. He went round to the boot of the car and pulled out the shovel and the sack of gravel. As he was working on the snow behind the back wheels he heard a tapping on the window above his head. Katarin had leaned back and was trying to attract his attention. She pointed to a low farmhouse set back a kilometre or so from the road.

"Tractor," she mouthed. "Get them to tow us out."

Sigmund shook his head. They were still too near the Palace. Peasants in this area would have seen Katarin passing on her way to the Novellnyi skating – he did not want to risk her being recognised. He scraped the snow from behind the back wheels and shovelled in gravel. Then he returned to the driving seat.

"We'll get out all right," he said. "No need to knock up the farmer."

"How very considerate you are, Sigmund. I see now why you're such a popular minister."

"Please, Katarin, stop getting at me, will you?" He started the engine. "I'm sorry I skidded the car. I'm sorry I drove too fast, I'm sorry I wasn't welcoming enough, I'm sorry this whole trip has gone so wretchedly wrong. . ." He engaged reverse. The automatic transmission on the car took up

186

sharply. They moved back a few millimetres, then the back wheels spun free again. "I'm sorry, Katarin. I really am."

He was at his worst, dirty, sweating, out of breath and anxious. But strangely he had not lost his temper. She began to soften.

"I'll drive," she said. "You get out and push."

Round at the front of the car he climbed a short distance up the low bank, bracing himself between it and the car's bonnet. He pushed while Katarin reversed. For a second the wheels slipped, then the chains found the gravel and the car shot backwards into the middle of the road. Sigmund fell flat on his face in the snowdrift.

Katarin parked the car and went back to help him. She hauled him out, and together they brushed the worst of the snow off his leather riding coat. They were both almost helpless with laughter. His comic disappearance into the snow pointed the silliness of their quarrel. They returned companionably to the car, he opened the door, and she climbed in. He stooped to kiss her lightly before closing the door and going round to his own side. The rest of the drive to Paskellnyi was idyllic.

Between the houses the car was suddenly noisy. Two men on horseback stepped into a narrow side alley to let it pass. The headlights shone in the eyes of dogs and on the averted faces of villagers. Katarin was fascinated by everything she saw, since she came from an industrial area and had never been so far into the mountains before. Her husband's country lodge which she had of course visited many times was down on the edge of the plains to the west, where a narrow escarpment provided caves and underground streams, and fine skiing in winter. The large low houses of Paskellnyi were unlike anything she had ever seen before, with their exterior stone staircases and their straw-littered ground floor entrances. The villagers, dressed in roughly-trimmed furs, were people from another century, people who had hardly changed in the lifetime of the Palace.

Sigmund drove slowly, so that she could see everything. They crossed the square with the thatched church and went on down the dirty main street. Then they were out of the village, the road steepening, and trees close around them again.

The house was lighted as it had been on Sigmund's first arrival that day. But there was no sign of Sorelle, who was keeping out of the way for reasons of her own. He drove into the garage and then led Katarin back onto the swept boards of the wide verandah. Then he turned her so that they could look out across the lake. Far out in the middle of the ice there was a long tree-covered island – one of Paska's footsteps on his way up to the top of the mountain at the beginning of time. Winds had cleared much of the snow from the ice and it shone with a hard, menacing stillness in the moonlight. The scene was as Sigmund liked it best, frightening as well as beautiful. Katarin held his arm close, and gazed out at the ice and the single island and the towering mountains beyond. Against this hugeness Novellnyi that she knew and loved was like a pretty snowscape in a glass ball. It surprised her not at all that the villagers had built their houses well away from the lake, hidden round the side of the hill. She would have done the same.

"You want us to go skating on *that*?"

"The island is nearer than it seems – about one and a half kilometres. There's a ruined chapel on it. I thought we might skate out and have a look."

"I wouldn't dare, Sigmund. Honestly, I wouldn't dare."

"It doesn't matter." He hugged her close. "It's far too late really. Let's go and see what Sorelle has got us for supper."

The small entrance hall was floored and panelled in plain unvarnished pine. There was a barometer, and a head of antlers serving as a hat and coat rack. A painted china clock stood on an ornately carved wall bracket and the space was lit by a single hanging oil lamp with a domed white glass shade. There was a smell of wood and of hot spiced vinegar. Sorelle must be busy in the kitchen. Sigmund helped Katarin out of her hooded jacket and hung it up.

"Well – what d'you think of it? Not a gold fitting in sight, I'm afraid."

"Sigmund, it's lovely." To be truthful, she found it a little bare. "Like a picture in a children's picture book."

"Much of the furniture was destroyed at the time of the Revolution. The villagers came down and made a bonfire out on the foreshore. I've always been meaning to replace it. As things are now it's probably a very good thing I haven't."

He led her through to the kitchen, their feet making a pleasantly definite sound on the bare floorboards. The old woman had propped one of her crutches against the wall and was leaning over the stove.

"Sorelle – this is Tanyi. Tanyi my dear, this is my second mother, the woman that paper insultingly calls an 'old retainer'."

Sorelle did not look up. It was as if she wanted to postpone the actual moment of meeting.

"Pleased to make your acquaintance, Comrade. You will be cold after your journey."

At first the conversation continued on this level, formal and defensive. Sorelle was unusually clumsy, almost resentful, her crutches continually getting in the way, the simplest tasks proving too much for her. Her behaviour was inexplicable – she was too intelligent an old woman to allow simple possessiveness to show itself in such childish ways. Sigmund had no way of telling if she recognised Katarin or not – either way she could still pretend ignorance, were it ever necessary.

In the face of the old woman's awkwardness Katarin behaved with unusual patience and restraint. She asked her

189

all the right questions: about Sigmund as a little boy at school, about the medal she had won in the Revolution, about the difficulties of her life in Paskellnyi. The interest pleased her, yet at the same time made her strangely distressed. She concealed this conflict as well as she was able, but the attempt only made her attitude even more inexplicable. Sigmund took Katarin – Tanyi – away as quickly as possible. Soon it would be bedtime: he was afraid that the delicate relationship between them was again in danger, that Sorelle's ambivalence would complicate reactions already perilously complex. He took her away into the old study, the big bare room lit only by a log fire in the stone fireplace.

Katarin's reaction was simpler than he had feared. Perhaps he had been over-watchful, sensing tensions where none existed.

"Poor old woman. . ." Katarin was different, changing, already softening away from the influence of the Palace. "She sees so little of you, and now I'm taking away even that little. No wonder she was prickly."

"She's not my mother, Katarin. She can't expect – "

"Shshsh. . ." She pulled him down beside her on the wide low shelf by the fire. "I thought I was Tanyi. Suppose she was listening at the door?"

"Not she. She has her dignity, if nothing else."

"Poor thing. Won't keep her very warm, that won't."

The fire burnt brightly, containing them in its warmth and noise, pointing the ice and silence of the mountains beyond, keeping them wonderfully safe from harm. Resting in each other's arms they watched the logs grey and flake like worn stones, the flames moving gently, the fire glow creeping away till the brief shapes dropped into powder. The sounds in the room were so faint, the watchers' ears so attuned to them, that when an owl cried in the trees behind the house the sound was as loud as a pain. Katarin sat up abruptly.

"I must have been asleep," she said.

"Not asleep. Your eyes were open. You were watching the fire."

"How d'you know?"

"I was watching you."

"Sigmund, what shall we do?"

"Do? The owl frightened you. There's nothing to do. Just lie here and then soon go to bed."

She leaned back against him and he pressed his face into her hair.

"Talking?"

"Quite useless."

"But it needn't be."

"Quite, quite useless."

They were both silent for a long time. After its single cry the owl had flown away. The only sound in the room was of the faint flames and the logs as they crumbled. The only sound anywhere. The only sound possible. At last Sigmund shifted. He got stiffly, reluctantly, to his feet. He helped Katarin up and together they went out into the hall. The kitchen door was open; they could see Sorelle reading by the fire. She laid her hand on the page.

"Going up, are you?"

"I hope we haven't kept you from your bed," Katarin said.

"Always read a bit in the evening. You know how it is – old people not needing so much sleep."

"Thank you for looking after me so nicely, Sorelle. Good night."

"Good night, Comrade Tanyi."

They went up the steep staircase. In the bedroom there was a half shutter on one of the windows, hardly more than a tiny carved peep-hole. Sigmund opened it and looked out. The moon was just setting and the valley lay impenetrably dark. But the lake was down there, and he could feel it. He could feel the sweep of the woods, and he could hear the earth creak in the cold. When he turned back into the room Katarin was already in bed. He closed the shutter and walked across the room to her side. She looked up at him very steadily, without smiling. He began to undress.

Downstairs Sorelle heard the door close. Then she heard his shoes thrown down onto the floor. She waited for a long time after that, her eyes shut for she was secretly praying. Then she put her book on one side, stood up laboriously, and went, leaning on the furniture, to the telephone in a corner of the kitchen. She asked for a number, waited until it answered, then asked almost in a whisper to be put through to a certain person. She found it difficult to make herself understood for at her age she was crying. The man she had to speak to was Marshall Tarsu.

Part Three

JANUARY

Twelve

ALTHOUGH IT WAS still dark, the main parade ground had been floodlit and the Guard was practising on it for the President's birthday celebrations. Snow had fallen the previous evening, but bulldozers and shovels had scraped the asphalt clean by the time the men had kitted up after breakfast. Snow was falling again now, in tiny hard flakes that blew about the parade ground like grit. The men marched and stamped and turned, swearing among themselves, the sound covered by the constant shouting of the five drill sergeants who ran around them in a state of near hysteria. If the President had to have an official birthday it should have been set in June or July when it would not have been such bloody torture for all concerned.

The Aide to the Minister of State Building, Boris Kils, listened to the distant marching and shouting, and guessed that morning had come. He had no precise idea of the time, neither was he aware of the weather. Except that he had been cold for so long now he knew he would never be warm again. The room he was in had no windows and had been brightly lit for the last week or more. Or less. He tried to concentrate on the sounds from the parade ground. They were a link with reality. He knew it would soon be the President's Birthday.

"Comrade Kils, I don't think you're listening to me."

"Indeed I am, Comrade Interrogator. You were asking about Poldi."

"If you hear, then you should answer."

"I'm sorry. I thought I had answered."

"That was last time. Today we are trying to remember something new."

He thought of last time, and all the other last times. The voice of the interrogator never varied, remained patient and sad. His questions recurred, their order jumbled, many of them meaningless. The face of his interrogator worried Boris very much – he knew it so well yet could never exactly place it. Colourless, with colourless hair . . . or perhaps that was only in contrast to his black trousers, jersey and gloves. The outfit helped him to concentrate on the face. If only the man would remove his spectacles. . .

"Remember something new? There's nothing new. I've told you everything."

"There's always something new. Every day something new emerges. You do not realise it, Comrade Kils, but your memory has improved over the last few . . . days."

"I'm glad to hear it. I really want to help. You must believe me."

"I do believe you, Comrade Kils. But how to make your friend Poldi feel the same? The things he tells us are sometimes so fantastic we – "

"Poldi was never a friend. We did business."

"State business. And you accepted bribes."

"I accepted bribes. I've told you I accepted bribes."

"You are corrupt, Comrade Kils. You are an enemy of the people."

The soldiers marched and counter-marched. Their idiot stamping got on his nerves.

"I hate the people."

"We need to find out why, Comrade. You must try to remember why."

There was a long pause in which Boris thought of people and wondered why he had said he hated them.

"How much were these bribes, Comrade?"

"I don't know the total. It worked out at ten per cent of the contract price."

"The Minister approved contracts on your advice. You were in a trusted position."

"I was in a trusted position and I abused it for personal gain. Does my wife know why you are holding me?"

"Tell me why you hate the people, Comrade."

"Does my wife know you are holding me?"

"You hold yourself, Comrade. Tell me why you hate the people and you can go free."

"That's impossible. I was in a trusted position and I abused it for personal gain."

"The President's Birthday, Comrade Kils. The time when amnesties are granted."

Boris thought about this. This was new.

"What do you want me to tell you? Help me to remember."

"At the time of the Revolution the people destroyed many beautiful things. That was wrong and stupid. Is that why you hate them?"

"I don't hate the people. I – "

"Corruption grows from a seed that is sown, Comrade. Somebody has to sow that seed . . ."

The marching had stopped. Outside the room there was complete silence. Inside the room one of the interrogator's shoes creaked as he rocked patiently backwards and forwards.

"I don't believe you hate the people, Comrade. Which is why I am prepared to recommend you for an amnesty."

"You say that because it amuses you."

"You are a small and simple man, Comrade Kils. Larger men will use you. Poldi used you. We need to know who else used you."

Boris's attention wandered. The creaking shoe reminded him of oars in rowlocks, of a summer afternoon when he was a boy. The fish had been jumping. There had been an overgrown water mill, the wooden troughs rotting from off the huge iron frame of the wheel.

"Tell me why you hate the people, Comrade."

"I don't hate the people. I told you. You believed me."

"Comrade Korda hates the people."

"Does he?"

"Does he?"

The creaking had stopped. Boris hated Comrade Korda and Comrade Korda hated the people. It was as simple as that.

"You're right, Comrade Interrogator. I've known it for a long time."

"The journalists were right in their accusations?"

"He couldn't have done it without me, you see. I handle all the appropriations."

"Tell me more."

The interrogator smiled sadly, and removed his spectacles. Boris recognised him at once, a man whom he had never heard to speak, the porter who replaced the books in the quiet room of the library.

At that hour of the morning President Borge was having breakfast with his wife. He interrupted his meal – as was quite usual – in order to answer an urgent telephone call from Marshall Tarsu. When he returned he seated himself without comment – again as was usual – and asked Katarin to pour him a second cup of coffee. His first had grown cold in his absence.

"And how are you this morning, my dear?"

"You've asked me that before, Orrin. I feel very well, thank you."

"Strange. I can remember asking the question. But I do not recall you answering."

"Then perhaps I didn't answer. Perhaps all these good manners bore me."

"I'll admit they're no more than a poor substitute,

Katarin." He drank his coffee. "I wish I understood you, Katyi."

"So do I."

"If you made it easier for me?"

"You still wouldn't be able to take enough time off from the affairs of state."

"Is it really that you're jealous? Honestly, I doubt it."

Katarin began peeling an orange. She wondered how much more of this she would be able to stand. During the two weeks since her husband's visit to Nass she had suffered torments. Sigmund she hardly saw – the Palace had swallowed him, every turn in its maze newly dangerous. Her husband – in many ways *he* was the Palace – had been as solicitous as the framework allowed. She had been for two rides on her own, and on one skating party to Novellnyi with members of the Central Committee and their wives. But thick snow had been frozen onto the ice so that even the area cleared by the soldiers had been lumpy and useless. She had been to a film in the Palace cinema. She had played piquette with the E.A. who had been attentive and had won every hand. And she had several times visited Maria who was still in hospital with shingles. Through all this she had waited in vain for some word from Sigmund, some sign that their relationship was still important.

"All this place runs on," she said suddenly, "is good manners and fear."

"You're very much mistaken, Katarin, if you believe that I am afraid."

"The Iron Marshall. I suppose the archive is already written."

"Katarin, I promised that we should have a holiday together." He leaned across the table and put his hand on hers. "After my official birthday I shall keep that promise. We will go away to my country lodge. I shall take no papers, nothing."

He was trying to convey something beyond the mere words. He was wasting his time. Communication between them was no longer even advisable. She waited out breakfast with him and after he had left she hurried into their sitting room, seated herself at the little modern desk, and began to write a letter. She had to contact Sigmund, she had to find out what he intended to do. But before she had written a dozen words she took the sheet of paper and tore it into tiny pieces which she threw away. Then she retrieved the pieces, carried them to the stove and burned them, crushing the ashes with the flat of the shovel. Apart from the risk, for her pride's sake she should never write such a letter.

She returned to the desk and again began to write, this time to a cousin of hers still living near Pol. She had decided to get away from Sigmund, get away from her husband, most of all get away from the Palace. A day or two alone and Orrin would realise how much better off he was without her. And Sigmund – would he not treat her leaving as an excuse to rid himself of a relationship that had become an embarrassment to him?

She was well rid of them both. She finished her letter, sealed it, and addressed the envelope. Then she hesitated – no doubt her letters were being opened. She decided to go out for a ride, so that she could post her letter in the nearest village. She phoned down to the stables for her horse to be made ready. Then she began dressing for the journey.

Marshall Borge stood for some minutes at one of the tall windows of his office. A telephone rang on his desk and he ignored it. After it had stopped he went through to the E.A. He found Novaks hunched at his desk, his head buried in his hands. The President had to speak twice before Novaks heard him.

"Raoul – Comrade Novaks . . . Are you sick, man?"

The E.A. sat up slowly, his clothes seeming to fill out almost as if a part of him had been absent. He looked up at the President, at first hardly recognising him.

"Sick . . .? No, not sick. . ." He gathered momentum. "Certainly not, Comrade President. I was only thinking."

"Glad to hear it, Raoul. For a moment you looked quite ghastly."

"It's thinking so early in the morning, sir." The joke was poor, but he was committed to it. "It always has a bad effect on me."

He knew he sounded feeble-minded. He shuffled papers on his desk, then stood up.

"You wanted me, sir?"

"Just had a call from Tarsu. Comrade Boris has broken: he's willing to give us anything we need against Korda."

"So there was something in it after all."

Raoul Novaks was completely himself. He knew very well that there was nothing genuine against Sigmund Korda. He also knew that the President was still too much of a soldier to be able to admit this.

"I don't like your implication, Novaks. Of course there was something in it. All we needed was proof."

"And now we've got it."

"I knew he'd break. These piddling little civil servants never have any guts, not when it comes to the pinch."

The E.A. wondered how tight the pinch had been. Tarsu's methods were effective, but seldom comfortable.

"And now?"

"Now we act. Send for Balenkov at once. And quietly find out where Korda is." Marshall Borge turned away, then paused. "Oh, and when Balenkov comes I'll see him out here. The interview is important: I'd prefer to have a witness."

The E.A. went with him to the door, closed it behind him and returned to his desk. He was amused. When the President said he wanted a witness he meant that he wanted to be within range of Tarsu's microphones. The operator along in the Communications Centre would be ready to record every word. When the arrest of a member of the Central Committee was being ordered the President was wise to take every precaution.

Since the E.A.'s secretary was still in hospital and he preferred not to accept a temporary replacement – especially with the example of Boris's Anna before him – he had to do his telephoning himself. He rang the main Guard Room first and contacted Colonel Balenkov. Then he rang the Education Office and enquired the whereabouts of the Minister, pretending to need information for the Department of Economic Security. As Novaks expected, the Minister was not available – most of his time recently had been taken up in organising some reception in his country lodge. On this occasion, however, he could probably be found in the library building where he had gone to inspect progress on the new extension. These were the two current obsessions in Korda's life: the reception and the library extension. From what Novaks knew of him, he would be in the library for the next half-hour at least. His greatest delight seemed to be to wander in and out of the ranks of new shelving or to stare entranced at the view from the new windows. . .

When Colonel Balenkov arrived, the E.A. called up Marshall Borge on the intercom. The President came through from his office immediately, carrying a presidential memorandum sheet. He closed the door behind him quickly – not before Novaks could glimpse the glass and brandy bottle on the littered surface of the huge teak desk. Novaks did not blame Marshall Borge: the coming day was not going to be easy. For many people its end would be very different from its beginning.

"Balenkov – good of you to come so promptly." The President shook Colonel Balenkov's hand, then seated himself at the E.A.'s desk. "Sit down, Balenkov, and listen carefully."

Colonel Balenkov's uniform permitted him a rigid perch on the extreme edge of an upright chair. He held his cap in both his hands. As a well-trained officer, he sat quite still. Raoul Novaks propped himself unobtrusively against the side of a high, silver-inlaid armoire. The President handed Balenkov the handwritten memorandum.

"Written confirmation of what I'm going to tell you, Balenkov. File it immediately. I have a difficult task for you, one demanding all your tact. I want the Minister for Art and Education arrested as soon as possible". A well-trained officer, Colonel Balenkov made no comment. "You understand that this is nothing more than a formality, and that the Minister is to be treated with respect and consideration. Enquiries are being made into allegations of financial impropriety, and – while I myself and the members of the Central Committee are convinced that these are unfounded – it is of course necessary to observe full legal formalities in the matter. It must not be thought that in our People's Republic today position or rank win any remission of the due legal process."

In case Balenkov should look his way, Novaks stared at the ceiling. Marshall Borge spoke his lines with admirable conviction. And all of them taped along in the Communications Centre. Novaks was puzzled, however, not yet sure of the President's plans. The newspaper articles had been surprisingly ineffective. Even with the testimony of Boris Kils – and the man would make a poor witness in any courtroom – it seemed unlikely that popular opinion could be swung substantially against Sigmund Korda. And proceedings that were not going to achieve this purpose would never be initiated. Therefore the only reason for this arrest was to frighten Korda, and in Novaks' opinion the other was not a man who would be frightened easily . . . Novaks suddenly became aware that he was being spoken to.

"Have you been able to find out where Comrade Korda is likely to be, Raoul?"

"He should be in the library, sir. He's looking over the reconstruction work."

"There you are then, Balenkov. Make the arrest as discreetly as possible. I'm sure there'll be no difficulty from the Minister. Place him under house arrest – in his quarters with two men on the door. I trust to your discretion as to whom you allow in and out." The President stood up. "That memo in my hand can act as your warrant."

Colonel Balenkov stood up also. The President walked round the end of the desk and took Balenkov's arm.

"A delicate job, Balenkov, and one for which you are ideally suited." He began to walk with the Guard Commander towards the door. "Korda is a reasonable man. Explain the situation to him and I'm sure he'll make no trouble." He paused with the Colonel in the middle of the room. "On your way then, Colonel. And good luck."

He led Colonel Balenkov out, not into the passage, but into his own private office. The E.A. gazed after them thoughtfully. If a man were on his way down to the library it was possible that the route through the President's office and down by the lift at the end of the corridor might save him a second or two. . .

Major Kohler was on the upper floor of the new library extension, discussing the recessed ceiling lights with Sigmund Korda. On delivery they had been found to be different from specification, and Kohler had been obliged to modify the fitting accordingly. He had worked at the design late into the night and had devised a workable alternative fitting. Sigmund was impressed. With Captain Felsen in charge, such a complication would have set the project back by a week at least.

"How soon will you have the windows sealed, Major?

The sooner I can get the librarians in labelling the shelves the better."

"You'll be delayed by the floors rather than by the windows, Comrade Minister. I wouldn't advise letting them be walked on till we've sanded and laid down at least three coats of polish."

"And when will that be?" Korda looked round and shivered. Tiny flakes of hard snow blew in round the unfitted window frames and the room was very cold.

"I'll say next Monday. Give the final coat a chance to go off all day Sunday. There'll be plenty of time to get things straight before the opening."

"One thing librarians can never have plenty of, and that's time. Still, we're well up to schedule, for which I'm very grateful."

He walked away between the free-standing shelves, stooping to pick up a long wood shaving which he curled round one finger. Major Kohler watched him for a moment, saw his clear pleasure in the shapes of the new panelling, in the smells of stone and paint and new wood. Comrade Korda was a man worth doing good work for – he showed his appreciation far more in deeds than in formal phrases.

Major Kohler had found the last two weeks a marvellous release after the insulting drudgery of Kitchen Duty. The Engineer Colonel had given him a completely free hand, hoping thereby to enable him to ruin himself. Captain Felsen had laboured under a work-plan that made only imperfect use of the available forces. Kohler had been able to recast the entire sequence, and so had caught up on the schedule and even clipped a couple of days off it. It was the sort of work he liked most of all.

During this time he had kept up twice daily visits to the Paul VII Passage. Its condition was worsening steadily: damp bloomed on the walls now and the noise of water beneath the floor was as loud as a wind in high trees. The passage had been taken off the itinerary of the regular inspecting officers and Kohler himself reported on it daily to the E.A. The pumping equipment had arrived from Dorlen as promised, and he had stationed the biggest pump in the main granary chamber. In this position it seemed to outsiders no more than a general precaution, yet it could easily be moved to the top of the vertical shaft down to the Passage when it was needed. Until the river melted there was nothing positive to be done about plugging the leak. Perhaps the Engineer Colonel was right – perhaps it would last his time out after all.

"Major Kohler. . ." The Minister was returning down the central aisle. "Major Kohler, a few days before the opening here I'm planning a small reception at my lodge in Paskellnyi. Writers, artists, musicians, educationalists, a few friends . . . I was wondering if, as engineer in charge of this fine work, you might perhaps find time to come."

"It's very kind of you Comrade Minister, but – "

"You won't be in the army all your life, Major. Educational building programme will always take up a fair proportion of the G.N.P. It would do you good professionally to meet men already active in this field. Frankly you'd be a fool to miss the opportunity."

"Thank you, Comrade Minister. If the duty roster permits it, then I'll be – "

"I'll see the Engineer Colonel. Duty rosters can always be adjusted."

Sigmund Korda was not particularly interested in the man's future as a civil engineer: he was, however, eager to obtain as many active supporters among the more senior officers as possible. There were difficult days ahead, in which he would need all the help he could get. He recognised in Major Kohler qualities of leadership and courage and loyalty – coupled with a certain lack of imagination – that might one day be very useful.

"That's fixed then. You'll be receiving an official invitation as soon as my secretary can get them out."

Major Kohler thanked him and the Minister took his leave. Kohler was bewildered and impressed. He had in fact never considered the possibility of a life for himself outside the army. He wanted no such thing – service routine gave him the sort of framework in which he was happiest. Yet he knew that promotion – on the Engineer Colonel's retirement, for example – would make him increasingly desk-bound and separated from the practical work he most enjoyed. A few years stuck in some office and he might be very glad to buy himself out and find more congenial work with some State Building Organisation. With that end in view this reception might give him some useful introductions. Comrade Korda was a remarkable man – not many Central Committee members found time to think of the careers of the men under them.

Major Kohler gave last instructions to his Engineer Sergeant for the fitting of the ceiling lights and then made ready for his morning visit to the Paul VII Passage. As he was leaving the library Colonel Balenkov came hurrying up the steps.

"The Minister of Education – is he here?"

"You've just missed him, Colonel. He left a few minutes ago."

"Did he say where he was going?"

"I'm afraid not, sir."

"Damn. Where's the nearest telephone?"

"In the librarian's office, Colonel. Just along on the left."

He watched the Guard Commander go along the corridor into the librarian's office. It seemed odd that Colonel Balenkov should have such urgent business with the Minister. Central Committee business of some kind, he supposed. Turning up his collar against the eddying snowflakes he continued on his way to the catacombs.

Katarin Borge had no objection to the snow. In fact she delighted in it. Life in the Palace was softening her, mentally as well as physically: there was no other possible explanation for the mess into which she had allowed herself to drift. She sat on her horse, waiting impatiently while the stable sergeant adjusted her stirrup leathers. The ride would clear her mind, force her to concentrate for once on something outside her own head, beyond the hothouse indecisions and forced significances of the Palace. By the time she reached the postbox in the village she would know – know without conscious thought, for once – whether it was right for her to post her letter or not.

"You're fine now, Comrade." The sergeant stood away and looked up at her against the grey dawn, creasing his eyes from the tiny snowflakes. "Don't go too far, Comrade Katarin. This may turn into a blizzard by midday. The President will say I shouldn't have let you go."

"Let me go, Prado? He knows bloody well you couldn't have stopped me."

She nudged her horse and set off through the streets to the Patriot's Gate. Few people were about; it was the sort of day when most of the Palace staff went between buildings by way of the catacombs. She had just crossed the Cathedral Square when ahead of her a man suddenly emerged from the turning to the library. He was lightly clothed and walked with his head up, defying the wind and the grits of snow. She reined in and tried to turn aside. But as she had recognised him, so at the same moment had he recognised her. He ran towards her.

"Katarin . . . Katarin, how good to see you."

"You talk as if I lived in another country."

"But you do, my dear. You do . . . You live in a country of human beings, while I – I live in a land of political automatons, inscrutable and treacherous."

He was in a flowery mood – things must be going well. He was the last person she had wanted to see – in spite of herself she found him irritatingly magnificent, warmed by a secret strength and able to draw her to him simply by standing motionless in the snow, his arms outstretched in an absurdly stagey gesture. Her horse danced sideways, annoyed to be kept waiting.

"It's quite obvious which country you prefer, Sigmund. Please get out of my way now."

"Katarin, you are angry with me. But what can I do? We stand poised on the brink of great things, Katarin. What sort of man would you think me if I lay and sighed for your lap, if I cast aside the — "

"You're disgusting when you talk like this, Sigmund." Which should have been true but somehow was not. "My horse is twitchy. If you don't get out of my way there might be an accident."

Suddenly she knew if he did not move to one side she would ride him down. His confidence, the way he used himself, was more than she could bear . . . Another man came striding through the snow from the direction of the library.

"Comrade Korda — Comrade Korda, a word with you, please."

Sigmund stepped out of her way and turned to meet the newcomer. Katarin urged her horse by at a trot, kicking up wedges of snow in the two men's faces. Whatever Colonel Balenkov had to say to Sigmund Korda was no concern of hers. She had left it all behind her: already she was a different person, a woman on a horse, feeling animal warmth and the snow beating against half-closed eyelids.

Thirteen

"Comrade minister, I must talk with you. Where may we go?"

"Talk with me? Why not the library, Colonel? It's not far."

"A place where we cannot be overheard, Comrade. What has to be said is not easy."

"You intrigue me. The Cathedral, then. Perhaps the holy atmosphere will make the saying easier."

He clapped the Colonel's shoulder and together they went on into the Cathedral Square and up the wide steps to the west front. The door hushed shut behind them. They went through the weather-brake outer chamber and into the gilded silence of the nave. Between the trefoil pillars the sound of their footsteps disintegrated into meaningless clatter and their lowered voices massed about them in sibilant confusion.

"Comrade Minister, I am here with a warrant from the President for your arrest."

"Arrest? My dear Balenkov, the President must be joking."

"Believe me, Comrade Minister, I wish he were."

Korda walked on a few paces without speaking. Far ahead of them, beyond the screen, the vast reredos glittered in the dim, snow-coloured light. The President was his friend – also a man astute enough to be aware of his position, of the strength of his influence throughout the country. This arrest must be a formality insisted upon by powerful enemies. Powerful, but not – so he judged – powerful enough.

"Tell me, Balenkov, you know who is behind this? Who was at the President's elbow when he signed that warrant?"

"Politics are not my sphere. The President would not tell me such things."

"Of course not. It was foolish of me to ask." Korda hesitated, then made up his mind. "Well, Balenkov, so I am to consider myself arrested. What next?"

"Close arrest in your quarters, with a guard on every door."

"That's not too bad. At least I shall be able to get some work done. This comes at a very awkward time, you see."

For all the Colonel's military stiffness, Korda could see there was something bothering him. Balenkov looked round furtively, as if even there he was afraid of being overheard.

"Comrade Minister, I beg of you not to take your arrest so lightly. There are men who mean to have your life. The evidence they bring is formidable."

"You said yourself you weren't a political animal. How can you – "

"I know what I am saying, Comrade. The case against you is strong. They have informers, men willing to swear your life away."

"How can you possibly know this?"

"The cells are under my jurisdiction. Also the interrogation rooms."

Korda looked up sharply. This began to make sense.

"You mean to tell me they've got some poor wretches to. . .?" Balenkov nodded. "This must be Tarsu's doing. And the President has had to go along with him. All the same – "

"Comrade Minister, the President is against you. You must believe me."

"Even if he is. . ."

Korda leaned against a pillar, tried to think. First the newspaper articles, and now this. The President must be mad to imagine he could be broken so easily. He knew too much, too much about the Palace, too much about Tarsu's methods. If they had informers, then they must be planning a public trial in Dorlen. In open court he would annihilate them. Surely they would never dare... Behind him Colonel Balenkov cleared his throat, the thin sound echoing unpleasantly among the painted madonnas.

"Comrade Minister, the President knows about Paskellnyi."

Korda felt little shock, hardly any surprise even. It had to happen. At least everything now made sense. The game was played out, the crisis now, sooner than he had expected, sooner than he had hoped. But that was in the nature of crises. He stood away from the pillar and turned to Colonel Balenkov. His plans were ready. He would prefer to have Balenkov as a friend, but he would outwit him if it were necessary.

"So it really is serious after all, Colonel. To screw the President's wife is undoubtedly a killing matter." He balanced on the balls of his feet. The Colonel was slightly older than he, but probably in better condition. "We were friends once – fellow officers ... is that why you're telling me this?"

"You have one chance, Comrade. And that is to escape now."

"I was thinking the same thing. You've been sent alone?"

"The arrest was to be discreet. You were to have come with me peacefully and quietly."

"Which I damn nearly did. So?"

Colonel Balenkov turned away and stared at an altar to the Blessed Virgin, tier upon tier of silver filigree against jewelled blue enamel. There was a smell of incense, even after twenty years.

"I can give you a count of five, Comrade. More than that I do not dare. We must have been seen coming in here together ... But for a count of five let the Blessed Virgin guard you."

"Thank you, Balenkov. I shall remember this."

"You have nothing to thank me for." He had swung round. He was shouting. "Nothing to thank me for. Nothing."

Korda stared at him, at his sudden intensity. Balenkov turned away again and lifted his eyes to the statue of the Blessed Virgin ... As he heard the other's footsteps slowly retreating down the aisle he removed his cap and flung it skidding across the worn stones till it came to rest against the plinth of a royal tomb. Then he took the front of his greatcoat and tore it open, ripping off the buttons. Finally he drew his pistol.

In the distance the door to the Cathedral opened and closed. Immediately he turned and raced the length of the aisle. In the outer chamber he checked. Carefully he opened the door a few centimetres. The snow was falling more thinly and he could see Korda hurrying away across the square. There were two messengers also in the square, and a parked lorry. He waited till Korda was almost at the other side, then wrenched the door open and flung himself out.

"Stop that man. Stop Comrade Korda. Stop an enemy of the people."

Aiming with great care, he fired three shots. The bullets chipped the wall by Korda's head and he dodged away, ran to the corner and was gone. Balenkov called to the messengers and the lorry driver.

"After him. See where he goes. He may be armed, so be careful. I'm calling out the guard."

He stumbled along the front of the Cathedral and made for the back entrance to the school. Just inside the door there was a telephone. Through a window in the next door he could see that lessons had just started. The children had not heard his three shots. As he waited for the operator

213

to answer he watched them stand to salute the flag. He asked to be put through to the President.

All incoming calls to the President went through the E.A. Comrade Novaks connected the Colonel and then hurried through into the President's office.

"... And don't bother with warning the gates, Colonel. He'll never try to get out that way." The President was frowning angrily. "Listen to me carefully, Colonel. He will try to escape through the catacombs. There is a secret passage under the river. Its entrance is in the Paul VII Passage." The E.A. made a small unnoticed gesture and quickly thought better of it. "Go there yourself at once. He must be stopped. To run away is madness. The whole country will believe him guilty if this gets out. He *must* be stopped."

The President replaced the receiver and sighed. He gazed across at Raoul Novaks who made no comment.

"You'd have thought Balenkov could manage a simple job like that, Raoul."

"You mean to say Korda has run for it?" Novaks feigned incredulity.

"I agree with you, Raoul. It doesn't look good. What innocent man runs away..." The President leaned back in his chair, pressed the palms of his hands into his eye sockets. "Between you and me, Raoul, I hadn't placed too much faith in this evidence Tarsu says he's got. I know his methods. But now ... well, what do you think?"

Novaks wondered why the President bothered. It was a good performance, but quite unnecessary.

"No sir, it's very difficult," he said.

Major Kohler was carrying out his inspection of the Paul VII Passage. Over the previous five weeks his readings for flexion in some of the flooring slabs were larger than he would have believed possible. They made some of the things

214

he had been taught in mining school sound very silly. Today a seepage of yellow water had accumulated at the far end of the passage to a maximum depth of nearly eight centimetres. As he stood quietly putting his level back into its case and watching the slow trickle across the floor, he heard a sudden crack from the vaulting above his head. Mortar pattered down, and some flakes of stone. He watched, fascinated, as a thin dark line spread down the curved masonry. It stopped where the root stones of the vault abutted the walls. There was no further movement, and no sound other than the rustling water in the tunnel below.

He collected the rest of his instruments and returned to the base of the vertical shaft. The lights still shone brightly at their four metre intervals – to the casual observer the passage would have seemed solid and utterly immutable. Major Kohler packed his instruments into their carrying bag and climbed the unsteady ladder up to the next level. He heard the distant sound of approaching footsteps. He slung the bag over his shoulder and tightened the strap.

A moment later Sigmund Korda rounded a corner in the tunnel. He was wearing an army greatcoat and boots – 'borrowed' from the Officers' Mess – and he walked with an assured, unhurried step. It would be some time before his pursuers caught up with him – the existence of this escape route was a closely-guarded secret. Balenkov would be wasting his time putting guards on the gates. Balenkov was a good friend.

"Comrade Minister – "

"Who's there? I can't see you – who's there?"

"Major Kohler, sir. Official tunnel inspection."

The two men faced each other, both of them undecided. Kohler was puzzled by the Minister's presence, dressed so, in a tunnel that only led to the Paul VII Passage and to the secret escape route. Korda was puzzled as to whether he dare trust Kohler with the truth.

215

"Well then, Major, don't let me keep you. I often look around down here. The ... the catacombs interest me."

"Of course, Comrade Minister." Still Major Kohler hesitated. "The condition of some of the passages is very poor, sir. I hope you will be careful."

"Thanks for the warning, Major. I shan't be going far." He was about to walk on. "One thing more. You needn't talk about our meeting down here. Not unless you're asked, of course."

"I'd have no reason to, Comrade Minister. You can rely on me."

The low tunnel jangled their voices. Above the jumble of sound Korda thought he heard the sound of careful footsteps behind him. He tried to push past the Major.

"Comrade Minister, the tunnel ahead is blocked."

"Let me past, Kohler. You don't know what you're talking about."

An army officer appeared, silhouetted hatless against the bright archway of light.

"The secret tunnel, sir – it's caved in. Completely flooded."

"You mean that?"

Behind them Colonel Balenkov was calling. Korda stared for a moment, seeing that Major Kohler was in earnest. Then he shrugged his shoulders. He turned and walked back up the tunnel towards Balenkov.

"It seems your help was wasted, Colonel. I'm not sorry. Running away has never been my – "

And Colonel Balenkov shot him four times, carefully, in the chest. The sound of the shots was deafening.

Major Kohler ran to the Minister's body, felt for his pulse. As he held his wrist the flicker faded. Already bloodstains had penetrated the thick material of his borrowed greatcoat. They ceased to spread. Major Kohler felt the cold smoothness of the stones on which he was kneeling. He became aware of the Colonel standing over him.

"An enemy of the people," Balenkov said. "He was trying to escape. You saw, Major. You will witness that he was trying to get away."

Kohler stared up incredulously. Even by the poor lights of the tunnel he could see that in Colonel Balenkov's eyes there were tears. The murderer wept. Balenkov walked very slowly back the way he had come. The smoke from his gun drifted like incense in the still cold air.

Fourteen

THE PRESIDENT WAS anxious for news. He sat quite motionless in his canvas chair and watched the meagre snowflakes, black against the sky, slip endlessly down past his window. In the room behind him the E.A. had been joined by Marshall Tarsu. They talked together in whispers.

"I should have gone myself," the Marshall murmured. "Balenkov's a good officer, but hardly the most tactful of men."

"The situation's gone rather beyond tact, I imagine."

"It needn't have done. Can't think what he can have said. No call for Sigmund to make a dash for it, no call at all."

"The President fears it may mean he's more guilty than we thought."

"Sigmund fiddle the books? Never be worth it, not in a million years. He was playing a far bigger game than that. Long term. Subtle." Tarsu dared speak his mind in one of the few places safe from his own prying ears. "He'd never risk everything for a few sticks of furniture."

"That's what I'd have said, Marshall. But how else do you explain – "

"Not my job to explain things. But I tell you one thing – " Tarsu's voice sank still further – "whatever happens, just remember I'm behind you all the way, will you? And the President, of course."

Novaks looked away, at the basalt clock and the walls

hung with weapons. Abruptly the President stood up. The face he turned to them was controlled to a point where even the movements of speech were painful.

"I must go and see what is happening. I have a premonition of disaster." He threaded his way between the many pieces of furniture to the studded leather door. "Please," he said, "come with me. If anything has happened to Korda the whole Government is in danger."

Tarsu joined him. As Novaks followed he suddenly felt sick, hardly able to breathe, the gilded ceiling pressing down on him, the walls crushing him. Out in the corridor he felt little better. The perspective of tiny chandeliers crackled like ice, dropping sparks as they passed along it. Doors slid by, and behind them whispering. Tapes gibbered in his head, recorded voices hideously distinct. He was going mad. The President walked ahead, not speaking, and Tarsu a pace behind him. Together they filled the entire width and height of the corridor. Novaks closed his eyes, followed their carpet-muffled footsteps, struggling with the demon. Around him the whispering grew louder ... Eyes now very wide, he ran to catch up with Marshall Tarsu and the President. Nobody noticed him. There was nobody to see.

... Later he found they were crossing the huge first floor foyer. Now there were people, but they moved to one side like bent twigs. He was a torrent, gross and unstoppable. The two men in front were also he. In the one endless moment he destroyed and was destroyed, he conquered and was conquered, he lived and was lived upon. The people round him bowed and jeered. He stumbled, thought he would fall. He was on the brink of the great marble staircase.

He was a man in a grey Palace suit and black Palace shoes. That which comprised himself, that much he had control over. He stopped on the second step down and smiled at someone who was standing near, who did not know him. Ahead of him Marshall Tarsu and the President had also stopped. They were watching someone across the blue tiles of the Entrance Salon. Novaks saw Colonel Balenkov, bare-headed, his overcoat hanging open. The Colonel seemed to walk for a long time without getting any nearer. Then suddenly he stood, looking calmly up, a step below Marshall Tarsu and the President. The Palace waited, as quiet as a windless frozen mountain.

"I have to report an accident, Comrade President. Pursuing Comrade Korda, I shot at him with the intention of wounding him so that he should not escape. Unfortunately my bullets must have struck a vital organ. Comrade Korda is dead."

To Novaks the scene stuck at that point, so that he was able to examine every detail. The guards opposite each other at the foot of the stairs amused him. In their formal detachment they could only gaze at each other and widen their eyes.

"Sigmund? Sigmund Korda is dead?"

The cry from the President was of animal anguish. It jerked reality into motion again. Novaks watched him link his hands and raise them high above his head. Without surprise, without emotion of any kind at all, he watched the President bring his linked hands down with all his force on the bowed neck of Colonel Balenkov.

"Accident, you say? Then I say murder, Balenkov. Monstrous, bloody murder."

Balenkov staggered, missed his footing, and fell. He rolled clumsily down the staircase. The guard he blundered into stood his ground.

"Murder, I say. Murder."

This time real stillness, not one of fifty men daring to move. No sound reached Novaks, only the blood pulsing in his ears. Then Marshall Tarsu stepped forward, down past the President.

"Guards, you heard the President. Arrest Colonel Balenkov.

Allow him communication with nobody. The charge is murder."

Novaks watched the Entrance Salon scatter into movement. Balenkov was being helped to his feet. The President had turned away and was leaning on the marble balustrade, his head bowed. Tarsu finished giving orders and ran lightly back up the stairs. He said something to the President that Novaks could not hear above the growing murmur of feet. The President nodded.

In a state of near-trance the E.A. received his instructions and carried them out with his usual quiet efficiency. He convened an emergency meeting of the Central Committee, phoning round to all the members available within the Palace. During the meeting he stood at the President's elbow, smiling faintly, suffering the agony of total recall, of knowing in detail everything that was about to happen, every word, every gesture. Of all those in the Palace that day it was he, Raoul Novaks, who had the most reason to weep, he who had the most cause for despair. His devil held him tight and would not let him go.

". . . but we are not here to pay tributes. There'll be time for those later. All of us have lost a colleague, and many of us – myself included – have lost a dear and personal friend. But this meeting has been called in order to decide upon immediate action. We must remember that our loss is political as well as personal."

Marshall Borge looked round the carefully serious faces. Tarsu had his hands resting on the table, one finger slightly raised.

"As this is primarily a security matter," the President said, "I shall call first upon Marshall Tarsu."

"Thank you, Comrade President." Everybody spoke sitting down. It was established Committee procedure. "The first thing I would like to emphasise is that whatever action we take must be taken at once. One sign of weakness or uncertainty and we'll have the reactionaries about our ears.

This is not just any murder. It is above all one in which it may be suspected that there has been official complicity. It might be suggested that Comrade Korda's great national popularity had been thought dangerous." He struck the table sharply with the flat of his hand. "Such a rumour must be given no chance to spread. No chance at all."

The Minister for External Security frowned.

"May I ask exactly what the people have been told so far?"

"It was necessary to issue an official statement immediately. With Balenkov's confession witnessed by so many people it was impossible to be sure of total security. Therefore I took the responsibility for putting out a short communiqué. I have the text of it here". Marshall Tarsu read from a single duplicated sheet. *"The Palace announces with deep regret the sudden death of the Minister of Art and Education, Sigmund Korda. Priority investigations are being carried out, and a further statement will be issued at 1300 hours.* That gives us ninety minutes."

"This confession of Balenkov's. . ." The Minister for External Security stared at the table in front of him. "People are going to think it very odd, in view of the complete lack of motive."

"We aren't here to judge the case, Comrade." Marshall Tarsu was very smooth. "But I do assure you we have quite adequate evidence as to that already."

"Which brings us," said the President, "to the question of a special court. I take it we are all agreed that one should be set up immediately?"

The Minister for External Security coughed. When he spoke his voice was barely audible.

"As long as we are convinced, Comrade President, that such a court will not bring to light any . . . undesirable items."

President Borge leapt to his feet.

"There are no *undesirable items,* Comrade Minister.

Colonel Balenkov's orders were clearly stated. We discussed them in this room only yesterday. The Colonel had them in his pocket when he was arrested. There can be no question at all of *undesirable items*. Our consciences are clear."

The Minister for External Security made a small gesture of submission.

"I was only thinking of Europe, Comrade President. Too much publicity is sometimes dangerous."

"And none at all is suicidal."

There was a murmur of agreement round the table. Marshall Borge sat down.

"I suggest convening the court at 1500 hours. That will give reporters from Dorlen time to get here. There must be no suggestion that anything is being hushed up."

Again the murmur of agreement. The President leaned back in his chair and spoke to the E.A.

"You'll get the necessary Authorities made out, Raoul? Have you been on to the Judiciary Building yet for the names of the judges available?"

Novaks had. He gave the Committee the names of five judges in the Palace at that moment, and three were chosen.

"Now to the question of prosecuting counsel. I'm sure I speak for us all when I ask you, Raoul, if you would be willing to act for the People?"

Raoul Novaks tried to control his shudder of acute physical nausea. He masked it with a slight bow.

"Not advisable, Comrade President. My friendship with Sigmund – with Comrade Korda is too well known." The first and only time he would use the dead man's first name. Deceit wormed through everywhere. "I fear there might be accusations of personal animosity were I to undertake the prosecution of his killer."

The snow had stopped. Outside the windows of the Central Committee Chamber the sky was lightening. But inside Novaks' head the demon crouched lower and bit deeper. He felt now that he would never be free again.

223

In return for his help, Boris Kils had been given a bed with blankets and a mattress. He was also allowed darkness. Warm and contained at last, after so long, he was sleeping soundly. So soundly that he did not hear the door of his cell open, nor the careless footsteps of a new political motive.

"Tell me again how you worked your system of double indents, Comrade Kils."

"Double indents?" Boris Kils turned over in bed, kept his eyes shut, seeing the brilliance beyond their closed lids. "Double indents. . ." He gathered his wits. "Well, you see, it was necessary to get the Minister's signature at the bottom of each individual indent, so Comrade Korda suggested to me that – "

"Open your eyes, Comrade. Look at me when I'm speaking to you."

"Comrade Korda suggested that I – "

"Tell me why Comrade Korda hated the people."

"Comrade Korda hated the people because they were stupid, because they misunderstood his work."

"That is the lie you told last time, Kils. Can you really not make up something better?"

Boris closed his eyes, then quickly opened them again before he could be ordered to.

"His high ideals were always being frustrated by – "

"We've been looking at some of the other lies you have told us about Comrade Korda. We think – "

"But you wanted – "

"We think you've been trying to save yourself by blackening another."

Boris began to cry.

"I told you what you wanted to know. I – "

"You told us what wasn't true."

"You wanted evidence. I gave it to you."

"Then it wasn't true?"

Boris covered his head with the bedclothes. They were ripped away. He had gone to bed only in his shirt. He started to shiver violently, from shame and fear.

"What sort of a man are you, Kils, to try to destroy the honour of a Senior Minister?"

"An enemy of the people. An enemy of the – "

"You told us what was not true?"

"Enemy . . . of the people."

"Then it wasn't true?"

"What more do you want?"

"There weren't any double indents?"

"No double indents."

"And Comrade Korda never suggested to you that you – "

"He hardly spoke to me. Except to laugh at me. To him I was only a . . . a . . ."

"Perhaps he knew you for what you were?"

"I must say it again?"

"You don't have to say anything, Kils. Nobody forces you to say anything at all."

Boris cowered on the bed, his naked knees drawn up tight to his chin, his arms folded awkwardly. He tried to think of his wife. He knew that he was as good as dead.

Amélie Korda had been called from her bed of pain. From Marshall Tarsu she had received the news of her husband's death. She had received the news with great dignity – dignity she had not shown since the day of her marriage. She sat very pale and upright, and behaved as was proper in the widow of a Senior Minister, with a Senior Minister's widow's pension. Her subsequent conversation with Marshall Tarsu, however, was wearing. Finally her strength failed her. That Sigmund should leave her now, alone and uncared for, was too much. He never had loved her, of course – not what she called love.

". . . I was attractive then, Marshall. I haven't always been the wreck you see now, the wreck he made of me. Ours was a garrison town, Marshall . . . I could have had anybody, anybody at all. Gregor Balenkov never forgave him, of course. Look at him – single to this very day. Now Gregor really loved me. Passionately. Would have died for me . . . I suppose I chose Sigmund because he was the handsomer of the two. How silly we are when we are young, Marshall. But Gregor – he's been like a lost soul ever since. How much he hated my husband nobody will ever know. I suppose he remembered me as I was, as I'd been in the old days at home with father . . . Never without an escort, Marshall – dancing, boating, picnics in the woods, the little notes exchanged, and never without an escort. And he had to watch what Sigmund was doing to me, how he was treating me . . . I refer to his women. Women, Marshall – the secretaries, the little bits of fluff, the disgusting chance liaisons. Can't you see what this must have done to a man like Gregor? Poor dear Gregor . . . I've seen him about the Palace, you know, giving me looks as of a man on fire. The passion in those looks, Marshall. Poor, poor dear Gregor . . . And now he's done this terrible thing. For my sake. Poor man. Poor, poor man. . ."

And she had wept.

Luckily for Marshall Tarsu, Major Kohler's evidence was more concise.

"Minister Korda was unarmed. I told him the escape tunnel was flooded. He turned and walked slowly back towards Colonel Balenkov, his arms by his sides. The Colonel shot him four times in the chest. He died instantly."

The Special Court sat at 1400 hours, the courtroom packed with Palace staff who could get away from their work and with news agency people of every nationality who had come from Dorlen in cars and buses and even on motor bicycles. The prosecution evidence was delivered very briefly: the official warrant to establish the exact terms of the arrest,

Major Kohler to witness the shooting, Amélie Korda to provide a motive, and President Borge himself to describe the prisoner's own report of his crime. The defence evidence was even more brief: counsel reported that the prisoner had remained obstinately silent since the moment of his arrest – therefore counsel could do no more than put forward a strong plea for mercy, citing the prisoner's distinguished army career and fine Revolutionary record.

The judges deliberated for eight minutes before arriving at a unanimous verdict. The prisoner had admitted the offence in the hearing of many witnesses. His plea of accident did not accord with Major Kohler's evidence and the court had decided to believe the Major. Motive, opportunity, and the deed itself were all proved beyond any reasonable doubt. To shelter behind the warrant and plead accident was despicable. Colonel Balenkov was found guilty of premeditated murder and sentenced to be shot. The extreme culpability of the circumstances denied him the right of appeal. The sentence was to be carried out strictly within the due legal process.

Colonel Balenkov would be shot at 1530 hours.

Fifteen

AT A VILLAGE the name of which she never discovered, Katarin had reined in her horse, dismounted, hitched the reins to a lamp-post, and hurried in to the post office. Her resolve strengthened by the inopportune meeting with Sigmund outside the Palace library, she was determined to post her letter, determined to get away from the brooding atmosphere in which she had lived for the last eighteen years. Its sickly weight of passion was destroying her, the power it offered and the price it exacted. With help from her family she would get away.

But the lip-licking post-master had been listening to the radio. His wet red lips were all of him she could ever remember – they told her of the radio announcements; first of Sigmund Korda's death and later of Colonel Balenkov's coming trial. They noticed her expensive furs – didn't she come from the Palace? they said. What did she think of such a thing? Had Balenkov been put up to it, did she think, and would he get off?

Katarin had not replied. Anything, anything might be true. She had left the post office, the letter to her relative near Pol still in her hand. Sigmund was dead, killed by Balenkov. All neat and tidy. But why Balenkov? She remembered her strange meeting with the man, months before, after that first skating party to Novellnyi...He had spoken confusedly of Sigmund's wife – could there really be a connection? She tore up her letter and threw it

away, the white paper unpleasantly grey against the un-
trodden snow. She needed to know who was really behind
Sigmund's death. If it were Orrin, she . . . if it were Orrin
she had no idea what she would do. Such an intensity of
personal emotion she had not thought him capable of.
Much more likely to be Tarsu, or the scheming E.A.

As she rode back to the Palace she looked into herself
and saw with surprise how small a part grief had in her
confused emotions. If she grieved at all, it was for
Paskellnyi – Sigmund had never been more than what she
had tried to find in him. Paskellnyi, on the other hand,
had been real, and the cranky devotion of old Sorelle. What
she felt most was curiosity, and anger, and a perverse new
respect for her husband.

The sun was near to the horizon, shining redly across
the plain under a weight of cloud that promised more snow
before midnight. As Katarin passed under the Patriot's Gate
the Cathedral clock began to strike half past three. Confused with the sound of the big bell came a short untidy
rattle of rifle shots. Katarin might have persuaded herself
that she imagined it, had not her horse shied slightly and
laid back his ears. Feeling calmly detached, she rode slowly
round to the tiny execution yard at the back of the Old
Barracks. A few people were already coming away; some
of them she thought must be foreign reporters.

In the yard itself a squad of soldiers was standing neatly
at ease. Marshall Tarsu and a young Palace doctor talked
together, alone in the middle of the black cobbles. Other
officials in long greatcoats waited at a distance, stamping
their feet. Two orderlies were carrying a loaded stretcher
away through a doorway in one blank side wall. Katarin
had no idea where it led. The execution yard was over-
looked by no windows; bare black walls surrounded it on
four sides only relieved by a tarred wooden screen placed
to take the impact of any stray bullets.

Katarin watched over the heads of the few remaining

onlookers. It was a black way of dying, at the bottom of a black well, under a black sunless sky. Marshall Tarsu noticed her and raised one gloved hand in polite greeting. He ended his conversation with the young doctor and started to come across the cobbles towards her. Already his lips were pursed, his face prepared for expressions of bland regret. Katarin dug sharp heels into her horse's sides and was away back along the narrow street, scattering people as she went.

She left her horse with the stable sergeant. She wondered if she cared too much what people said – she wanted to ask for Sigmund's horse. One thing was certain: Amélie would not want it.

"A bitter day for the Palace." The sergeant loosened her horse's girth strap. "Two good men gone. Often goes that way of course. They're saying it's on account of a woman – too much sense in those two, I'd say."

Katarin remembered she was the President's wife.

"We'll know the truth when the official transcripts of the trial are published," she said a little heavily. "Till then it will be best if we all reserve our judgement."

She left the stables, took the lift up to the third floor, and went straight to her husband's private office. He was alone at his desk, strangely insignificant against the barbaric magnificence of the room around him. When he saw her he got to his feet and came urgently across the room. He tried stiffly to take her in his arms. They stood together in a wilderness of over-stuffed furniture.

"They tell me you've been riding, my dear. Such terrible news to come back to. Such terrible news."

She resisted him. He held her as if he were a French general about to decorate her for courage beyond the call of duty.

"Tell me what happened, Orrin. What really happened."

". . . My dear, I have a busy afternoon ahead of me. So many formalities. . ."

"Colonel Balenkov is dead. I saw them carrying his body away."

"I know. We had to act decisively. Poor man." Marshall Borge sighed. "Personally I think he must have gone a little mad. But then, Sigmund also – "

"We are not overheard here, Orrin. You must tell me the truth."

"Katarin . . . Katarin, my dear, sit down. Sigmund was a friend to both of us. You deserve the truth."

She sat down as she was told. Even now he did not know they had been lovers. To tell him now would be pointless, vicious even. Sigmund's death had been political – that is to say, it hardly concerned her. But because she was the President's wife she listened to what the President told her.

"Certain elements in the administration, my dear – no need to go into personalities, no names, no pack drill – were worried by Sigmund's great popularity. They saw this as a nascent personality cult, and as a threat to democratic government."

"*They*, Orrin? How about you? Didn't you agree with them?"

"To be perfectly frank with you, Katarin, no. I have always been convinced that Sigmund was too wise to misuse the popularity his great personal charm gave him. Did I see Sigmund as another oppressor, another Stalin? Of course not." He walked away a few paces, then hurried and sat down beside her. "I know I shouldn't have agreed to the scheme, Katarin . . . But government is a balancing act – of giving in to peripheral pressures while remaining steadfast at the – "

"Scheme? What scheme?"

"A little rumour was started." Marshall Borge made an apologetic, dismissive gesture. "You read about it in the papers. Just enough to shake his reputation, we thought."

"So it was you. . ."

"When he proposed to turn even this to good account by means of this reception . . . What with that and the international opening of his library extension, it was decided – " again the apologetic gesture – "it was decided to try something a little more drastic."

"Such as an accidental shooting, I suppose."

"That is insulting, Katarin. We obtained evidence against him, poor evidence, evidence that would not stand up to detailed scrutiny. Armed with this, I ordered Sigmund's arrest. He would stand trial, the evidence would be found inadequate, he would be acquitted. Our legal system would be vindicated, and a little, just a little of the mud would stick . . . That is the scheme I agreed to, Katarin."

"But something went wrong."

"Yes. Sigmund panicked. He ran away."

"Perhaps he didn't trust you."

"Perhaps we none of us trusted each other." Marshall Borge was silent for a moment. The hands of the huge basalt clock crept round to four. "But he hadn't done anything. With his innocence and his public position he was unassailable. He must have known that."

"Perhaps he was guilty of things you haven't yet discovered."

"That seems the only possibility. But surely not Sigmund . . . An open personality, didn't you think?"

She could not answer. It was as if Orrin were begging for reassurance. He seemed old and worn – at the apex of a triangle a man had so little freedom of manoeuvre. Still she did not altogether trust him. Perhaps that too was the price of their position.

"Balenkov shot him while he was escaping?"

"Balenkov was unhinged. From Sigmund's wife we have evidence that Balenkov was deeply, perhaps insanely devoted to her. A gun in his hand, a sudden opportunity . . . it seems the only explanation."

"Promise me, Orrin. Promise me you had nothing to do with this."

"He was a friend to us both, Katarin. How could I face you, how could I face myself, with that on my conscience?"

He clasped her and buried his head in her shoulder. She let him. She put her arms gently round him: he was a victim as much as Sigmund, as much as any of them. More than most Sigmund had deserved to die — but then, so had she. It was Orrin, though, who bore on his shoulders the guilt of ultimate authority. Had he sought power, or had not power lain in wait for him . . . ? She knew she would never have gone to live in Pol: she loved the Palace too much. She hugged Orrin to her, and told him how she trusted him.

The devil in Raoul Novaks' head had gone at last, leaving him clearer and colder-sighted than he had ever been before. The devil had gone on the first stroke of three thirty from the huge Cathedral bell. The death he needed, but that he was not part of, had been accomplished. For him, as for others, Colonel Balenkov alive had been dangerous. Now he was dead, his loyalty no longer the only consideration that kept him from speaking . . . Novaks sat quietly at his desk, sensuously delighting in the help that had come from even the most unlikely people. His eye was caught by the tape recorder at his elbow. He decided it was time he went in to see the President.

He switched on his own microphone hidden in the President's office. He wanted to be sure that the President was alone.

". . . Balenkov shot him while he was escaping?"

Novaks was surprised to hear Katarin's voice. He had thought her still out riding.

"Balenkov was unhinged. From Sigmund's wife we have evidence that Balenkov was deeply, perhaps insanely devoted

233

to her. A gun in his hand, a sudden opportunity . . . it seems the only explanation."

"Promise me, Orrin. Promise me you had nothing to do with this."

Novaks laughed aloud.

"He was a friend to us both, Katarin. How could I face you, how could I face myself, with that on my conscience?"

Novaks heard a sound very like muffled sobbing. Then Katarin's voice in a murmur he could not distinguish. He rose to his feet and swung the tape recorder down off the desk. He would never have a better moment – two birds with one stone. The results would be interesting.

The scene that he interrupted when he entered the President's office was very touching. Two simple human beings in a basic attitude of tenderness amid all their gaudy glory. He put the recorder noisily on a side table.

"So they've shot Balenkov," he said.

"Do you not usually knock, Raoul?" The President moved away with dignity from his wife.'

"Balenkov is dead."

"The price a soldier pays for murder."

"I must correct you, Comrade President. The price a soldier pays for being an assassin."

"What are you saying, Raoul? I find your manner offensive."

Filled with a sudden dark premonition, Katarin got up quickly from the sofa and went to where the E.A. was standing, fiddling with his machine.

"Need you trouble the President ? He's – "

"Just one short item, Comrade Katarin. After this it need never be mentioned again, I promise you."

"From your expression you think this is going to amuse you, Novaks."

"Amuse is an unkind word . . ." He started the tape recorder. "With your permission, Comrade President?"

234

"What is it? What is it you're wanting my permission for?"

He sounded querulous, like an old man. He was stopped short by his own voice, stronger, younger, coming from the tape recorder.

"... *on your way then, Colonel. Good luck.*" Footsteps approached, a door closed, and the President's voice was suddenly much louder. "*I brought you in here, Colonel, because I need to have a private word with you.*" Then sounds of movement, of papers being sorted. "*Your record is excellent, your loyalty unquestionable. I predict a distinguished future for you, Colonel Balenkov.*"

Marshall Borge was on his feet. The tape reels continued to turn, their message lost under his angry protest.

"However you obtained that, Novaks, it must be destroyed at once. I thought Tarsu had left me free of his infernal bugging machines."

"This has nothing to do with Marshall Tarsu." The E.A. stopped his machine. "This is between you and me only. And your wife, of course."

Marshall Borge stood in silence for a long time, recognising the power Raoul Novaks had won for himself. It was deserved power: winning it had taken patience and foresight. Finally Marshall Borge spoke.

"No doubt you have some sort of agreement in mind, Raoul. I don't see that it need involve Katarin."

"Please yourself, Marshall. As you say, I have an agreement I would like to – "

"No!" Katarin looked incredulously from one man to the other. "No, Orrin. I must know what is on that tape. I can't just be bundled out of the way like an ignorant peasant."

"Please, Katarin." Marshall Borge kept his dignity, even *in extremis*. "There are episodes in most people's lives of which they are not particularly proud. It is seldom to anyone's advantage to pry into these."

"The Marshall's quite right, you know." Novaks spoke from strength, his manner slightly mocking. "Once you've heard this you'll wish to hell you hadn't."

She wished she could show him he was wrong. She wished her marriage was after all based on the sort of trust that would make it possible for her to go from the room and leave the tape unheard. But in her heart she doubted if there were such marriages, and so did he.

"I'll hear it through, Novaks."

The E.A. stooped over the recorder and re-started it. Darkness was falling so that in the big room they were to each other hardly more than shadows. The recorded voices were thin and false, but unmistakable. The tape took up where it had left off.

". . . .*necessary to present the arrest in such a manner that Korda dare not stay in the Palace. You might even plant the idea of escape by offering to be his accomplice. When he runs, then you can kill him. Make sure there are plenty of witnesses, Colonel. The prisoner resisting arrest. Plenty of witnesses.*"

"*I understand, Comrade President.*"

"*The man is an enemy of the people, Balenkov, so you need not be squeamish. This manner of execution is only necessary because of the false way he has insinuated himself into the hearts of the peasantry.*"

"*I obey orders, Comrade President.*"

"*Let me be frank with you, Colonel Balenkov. These orders are dangerous and secret. If you are brought to trial, I can promise you will be acquitted. But let one word of this conversation leak out and you are a dead man. I should deny everything and charge you with gross and treasonable perjury. On the other hand, play it my way and I foresee a great future for you.*"

Raoul Novaks stopped the machine. When he spoke his voice was strangely real.

"There is all that matters . . . I have copies of the tape," he added. "Should anything happen to me they would get into inconvenient hands."

Katarin had backed away: from Novaks, from her husband, from the vile machine with its tinny echoes of iniquity. Her back against the far wall now, she groped for understanding.

"Why?" she said. "Why, Orrin? Why?"

"My dear Katarin," the E.A. was quiet and serious, "political expediency will do many things. It turned your husband into a murderer. It has turned me to blackmail."

President Borge walked ponderously to his desk and sat down. He struck a match and lighted the oil lamp by which he preferred to work. Behind him the windows turned black and the slow dark clouds vanished.

"You're a mean, self-pitying bastard, Raoul. You know so much and you know so little. *Your* neurotic little life may be bounded by political expediency. Mine is not. Politics may have governed the mechanics of Korda's death – they had nothing to do with the reason. The reason lies with my wife, Raoul, whom I loved once and who is a whore. A whore, Comrade Novaks – how's that as a political reason for murder?" He swung round to face Katarin, his eyes deeply shadowed in the light from the lamp. "There's my reason, Katarin. Paskellnyi is my reason."

Orrin, whom she had so recently held in her arms and comforted. Orrin, who had lied to her at the very centre of what was to have been their marriage. Orrin, who had cheated where cheating was impossible.

"And you'll say that I lied to you, Katarin. I needed to lie. I needed you back so that the Palace would see. I needed you back, Katarin, so that one day I could humiliate you as you have humiliated me."

She fell across the room at him, a dagger in her hand from the wall behind. His paper indignation, his vindictiveness, what strength he had, he was nothing before her blind, agonised sense of wrong. She stabbed his chest and struck a rib, withdrew the dagger, stabbed again. He struggled hardly at all, his courage gone, his mind pre-occupied with irrelevancies like dignity and the unprotect-ing hands of Raoul Novaks. Katarin stabbed him once more and he fell forward across the desk, dying. Novaks rescued the oil lamp from where it teetered.

"I have a doctor," he said carefully, "who will prepare him for his coffin and give us a death certificate. Sudden heart failure, I think. Today's strains have been consider-able. He was, after all, no longer young."

Katarin disengaged herself and drew away, the pain in her changing, chilling her now so that eyelids blinked cold over colder eyeballs. And her understanding returned, sharpening till it too was a pain.

"You'll need my support," she said, "if you are to become President."

"A lot of nonsense is talked about support. The support of the army, the support of the people . . . Myself, I have the support of the Palace, and that is all I need."

He moved Marshall Borge back so that his blood should not stain the desk. Katarin watched from a great distance.

"If I were to stand trial," she said, "there would be unsatisfactory repercussions."

"My dear Katarin, there's no chance of you standing trial. You know that." He turned the lamp down, for it had begun to smoke slightly. "I think we will get on well together, you and I. We have so much in common. One day we might make a match of it. After a decent interval."

She had never thought of Raoul Novaks in that way before. Therefore, within the demands on each other that the Palace had taught them to make and not to make, she conceded that he might be right. All she knew of him was his intellect and the stillness of his body. Both these she believed to be impenetrable. So he might be right.

In the catacombs Major Kohler, his career as a civil

engineer aborted in the second hour, was starting unimpressed on his evening inspection of the Paul VII Passage. He did his work, and others did theirs. It was on this framework of duty that all his competence was based. In court that afternoon he had witnessed to a truth he knew to be severely limited – his respect for Colonel Balenkov alone was enough to tell him that. Limitations on truth were both inevitable and desirable – without them chaos.

He measured the slope of the floor. The rate of seepage down the walls had increased: the sump at the far end was ten centimetres deep now, deepening even as he watched. The water in it had stagnated and grown scum under the yellow electric lights. There was a new smell in the passage, noticeably organic. In one place a root stone had cracked, transmitting its distortion to the masonry below. At any minute the structure might collapse altogether. Nevertheless, his panic of a few weeks ago had obviously been a great foolishness.

He made up his notes and returned to the base of the shaft. In his position he should deal with events only as they happened. This realisation was a great source of comfort to him.